EBURY PRESS

IMAGINARY RAIN

Vikas Khanna is one of the most beloved Indian chefs in the world. He is an award-winning Michelin-starred chef and the host of highly rated prime-time shows, such as *MasterChef India*, *Twist of Taste* and *India's Mega Kitchens*. Khanna has been a guest on Gordon Ramsay's *Kitchen Nightmares* and *Hell's Kitchen*, as well as *The Martha Stewart Show*, *Throwdown! with Bobby Flay* and *MasterChef Australia*. Khanna has hosted events for former US president Barack Obama, the Dalai Lama, Pope Francis, Prime Minister Narendra Modi and many other world leaders and celebrities. In 2015, Deutsche Welle named Khanna as one of the world's ten most iconic chefs of all time. Khanna has received rave reviews from the *New York Times*, Condé Nast and the *Wall Street Journal*. He works with several foundations worldwide to support the fight against malnutrition in India. He lives in New York City.

ALSO BY THE SAME AUTHOR

My Great India Cookbook

My First Kitchen

Barkat

IMAGINARY RAIN

A novel

Vikas Khanna

Bestselling author and Michelin-starred chef

An imprint of Penguin Random House

EBURY PRESS

USA | Canada | UK | Ireland | Australia
New Zealand | India | South Africa | China

Ebury Press is part of the Penguin Random House group of companies
whose addresses can be found at global.penguinrandomhouse.com

Published by Penguin Random House India Pvt. Ltd
4th Floor, Capital Tower 1, MG Road,
Gurugram 122 002, Haryana, India

First published in Ebury Press by Penguin Random House India 2023

10 9 8 7 6 5 4 3 2 1

ISBN 9780143455356

Typeset in Minion Pro by MAP Systems, Bengaluru, India

www.penguin.co.in

To my Biji, Bimla Khanna, who taught me the magic of cooking

To my mother, Bindu Khanna, and her Lawrence Garden
(our Curry Bowl)
To her devotion to Indian cuisine, for which she won a Michelin star through me

To Shabana Azmi, who agreed to play Prerna and learnt how to cook for the part; I owe you everything for your faith in me

Was the rain real? Was it water and tears?
Prerna didn't know. All she knew was he had gone,
and all she had left was this rain . . . Or whatever it was.

Contents

Prologue

Dust swirled around the sandstone pillars of the Jama Masjid, as the sun made its white domes glow. It was 1975 in Old Delhi, and an excitable crowd stood huddled around a transistor radio, waiting to hear whether India had successfully launched its first satellite, Aryabhata, named after the Indian astronomer, into space. Amid the traffic and flag-waving throngs, a young girl, who couldn't have been older than ten, with the complexion of dried sugarcane and the rounded, hopeful features of a cherub, held a ragged bouquet of orange paper flowers in her hands. 'Flowers. Buy my beautiful, magical flowers,' she pleaded with the crowd, as they steadfastly ignored her.

But she wouldn't give up. She moved from group to group, and up and down the road, hoping to find someone to sell her flowers to.

'My dear girl, how much are your flowers?' inquired a voice from behind, suddenly.

'Ten rupees,' she said promptly.

'That's more than the cost of the average flower on this street. What's so special about your flowers that they cost more?' the moustachioed man asked, hands on his hips, leaning back in admiration at the girl's confidence.

'Well, not all flowers on the street are magical like mine. Do you want to buy one of my magical flowers or not?'

Karanjit threw his head back and laughed. 'Such confidence for so small a kid. Magical flowers, eh? Child, what is your name?'

'Prerna. You know what else is magical?'

'Besides your charm, I can't imagine what else. Why don't you tell me?'

'Sir, if I close my eyes, I can make it rain!'

'Oh, really?' Karanjit dug around his pockets, pulling out some change. 'Give me four flowers. One for me, one for my daughter, one for my mother, and one for you—for your own good luck.'

Prerna smiled and closed her eyes for a moment before picking four of the best flowers from her bunch for him.

'Don't close your eyes too long on the street or you will get hit by traffic.' Karanjit laughed as he handed over some coins. 'And I will wait for that rain. Delhi certainly needs it. This drought is killing us.' He took the flowers and then dug out more change from his pockets. 'Magic girl, here. Go to the bookseller and buy yourself a book so you can learn the ABCs. Then go to the shoe seller and buy yourself some new slippers; yours are getting old and worn. And, if it does rain any time soon, they are sure to get destroyed.'

Prerna looked down. The man was right, and she would be glad to have new slippers. By the time she looked up again, he had melted into the crowd. 'Flowers. Buy my beautiful, magical flowers!' She went back to selling her orange paper flowers.

A few days later, Old Delhi wore a different look. Gone were the crowds and the dazzling sun. The weight and ferocity of the monsoon knocked down the diminutive flower seller to the road, along with half of Old Delhi. She clung to her book for dear life as the wind howled, threatening to rip apart her new book, an English alphabet primer. She had bought it from the local book wallah, who sometimes competed with her for sales at traffic lights. The heavy rain beat down fiercely, soiling and soaking her feet, clad in her new, pink satin slippers.

Prerna cautiously opened one eye, only to see a rusty streetlight toppled over by the monsoon wind. A shadow passed over her small, shivering form. She looked up to see a moustache dripping with water and the kindest pair of eyes she'd ever seen. A pair of hands reached down as if from heaven itself. 'Come, come, child. Come out of the rain,' the man said gently, as he lifted her into his arms, and for once, she felt weightless—weightless as if she were a balloon. Holding the shivering little flower seller in his warm arms, Karanjit passed through a grand door.

And just like that, Prerna had a home.

It seemed to take only a few more closings and openings of Prerna's eyes for her to grow into the softer skin of being someone's daughter. One day, she opened them to stare in wonder at the bunch of pink and blue balloons surrounding her, as Karanjit sat making croquettes and besan (chickpea flour) laddoos—the poor person's sweet. It was Karanjit's younger daughter, Reema's birthday.

As Karanjit guided Prerna on how to roll out the dough, the little princess, Reema, was having the lice brushed out of her soft hair by Prerna's step-grandmother, Devi. The scowling old woman, mouth and eyes cinched up, as bitter and wrinkly as a bitter gourd, lorded over Karanjit, though she stood barely as high as her son's chest, as he instructed Prerna on how to give the final touches to the laddoo.

'Very good, *beti*, now knead a little more honey into the chickpea flour and then the laddoos will be perfect. Perfect and sweet, like you . . . Reema?' Karanjit said softly to his youngest, somewhat spoilt daughter.

'Yeah?' asked Reema, wincing with every stroke of Devi's comb, brushing the fallen lice off her knees.

'How many laddoos should your sister and I make for you?'

'Six,' Reema said firmly. 'Because it's my sixth birthday.'

'Wonderful!' exclaimed Karanjit, smiling at the doughballs rather like he did when he was honking cows off the road. Prerna rolled her eyes as her hands deftly worked the dough.

'Ouch, *Dadi*, You're pulling too hard!' gasped Reema, yanking her head away and turning to glower at Devi.

'Ungrateful child! Stay still! You can't have a birthday party with so many lice in your hair! And don't let your black sister and her black hands get too close to you.'

'Ma!' Karanjit interjected. 'Give Prerna a break for once. Look at the perfect laddoos she's making!'

'Karanjit, why on earth are you wasting your time teaching this dark girl anything?'

'Ma, she's my eldest daughter! It's just her second attempt and look how perfect her laddoos are!'

Devi didn't even bother to look up, as her hands expertly brushed through Reema's hair. 'Don't show me anything this girl makes. As long as I live, I will never eat anything her dark hands touch; no matter how sweet or round,' she said bitterly.

Prerna was used to Devi's taunts. Only Karanjit's warmth and kindness kept her from retorting. So she kept her head down and continued her work. Rolling out the laddoos was far more exhausting than Prerna expected, yet she thoroughly enjoyed doing it. It made her thirsty, this vigorous rolling of dough, so without thinking anything of it, she reached over to a glass of water placed on the table. The old prune bit her lips for a nanosecond and then exploded, 'Karanjit! What kind of son did I raise? I will never eat anything made by this girl's black hands and here she is drinking from a glass?' Before Prerna could even drink one drop of water, Devi reached over and snatched the crystal glass out of her hands.

'Don't touch the glass!' she screamed, tackling the girl. Devi was almost on top of Prerna, a couple of lice threatening to fall off the brush in her hand on to the dough. 'How many times have I told you to use a steel glass?' The crone grabbed a steel glass from the small shelf above the counter behind them. She held the glinting cup in front of Prerna's face. 'This is a steel glass. You will only drink from this, understand?'

Prerna reacted just in time and moved out of the way—this had happened many times before and she knew what would happen next—as Devi drew her arm back and threw the glass past her head.

'I'll do what I did with that black dog your father brought home! I'll throw your black skin back out on to the streets!'

Prerna watched the tumbler sail past her head, out of their kitchen and into their garden. She knew she would inevitably be the one to retrieve it if only to save her father from more of his mother's wrath.

* * *

The years flew by. Prerna learnt much from Karanjit—not just the art of cooking, but his kindness and compassion were lessons she knew she'd hold on to, forever.

Being the eldest daughter to a nurturing, progressive father meant Prerna would be expected to take on more responsibility as she grew up—not just in the family kitchen, but behind the wheel of the family car too, quite literally. But when Prerna became old enough to drive and her feet could reach the pedals, she summarily failed her driver's test, much to her and Karanjit's disappointment, but to Reema's and Devi's delight.

Karanjit sat in the driver's seat of their trusty Maruti, Prerna sobbing next to him, Reema smirking at the back. Flecks of grey spiced Karanjit's otherwise dark moustache and thinning hair. Other than these small hints of age, the years had been kind to him, for he still appeared as fresh-faced and graceful as ever. He smiled through the cracked windshield, scanning for obstacles as he navigated the bylanes of Old Delhi—and obstacles there were many. They had to expertly avoid the potholes lining the roads, keep an eye out for smoke from the bubbling cauldrons of tea in the roadside stalls that could obscure their vision, look out for vendors and beggars who could suddenly dart into their path, and, of course, there were always a dozen cows, lazily sunning themselves bang in the middle of the roads. Karanjit loved the cows though. The sight of one cow was enough for him to break into a wide smile, and he'd lovingly honk at them from within his beat-up Maruti. He would wait patiently for the animal to move and would never get irritated, no matter how long they took to clear the way for him.

Karanjit turned to his teenager, who had blossomed into a beautiful young woman. Prerna looked like a vision in the soft light of the dying sun, her green saree complementing her sparkly eyes and fresh face. However, sobs racked her body as she stared out moodily at Karanjit's beloved cows.

'Don't cry, beti, my sweetheart,' Karanjit said. 'Mistakes are bound to happen, especially the first time you try to drive.'

'I barely made it ten feet!'

'Most people have accidents the first time,' Karanjit lied.

'I want to be perfect at everything!' Prerna cried harder, resting her chin on the window frame. The buildings speeding past made her feel dizzy, but maybe her tears would stop if she felt sick, she thought.

A sharp laugh came from the backseat. It was Reema. Prerna turned around to glare at her younger sister.

'Father, that was the first and last time I will ever ride in a car that Prerna drives,' squealed Reema, as she checked herself out in a hand mirror. Unlike earthier Prerna, Reema was skinny and naturally fashionable, several shades lighter than Prerna and already covered in knock-off Chanel and Prada. No one in their small family knew where this child had inherited her sense of style from, but it was there. Only twelve, she already hid her face behind stylish sunglasses.

'Leave me alone,' Prerna said coldly, still fighting back her tears.

Reema leaned over. 'You're a terrible driver!'

'I know,' cried out Prerna. 'I know!'

'Sit down, Reema! Leave your sister alone,' Karanjit said, honking at another cow crossing the road. 'She did her best and that's what counts. Not every woman takes the risk of driving. At least your sister took the risk. Eventually, she will learn.'

Karanjit took one hand off the wheel and softly brushed the tears off Prerna's cheeks.

But Reema was relentless. 'I don't care if she did her best; her best was terrible! I thought I was going to die! Just promise me you'll never drive again.'

'Sit down, Reema! You're going to make me hit a cow!'

Reema fell apart giggling behind them.

'And, honestly, Reema,' continued Karanjit, 'you should encourage your sister. Stop scaring her. One can't be good at everything. We all know Prerna's skills are with food.'

The three were silent for a while.

Karanjit then reached out and touched the little pendant of the Golden Temple that hung from his rearview mirror.

'Daughters, let me tell you something . . . Life will always be okay. Those who lose hope can never win. When I was younger, I would work hard all day in a dirty metal utensil factory. But you know what? I knew that with every utensil, fork, knife, spoon, or even steam table or tandoor I made, I could save money for my education. At the time, I didn't have much money to feed myself, so I would walk across Amritsar for my one meal per day at the Golden Temple. That's all I needed . . . That simple meal of dal, vegetables, roti and kheer at the langar (the community kitchen of the Sikhs). It was a simple life—except for the kheer, which was always made with saffron. I praised God with every bite I took. Everyone there, thousands of people from every walk of life, were given the nourishment that they needed. I could have never come to own my own small utensil factory if it wasn't for that one meal a day that gave me sustenance, energy, and hope.'

Reema covered her ears and squealed, 'Papa, not again!'

'Not again what?' asked Karanjit, beaming at a cow.

'You always talk about Amritsar and the Golden Temple, but you never take us there!'

'Let Papa drive,' chided Prerna. 'I trust Pita ji will take us there one day.'

'Don't listen to your little sister. She's a little princess, she doesn't know how to be anything else,' Karanjit whispered into Prerna's ear, making sure Reema couldn't hear. 'Don't blame her. It's my mother's fault.'

Prerna smiled. She always loved it when her father confided in her and only her.

Reema again leaned into the front seat, glaring at them. 'Don't talk about me, you two! And Prerna, he's *my* Pita ji, not yours.'

Prerna buried her face in her *pallu*.

'Reema, stop it! That's cruel. You are both my daughters. And we're not talking about you anyway, I am trying to cheer Prerna up,' Karanjit said. 'Prerna, life will be okay.'

Behind her pallu, Prerna closed her eyes as she sniffled. *Would life really be okay*? She wasn't always so sure.

Suddenly, Reema began kicking the seats in front of her, a habit that irked both Prerna and Karanjit. 'Well, Papa, when will you take us to the Golden Temple?' she demanded.

'Be patient. I will not only take you to the Golden Temple, I will take you to see the whole of Amritsar, and then across the entire India,' Karanjit said.

Prerna pulled out her head from her pallu and turned to her father. 'Really, Papa?' She rarely questioned her father, and for a second, Karanjit's smile fell. But then a cow lumbered past, distracting him.

'Listen,' Karanjit continued once the cow finally moved out of the way, 'when I take you around the whole subcontinent, you know what you will experience?'

'What?' Prerna asked.

'A lot more than I experienced at the Golden Temple.'

'Really?' Reema pulled off her knockoff sunglasses to show her scepticism.

Karanjit smiled. 'You doubt me today? Remember what I said about having hope? Life will turn out okay.'

He directed his last comment to Prerna, making her smile.

'No, I just feel bad because I am such a lousy driver,' sighed Prerna.

Reema, who had pulled on her sunglasses again, suddenly popped in between them again.

'Can we buy a new car?' she asked abruptly. 'This jalopy is no good for our travels around India.'

Karanjit laughed. 'Be content with this car, Reema. It's old, trusty and faithful—just like your Papa.'

Prerna watched the familiar roads outside their car speed past. She wondered if she'd ever be able to drive again and if what her father had said about the Golden Temple was true.

ONCE UPON A TIME IN NEW YORK CITY

Chapter 1

Saffron and Curry Leaves in Staten Island

The sun lazily bounced off the tarmac as Prerna and her husband, Manish, sped past suburban Staten Island. American flags fluttered on the porches of Bay Terrace and boards in front yards proudly proclaimed that the owners of the houses had lived to see the turn of the millennium.

The couple lived in a simple, two-level, white-painted house. Prerna kept a small, manicured garden—a far cry from the weedy, neglected sidewalk outside. It reminded her of her childhood, but she preferred the grit and diversity of the city. Manish, however, didn't—he was a man of small pleasures, such as lying on the sofa and watching cricket, or enjoying a barbeque at a neighbour's house.

Sometimes, Prerna marvelled at how much Manish reminded her of Karanjit—they had the same moustache and high forehead—but he couldn't be more different from her father. For one, he barely smiled, whereas Karanjit was inclined to beam at absolutely everything.

'Work, work, always driving you to work. And at the same time every morning, every day,' grumbled Manish, as he steered the car down the last length of Hylan Boulevard before veering off to Bay Street, which runs alongside Upper New York Bay. The road would take them to St George for Prerna's early morning shopping before she caught the Staten Island Ferry to work.

'That's the restaurant owner's life in New York City,' Prerna said. 'I'm sorry, but you know we can't afford to live anywhere else. And here, we have more space. Especially with the state of affairs at The Curry Bowl.'

'I know.'

'Can you drive a little faster? I don't want to miss the freshest herbs and spices at Khanna and Sons in St George—they sell out so quickly. If we don't get there early enough, Shriman Khanna will try to sell me his old, wilted herbs and stale spices. I can't have that. I can't miss my ferry either.'

'Driving as fast as I can, dear.' Manish threw up his hands. 'Traffic! You don't drive, so maybe you don't understand that.'

Prerna glared at her husband and was about to retort sharply when a bicyclist veered in front of their car. 'Manish! Watch out for that bicycle!'

Manish honked at the errant bicyclist and rolled down the window. 'Get to the side of the road! You are going too slow for the traffic!'

The bicyclist glared over his shoulder, flipping them off as the Nissan sped past him.

'Don't worry, I'm an excellent driver.'

'You remind me of my father; he would smile and honk at all the cows in Old Delhi—only you don't smile when you honk and there are no cows crossing the roads in New York. It's just aggressive people in aggressive vehicles.'

Manish pressed on the accelerator as they closed in on downtown St George. 'My courier business is starting to trickle off. I'm not sure why. I gave a lot to the Indian community downtown—the best prices, taking risks on some of the rules for people like Dr Annu. I feel that they are not appreciating what I've done for them,' Manish sighed as the traffic lights in front of them turned red.

'Take it easy. Businesses are still recovering from 9/11. It's for everyone. We can talk about that later; I really need to get to the spice market now,' Prerna responded.

'Always about you; never about me!' Manish stepped on the gas again, and soon they were in another world. Soon Manish pulled over on the uneven, ragged curb and kissed his wife on the cheek.

'Be careful in the city and have a nice day,' he said.

'A nice day for me is running my restaurant and making my customers happy, even if it is for the last time,' Prerna laughed as she slipped out of the car and headed towards her first destination on Victory Boulevard.

Her walk revealed a slight limp and a rhythmic flick of her wrist as she strode down the cracked, gum-stained sidewalks of Staten Island's gritty downtown—her bag swinging from her shoulder. The sari she wore was just a little more sober than the ones she wore as a teen in New Delhi, and rather than sandals, she now wore white sneakers. She had adapted. After so many years of cooking, her 'chef's wrist,' the carpal tunnel syndrome, which always seemed to flare when she was stressed or entered dark spaces in her mind, nagged at her. She had the chronic tendency of reaching over and massaging it with her thumb whenever she could, which was quite often.

Prerna rounded a corner, avoiding the more aggressive drunks, but offering the politer drug addicts or poor opioid zombies whatever change she had on hand. From what Prerna knew about America, St George and Tompkinsville areas were like San Francisco, with a couple of black eyes added on. It sharply contrasted with the neighbourhood she and Manish had settled in, which was more like white-suburban middle America, but with far less space. The progressives who lived there were getting rusty and becoming increasingly conservative, leaving most immigrant families to suffer the forces of gentrification. Many couldn't afford to live there any more. In this way, Prerna and her family were lucky that she was a small business owner—one with a loyal clientele. In contrast to the grit of downtown Staten Island, the area's low hills, its steep streets dotted with regal Victorian and Craftsman mansions (most of them sliced and diced into apartments), which seemed to lord over the beautiful, usually placid harbour, hinted at a deeper history than the area was given credit for.

As she approached her destination, Prerna heard the booming horn of the Staten Island Ferry and felt the moist harbour breeze ruffle her hair. Before entering the spice shop, Prerna hesitated a moment, pressing her phone to her ear—not only to look occupied and tethered to safety amidst the last stretch of the dangerous block but to speak to her most trusted staff member, Dilip.

'Dilip, good morning. I'm on the way; I just got to the Khanna's . . . Yes, that is correct, I will get curry leaves, okra and raw mangoes . . . If their saffron is cheap and of good quality, I will get a bunch of that too. See you soon!'

As Prerna entered the store, she took in the tall shelves stacked with colourful jars of pickles, the mountains of spices kept behind the counter, the unopened sacks of herbs that called out to her from the corner, and the aisles and aisles of utensils. What always seemed to be missing, however, was the absolute, uplifting freshness of the products Prerna and her father always discovered together while shopping in the markets of Old Delhi—a freshness that seemed to cleanse the air.

The shopkeeper, Aadesh, and his assistant, Adarsh, looking for all the world like twins with their bushy moustaches and matching off-white kurtas, sat behind the counter, warily eyeing her. Prerna made her way past the spices, assessing everything from the green and red chillies, the round purple brinjals, the glistening karelas and okra, and, of course, reserving her sharpest judgement for the saffron and curry leaves. Her frown seemed to deepen with each vegetable she picked up. 'Aye yi yi,' she said, levelling her eyes back at the shopkeepers.

Aadesh laughed. 'Good morning, ma'am. Fresh vegetables and spices today?'

'If that's what you call them. Maybe . . .' Prerna folded her arms, deciding which products offered by Khanna and Sons she was willing to risk her hard-earned restaurant funds for, and especially her loyal customers' taste buds. As the sons of Khanna stood behind the counter, rolling their eyes at her, her phone rang. 'Hello, Manish. How was the traffic on the way home?'

'Terrible as always. Too many bicycles on the road these days.'

'I know. What is it?'

'Prerna, where is my jacket?' asked Manish.

'Which jacket?'

'My millionaire jacket!'

'Oh, that jacket. I ironed it last night, and it should be hanging to the left of the kitchen cupboard where I always hang it, ji.'

'You know, it's my big day today, Prerna. I will return today wearing my millionaire jacket! I plan to come home from court with a large sum of insurance compensation. I deserve it. Bloody because Bay Terrace doesn't maintain its streetlights, I tripped over a crack in the sidewalk a few months ago and almost broke my hip and neck. You know I've been in pain for months. I deserve the compensation! I plan on wearing the millionaire jacket as I strut around after the hearing, when I receive the final settlement figure.'

With his dwindling courier business, Manish had recently begun taking monetary advantage of any accidents he suffered—whether or not he actually suffered them. Prerna was sympathetic to her husband's desperation, but in a way, life was hard for working-class Indians in New York—so she couldn't really blame him for trying to make a quick buck, though not in the best possible way.

'I wish you the best, ji,' Prerna said. 'Speak to you later. Let me know how it goes at the court.'

Prerna sighed as she strode over to a small heap of okra, pinching at a few pieces to check their ripeness.

Adarsh, the younger of the twins, trying to impress his older brother, was on to Prerna instantly, trying to pick the okra from her fingers. 'Ma'am, how many times have I told you not to pick and choose your okra so much? You take away all the good ones and leave behind the rotten ones.'

Prerna was taken aback. 'What do you expect? I run a restaurant! I can't serve my customers rotten okra.'

'Ma'am, I understand, but okra costs two dollars for one pound . . . In bulk!' he said, trying to work the individual okras back into the pile.

'How can you survive on such tasteless and bad-looking vegetables, Adarsh?' retaliated Prerna at once.

Adarsh glanced over his shoulder to look at his older brother, who nodded his approval for what came out of the younger twin's mouth next. 'You don't need to shop here then, ma'am.'

'Adarsh, there aren't any other options nearby! And you and Aadesh take full advantage of this fact. If you get fresher okra, of course, I wouldn't complain about the price. Anyway, please pack five pounds for me.'

Adarsh grabbed a brown bag from behind the counter and began to pack her okra for the day. Meanwhile, Prerna reached over and picked up a small fistful of curry leaves from an adjacent pile and brought them under her nose, taking in their fragrance. She immediately pulled a face. 'Ew! These kadi patta leaves aren't fresh either. These must be American.'

Aadesh placed his hands on his hips and glared at her. 'Ma'am, we have what we have. Take it or leave it.'

'Oh well, I have no choice,' Prerna sighed. 'Curry leaves from India always smell good . . .'

'Well, why don't you get them from India then?'

'You know that's not practical when you are running a small restaurant,' Prerna explained. 'Let's stop the chit-chat here. Give me eight ounces of curry leaves and four fresh mangoes. All I see in the bins are the old, shrivelled stock. I know you have to make a living, but I can't use the old ones. Can't you come up with some fresh produce for me? You must have some around here somewhere. Please?'

Adarsh scurried to the back of the store and came back with some fresher mangoes, as well as another load of fresher okra.

'I knew you had fresher products hidden away somewhere!'

'Delivery just came in,' he offered lamely.

At the cash register, Prerna spied the saffron in its small glass vials. 'Oh my lord! Twenty-four dollars for these tiny containers?'

'Not twenty-four, ma'am, twenty-four ninety-nine.'

'Patel Market sells the same amount for eighteen!'

'Well—'

'You're right, I should get my saffron from them too.'

'Khanna and Sons offer saffron of a much higher quality. And our saffron does come from India, see for yourself!' Aadesh opened one of the vials and handed her a few strands of saffron. She gingerly felt its texture, checked its colour, and placed a few strands under her nose. A sweet and musky smell wafted up to her.

'That's more like it! Okay, give me five vials of your "highest-quality" saffron, sir. I'm making a saffron kheer at the restaurant today.' Prerna smiled, suddenly pleased with the day's purchases.

Chapter 2

On the Ferry, On the Subway

Prerna rushed to the St George Ferry Terminal—her okra, curry leaves and mangoes nearly spilling out of her bags. With her free hand, she clutched her handbag—her only stylish accessory, a knock-off Coach handbag from Reema. Fashion didn't matter to Prerna. All that mattered was food.

She pushed through the mass of human bodies—dour businessmen in grey overcoats, excitable tourists in their colourful shirts and shorts, rough-handed and sleepy-eyed workers who looked as if they could do with more sleep, preppy college students, pushing their bikes or scooters to the ferry, and the occasional eccentric who defied category. Like a colourful school of fish, the crowd squeezed in from the streets and parking lots surrounding the terminal. Once inside, they all swam through the massive glass gates leading to the ferry gangplank, on to the Staten Island Ferry.

Prerna preferred to ride at the front and would go to pains to arrive early enough to ensure she got a place to sit aboard one of the deep, burnt-orange vessels—the colour of mace—which reminded her of the vegetables she seared in her tandoor. She could almost smell the rust of the ferry.

She never learned the name of each boat, but she preferred the older models, which featured what she thought were mid-century bathroom fixtures of wood and brass. Best of all was the fact that her picturesque twenty-minute commute, though sometimes packed and frantic, was free—and Prerna loved a bargain!

Clutching her bags of fresh Indian herbs and spices, her mangoes and okra, Prerna pushed through the crowd towards the bow and ascended the stairs to secure her favourite spot for the twenty-minute water journey—the deeply-worn, shellacked benches of the upper deck, whose visible layers of exposed paint and scratches revealed much history. This position gave her a marvellous view of the Statue of Liberty to her left and a fine view of the immensity called Manhattan.

The waters were choppy that day, with the rising sun rapidly dispelling the last vestiges of the fog. Seagulls and security helicopters appeared to give chase to the lurching ferry, and soon their only companions were the occasional military ships, oil tankers, barges, luxury speedboats and other boats.

It was a beautiful sight that Prerna would never miss taking in—the Statue of Liberty, thrusting her torch in the air from a distance. To her, it didn't matter what others thought of the statue, what mattered most to her was that Lady Liberty was just that—a woman offering freedom. Prerna was content to view her from a distance, for no money whatsoever. She held her thumb up to measure the statue's height from where she stood, only as big as a piece of okra.

She then peeled her eyes from the view of Lady Liberty and the ocean life and saw she was sitting amidst a varied group of people. A blonde sat to her right, pampering a Havanese puppy with pink ribbons in its hair. The woman vaguely, very vaguely, resembled Brigitte Bardot—her bleached hair and smear of pink lipstick gave the superficial impression that she was thirty rather than pushing seventy. If she weren't on the ferry, she would have easily been hanging backstage with Mick Jagger, or even Pandit Ravi Shankar.

On Prerna's left sat a mild-looking college kid, with a trimmed 'millennial' beard, his oxford shirt buttoned all the way to the top. He was probably a graduate student at Pace University. Prerna knew the type—students from Pace often came to her restaurant for lunch takeout. The kid was absorbed in listening to whatever was playing on his iPod, but smiled at Prerna when she shifted her fragrant bag of curry leaves from under the curious nose of the Havanese next to the kid's legs to make room for others to sit. A woman carrying a baby approached. Prerna and the baby made gleeful eye contact. The child waved and Prerna waved back. She had a way with kids. As the mother settled down into the empty space, the child, drawn by Prerna's kind eyes, reached out to her. Prerna smiled.

As the ferry inched closer to the Manhattan skyline, Prerna closed her eyes, lowered her nose into her bag, and smelled the fresh mangoes she had bought. Underneath the sweet scent of mangoes, she could also smell the acidity of lemon—even though she hadn't bought any that day. She was instantly transported back to their home in Delhi, where Karanjit sat at the dining table, making her smell different vegetables and fruit, so she would recognize their scents. For a moment, it felt as if he was right next to her, smelling the fruits alongside her on the ferry. He smiled at her, but instead of hearing the honk of his old Maruti's horn, the deep, bone-shaking bass of the foghorn sounded. Prerna was startled out of her reverie, and even though all she wanted to do was close her eyes and linger on the memory of her father, she busied herself gathering her bags. It was time to get to work.

'I live and work on the islands,' Prerna, who had grown up in the interiors of India, far away from any oceans or seas, would sometimes repeat to herself.

In the bustle of Manhattan, she could easily forget her roots—especially when she looked up and saw the glistening buildings standing tall beside the worn historic buildings, the latter's exposed brick rubbing against the sleek steel and bright glass of the former, as if Manhattan wore a pair of immense mirrored sunglasses. But the inevitable smudges on these glasses could be seen as you neared them.

Prerna had reached Lower Manhattan, the place in which she had spent over two decades, running her own restaurant.

The ferry, with another deep bellow of its horn, thudded to a stop as Prerna stood up, embracing her collection of bags. She waved and smiled at the baby, who was delighted to wave and smile back, before making her way across the upper deck and down the crowded stairs to wait for the ferryman to release the rope that signalled it was safe for them to disembark.

Soon, she was out of the ferry station and on her way to her favourite place on Earth, her small Indian restaurant in Lower Manhattan, The Curry Bowl.

Prerna felt her usual urgency to get to work, but on this day, she did not immediately step into the subway entrance. Instead, she increased her pace and headed towards Broadway, through a park planted with a grove of plane trees—trees she had never taken the time to admire. Their trunks looked almost like the trunks of the huge elephants she might have recognized from her home country, or like pythons that had suddenly frozen on their way to heaven. Prerna left the park and found herself near the world-famous sculpture, the Charging Bull. It never failed to puzzle Prerna that this was a culture that revered a cow enough to cast it in bronze but still happily devoured its flesh. But she also understood that the bull represented several things to other people—the bullishness of desire, greed, hope and persistence. She watched as a group of tourists took pictures of the bull, one of them even climbing atop it. She knew Karanjit would have loved the bull—he never failed to honk at them from his trusty Maruti, laughing joyously as they grudgingly made way for him. (Later, another sculpture would be erected, that of a little girl with a ponytail and skirt, hands on her hips, defiantly staring the bull down. Prerna's bet was on the girl.)

She had another monument to pass before she reached work—a museum dedicated to the natives of the country. Prerna knew the chequered history of the country she had made home. And she knew it was made that much harder for a woman immigrant. She found the museum fascinating, having visited it a couple of times. The original peoples of the land of liberty and their various tribes somehow reminded her of India. Where she fit into this complicated scheme as a brown Indian woman, she didn't know. But she never let it bother her, or stop her from surviving or doing what she did best—preparing delicious food to feed others, no matter who they were or from where they had come.

Staring at the entrance of the museum, Prerna was suddenly overcome by an urgency to get to her restaurant as soon as possible. She cut back to her usual path and, as she had done every day for over two decades, subjected herself to the grime and odour of the subway—descending into the Line 1 Train to sit amidst another tightly packed transport with her purse and bags of groceries that took her from South Ferry to Cortland.

Somewhere in between, as the subway ground to a stop, and as everyone groaned or fidgeted, Prerna's wrist pulsed with pain once again. As she tried to massage her wrist with her thumb, she thought about the boy.

The boy with the smoothest brown skin and eyes that danced and sparkled like hers. He was already as handsome as her father, and just as trustworthy, just as restless, just as rakish, even when he was barely awake.

'Maji! When I grow up, I am going to be a very rich man,' Karan said—his voice so close, she was sure he was on the train next to her. Prerna sighed and smiled.

'So rich you will forget your old mother?' she asked.

'So rich that I'll never forget you. You're not old, Maji, you are like my sister!'

'Karan! I only wish I was that young.'

'Ahhh, Maj, why be so cheesy all the time?'

'Time for you to sleep now, future rich man,' Prerna said, tucking Karan into his small bed, covering him up to his chin. It was the same blanket she had swaddled him in as a baby—with its motifs of peacocks, herons and kingfishers, flying, strutting and diving into reedy pools and fresh springs.

'What about my pillows?'

'You have a pillow already; look behind your head!'

'I can't sleep without my pillows.'

'How many do you need, picky boy?'

Karan held up three fingers.

'Only three?'

He changed it to four fingers.

'Okay, your other pillows are in the laundry, but let me see what I can do.'

Prerna vanished into the hallway and returned with three more brightly patterned pillows. He was a loving and polite child but had his quirks and Prerna loved him all the more for it.

She arranged the pillows around him, as he pulled off the one from under his head and placed it next to him.

'I like to lie flat,' he explained.

'Okay, satisfied? Will you finally be able to sleep now?'

Karan nestled into his pillows. 'Maji, when I am an old, rich guy, I will open a big Indian restaurant for you in New York.'

'Where will you get the money from?'

'I told you, I'm going to be rich. I am going to open your restaurant, so Chacha David won't ever insult you again!'

'Chacha David's insults are like peacock feathers—they just float off from over me.'

'You'll be the queen, ordering everyone else around. And then your hand won't hurt any more.'

Prerna was transported back to the present, as the pain in her wrist flared again.

'And who will do the work of making the most delicious Indian food in Manhattan that no one knows about?' she teased Karan, as he snuggled deeper into his pillows.

'Not you, the queen can't work.'

'The queen doesn't trust just anyone to make her recipes . . .'

'We will hire the best chef assistants for you, Maji, and one day, you will become the best, most famous Indian chef in New York. Promise!'

Prerna laughed and stared into her son's eyes. 'Karan, all I want to do is to take you someday to the Golden Temple in Amritsar, where my father learnt how to appreciate food and what it means to people. Deal?' Karan didn't blink. Finally, he yawned.

'Now, my boy is tired.' Prerna stroked her son's hair and caressed his cheek. 'All your crazy ideas have exhausted you. Go to sleep.' She stood up to leave when suddenly her boy called her back.

'Maj?'

'Yes.'

'Come here and close your eyes.'

'You know I don't like surprises!'

But Prerna did as she was told. Sitting back on the bed, she closed her eyes. She felt a soft, cool and soothing mist on her cheeks. She opened her eyes. Karan held a small white portable mister—a spray gun with a tiny fan attached—in his hand.

'It's raining,' Karan laughed, as he set the mister down.

'Silly boy!' smiled Prerna, wiping the mist off her cheek.

'Silly boy says goodnight!' said Karan.

Prerna turned Karan's lamp off. 'Good night, please don't be late for school tomorrow.'

Karan groaned. 'Can I stay home tomorrow?'

'Absolutely not. I don't want you to turn into a delinquent.'

'What's a del . . .?'

'A bad kid.'

'I'm not the bad kid.' Karan seemed to startle himself awake. 'The other kids at school are the bad ones. Deli—whatever the word was. Calling me names I don't want to repeat, teasing me about being Indian or darker than them or even smarter than them!'

'Karan, shhhh . . .' Prerna placed her finger on his lips and stroked his cheek, hoping to calm him down. 'Don't worry. They will grow out of it. That's natural with boys your age. You want me to call the principal of your school?'

'That will probably make it worse. They'll call me a snitch. Maj, this is serious. I don't think you understand!'

'I do understand. I experienced some of this when I was your age. Life will take care of itself. Try to be strong and ignore those boys. Now go to sleep, Mommy needs her rest. She also has to wake up early.' The last thing Prerna remembered of that night was turning off the light next to Karan's bed.

Prerna floated back to the present to see the subway moving again. Soon, she was on her way out of the WTC/Cortland station—which once lay in the belly of the World Trade Centre—with the throngs of commuters rushing to work.

Chapter 3

A Good Morning at The Curry Bowl

The pain subsided in Prerna's wrist, along with the memory of her son. Rushing now, she took a sharp turn on to Fulton and reached the dented steel gate that covered the front of a hole-in-the-wall Indian restaurant: The Curry Bowl. Its only external pretence was a lofted white plastic sign with red-and-blue lettering that lit up at night. Prerna searched her handbag for her keys and scanned the white official certificate with a large blue 'A' on it, The Curry Bowl's top NYC health department rating, plus copies of a few positive Yelp reviews. There were also a few articles—some of them featuring Prerna herself, although she was a bit camera-shy—carefully cut from newspapers.

Prerna set her collection of bags down and unlocked the metal gate, flinging it open with all her might. She stepped in to open the front door of her restaurant, which stood in the middle of an off-white entrance, hidden behind the steel roll-up, that vaguely resembled the entrance of the Golden Temple.

Once she managed to unlock the door, Prerna lifted her bags and entered The Curry Bowl's deep-red wallpapered lobby, which was decorated with posters of the Golden Temple and the Taj Mahal, a photo of Karanjit, a little box of cinders and sand for candles and incense sticks, a brass bowl filled with cumin seeds, and a Ganesha idol occupying a small mandir.

The crimson lobby gave way to the lime-green and deep turmeric-yellow walls of The Curry Bowl's dining area, adorned with another, grander depiction of the Golden Temple in Amritsar, below which was written a prayer.

The Curry Bowl's dining room was a simple but efficient and friendly affair of tables and chairs, and a glass-covered steel buffet, which later would be filled with steaming, enticing food, beckoning customers to take some more. Prerna didn't love describing her selections as coming from a 'buffet'—for to her, the word carried no dignity. It always gave her some vague, cringeworthy visions of a suburban Western town she had once driven into, where the food from the buffet she had visited, some truck stop, was heavy, tasteless and unhealthy—a far cry from what she preferred to prepare and serve.

She entered the kitchen and turned the fluorescent lights on. The small, cluttered space was painted in hues of green and orange, and featured two counters with two cutting boards, a single frying station and a walk-in cooler, but it was dominated by a big-bellied Buddha of a tandoor with a big welcoming mouth. Prerna loved watching it fire up and glow every time she opened The Curry Bowl, as though it was breathing a fire that would keep everyone warm.

She took her bangles off her wrists, drew an apron over her sari and put a hairnet on, before unloading and organizing her groceries. Then she turned on the main gas and sparked all of her blue fires to life. These were the daily rituals for Prerna, for so many years, and she preferred to do them alone.

She clasped her hands together, touched them to her forehead, and then let her eyes rest in the air, contemplating what she would offer on The Curry Bowl's last menu and last morning buffet.

It was then that Iqbal, her diminutive Bangladeshi kitchen assistant, appeared, rushing in from the main entrance. 'Sorry I'm a few minutes late, ma'am!'

'Late? You're not late, Iqbal, I am always early. Let's get to work.'

Iqbal leapt into action and began the day's prep, without missing a slice or skewer, knives and flames flashing all around Prerna, with Iqbal performing a culinary carousel—cutting onions, chopping garlic, grating ginger, whisking yogurt, grinding fresh spices with a mortar and pestle, adding pinches of the fresh saffron, then adding oil to the hot pans to fry mustard seeds and curry leaves, squeezing the juice from lemons, rolling the dough for and shaping samosas after filling them, heating milk, grinding the spices to fill the spice containers, seasoning the fish—red snapper today—and then searing it, deseeding and chopping red and green chillies, cutting potatoes and boiling them, peeling, slicing, then pureeing fresh mango, making missi roti dough and packing it in plastic to let it rest, roasting eggplant, scoring the tomatoes, skewering chicken pieces and grating a coconut. As Prerna's main assistant chef, Iqbal was a wonder to behold and a testament to her skill as a cook and a teacher.

The rising aromas of Indian cuisine, which Prerna's nose never tired of, reminded her of Karanjit's near-constant cooking pontifications, which he always gave titles to, like 'Power of Spices', 'Value of Salt', 'The Sacred Fire,' or 'Menu of the Day'.

Finally, lighting the clay belly of the tandoor Buddha, with an electric snap and a whoosh of flame, signalled The Curry Bowl was open for business on time—even though it was the venerable restaurant's last day.

Soon, the first order of the day rang out on The Curry Bowl's well-worn wall phone. Prerna picked it up before the second ring. 'The Curry Bowl. Good morning. How can I help you?' she asked, her eyes dancing with anticipation.

'What's the lunch special today?' asked the first caller.

'Please hold on a minute, sir,' said Prerna, then covered the mouthpiece with her hand, which was still moist from helping Iqbal prepare the day's food. 'Iqbal, remove five limes from that bag and finely chop ten tomatoes.'

'Yes, ma'am,' said Iqbal, getting down to business at the kitchen cutting board.

Prerna placed the phone between her shoulder and the side of her chin, so she could turn off the gas of the burner on which she had been caramelizing onions and then turn off the blender in which she had been pureeing spinach. She turned back to the call. 'Sir?'

'Yes, I'm still here. What's the special today?'

'We are doing a lunch box of fish moilee, snapper with a special coconut curry from Kerala. Only $7.95. You will love it.'

'Yum! I always love The Curry Bowl's food. I'll come in later for takeout.'

'See you then.' Prerna massaged her right wrist as she spoke, wincing.

'Your wrist still hurts, ma'am?' asked Iqbal, having already carried out Prerna's instructions.

'It's fine.'

That was when Prerna's other assistant, Dilip, appeared, already dapper and ready for work in his white apron and hat. Dilip was older, balding and more grizzled than Iqbal. He was in his mid-fifties, a slightly portly man with a faded red bindi always gracing his brow, more wizened than his fairer-skinned and younger counterpart, who always seemed to kneel on his prayer rug between meals and service, sometimes to Dilip's consternation, especially during the lunch rush. Despite their religious differences and a few divergent habits, Prerna's main cooks manned her kitchen like brothers, out of love and respect for her food.

The two community-college-culinary-school-educated cooks she had saved from their institution in Queens might not have been the chefs in Karan's dream restaurant, but they were reliable and talented enough to meet her standards. And they were always on time, unlike some of Prerna's other staff.

'Morning, *Didi*, you haven't soaked the rice yet?' asked Dilip, rolling up his sleeves, revealing thick forearms.

'I'm ahead of you, Dilip; I already cooked it,' Prerna said. 'The rice is in the oven. Please check the morning catering order we received yesterday and start the prep.'

'On it!'

The phone rang again and Prerna picked it up, squeezing it between her ear and shoulder so she could keep working. 'Sir, the lunch box special always comes with rice. With rice, the fish moilee would be $7.95, with naan or roti, it is a dollar extra,' she explained. 'The chicken tikka or vegetable korma box is $6.95 with rice, and one dollar extra with naan.'

'Delicious. What a deal!' said the caller.

'Well, we wanted to offer something special on our last day.'

'Your last day?'

Prerna hesitated before answering. 'Yes. Unfortunately, we have lease issues.'

'Too bad. You'll be missed. What are your hours today?'

'We usually open at 11.30 a.m. and close at 7.30 p.m. But given the circumstances, we are only offering the lunch service today.'

Dilip leaned in as Prerna spoke. 'Didi,' he whispered, 'you should have had me make the naan dough; why did you do it? Now your wrist will hurt all day.'

Prerna took down the order and hung up.

'Don't worry about my wrist, Dilip,' she said. 'Is Nazim here yet? And where's Parminder?'

'Just got here, ma'am,' said Nazim, a fatherly man of roughly Prerna's age, who had left his family behind in Allahabad so he could give them a better life with the dollars he might earn in America.

'Nazim, please make ten glasses of mango lassi,' said Prerna. 'And don't forget the raita!'

'Right away, Prerna.' Nazim was the only member of her staff who called her by her first name—he often behaved like her older brother, rather than the maître d', the assistant floor manager and backup prep cook that he was.

Dilip chimed in from his place at a table. 'Your darling Ruchi hasn't shown up yet?'

'Ruchi already called. She'll be late. Some final project submission today for her journalism class,' said Prerna. 'She probably didn't even sleep.'

'Didi, why do you hire these young students?' asked Dilip, organizing the catering order, then frantically listing the day's menu under his breath before jumping to the first takeaway orders. 'These students are really good for nothing.'

'Hush, Dilip!'

Nazim blended the mangoes into lassi, then vigorously went at grinding the handful of roasted cumin seeds he had grabbed from their container. He slipped out a large cucumber so he could grate it into the blender along with the ground seeds. After a whirr of blender noise, he displayed the chopped and blended food items, a large, cool and savoury whirlpool of raita, for Dilip's approval. 'Lassis done. Dilip, is this raita enough?'

Dilip was too busy brooding over the oncoming orders and sipping the chai Prerna had prepared for him. So Prerna assessed the quantity Nazim had prepared even before he could respond. 'Enough raita already, Nazim! Only a few customers like cucumber with cumin.'

'Sorry ma'am,' said Nazim. 'I won't make any more. I'll get started on the yogurt curry.'

'Perfect.'

The phone kept ringing, and between orders, Prerna spooned all the food she and her team had prepared so far into the sheet pans that would be fitted into the steam tables for the buffet. The aromas were already filling the space and drifting out of the entrance on to Fulton Street. *Guerilla marketing!* Prerna thought to herself. No one in the vicinity could resist inquiring about the aromas once they started wafting down the street. That was how The Curry Bowl had first made its mark.

'Okay, guys, let's ramp it up. I've already made the dough balls for naan and have prepared five missi rotis from the remaining cornmeal in the bins. Oh, Iqbal, when Parminder finally arrives, can you ask him to prepare the potato filling for the samosas?' asked Prerna.

'Absolutely, ma'am,' said Iqbal. 'I love bossing that latecomer around. Serves him right.'

Prerna smiled but said, 'No conflict on our last day.'

'I know . . . just wishful thinking,' said Iqbal.

Finally, Parminder entered through the back door and appeared in the kitchen in his typical lackadaisical and dishevelled fashion, his shirt untucked and his face wearing the same dissatisfied frown and disrespectful glare he had on every day.

'Look who's here!' said Iqbal, smirking. 'Prerna needs you to start on the samosa filling asap. Since you're late again . . .'

'Back off!' snapped Parminder, though he immediately grabbed handfuls of potatoes, garlic and chives, and slammed them on the prep table.

'You haven't shaved again today, Parminder,' Prerna said.

Dilip exploded in his characteristic laugh that sounded like a cat hissing. 'For that, he would have to miss work for an entire day!' Dilip said. 'Look how thick his beard becomes even after one day.'

All eyes went to Parminder's beard, which was truly a bramble.

'Why should I shave every day? It's not like this is a Michelin-starred restaurant,' mumbled Parminder.

Every other staff member fell silent, except Prerna, who only smiled. She was too proud, and at The Curry Bowl, she was in her element, too confident to seethe. Instead, she changed the subject. 'Parminder, please ensure that none of the naans are undercooked. We had our first three complaints yesterday. Undercooked naan tastes like adhesive.'

'Prerna, it's the last day of the restaurant. What does it matter now?' asked Parminder. 'The gate will be locked and we will all be out of work. Buh-bye.'

'It matters to me, Parminder. Don't be so callous. We still have to take care of our customers until then.'

Parminder slammed more potatoes on to the counter.

'Didi, I will get the orders ready; you get the restaurant ready,' said Nazim.

'Okay.'

'The fish moilee has turned out very tasty today!' said Dilip from the kitchen.

'It's what we are known for,' said Prerna, placing the kheer she had planned for the day into a large tub. The sweet Indian dessert of reduced milk, rice, sugar and saffron was usually offered to god as prasad.

The phone would not stop ringing, even before the official lunch service began. Word was spreading.

'The Curry Bowl, good morning,' said Prerna. 'How can I help you?'

'Hi! I'd like to order the chicken tikka lunch box with rice and naan. For pickup.'

'Okay, $7.95.' Prerna covered the mouthpiece with her good hand. 'Dilip, prepare the gravy for the chicken tikka.'

Dilip raced into the prep area. 'Yes, Didi. Right away.'

'Sir, it will be ready in thirty minutes.'

The phone rang once again, almost immediately, a delivery order for the next day. 'No, ma'am, I'm sorry, we can't deliver tomorrow,' explained Prerna. 'Today is our last day. The Curry Bowl is closing.'

'My lord, no! Well, I will have to come in and order later today then!' said the woman at the other end.

'Will be great to have you,' said Prerna. 'Nazim!' she hissed. 'Switch on the steam tables; we are behind schedule.'

'But it's our last day!' Nazim said.

'First or last day, it doesn't matter. The Curry Bowl always opens on time. That's what set us apart.'

'Absolutely, Didi,' said Nazim. 'But that's not what sets us apart—it's your excellent recipes.'

Prerna gave him a quick smile and returned to the call. 'Yes, ma'am, after more than twenty years.'

She suddenly felt faint, as tears pricked at her eyes. For two decades, she had given the restaurant her everything. And now she would have to close it. The phone nearly slipped out of her hands, but she steadied herself. Prerna straightened her sari beneath her chef's smock and fixed the phone back under her chin. 'Yes, ma'am. Thank you. I have mixed feelings. It's hard running a restaurant in New York, especially if you are a woman from India. But we had a good run. Continued blessings to you,' Prerna concluded before hanging up.

She regained her composure and carried the large bowl of kheer to the refrigerator, where she placed it as though it were an offering next to the cups of lassis. She spooned out a small bowl and walked into the lobby. She stood before the Ganesha shrine and gazed at the photo of Karanjit on the wall. Nazim came out from the back to turn up the steam table, while Iqbal frantically cleaned the chairs and tables with a cloth, then placed napkins in their holders and a pitcher of water on each table for The Curry Bowl's last lunch.

Chapter 4

A Gift for Nazim

Prerna lingered near the altar, preparing to do her morning prayers under the picture of her father. She was lighting a special oil lamp and a stick of *nag champa* incense to purify the entrance for the customers who were sure to arrive. Nazim stopped cleaning the steel glasses and joined Prerna in the lobby. He held a small picture in his hand—a pretty young woman in a sari, his beloved daughter, smiled out of the photo. Next to her stood a good-looking young man in a sherwani. Judging by the shine in their eyes, the young couple were absolutely smitten with each other, tightly holding hands.

Prerna concluded her prayers and bowed to her father's image above. When she saw the picture Nazim held out for her, Prerna was stunned. 'Nazim!' Prerna gasped, shaking her head. 'What you left behind to end up working with me . . . I'll never take for granted.'

Nazim closed his eyes as he nodded. 'Yes. But it's always been my pleasure.'

'Our Ruksana is looking so beautiful.' Prerna's eyes slid from the engagement picture and looked straight into Nazim's, who was crying.

'When did she get engaged?'

'Last week, Prerna,' said Nazim. 'Her husband-to-be is a doctor from an educated family. She has grown up so fast, and now I am relieved she has some hope and opportunity in her life.'

'Oh Nazim, that is absolutely beautiful! Both your daughter and your sentiments.'

'Yes. Ruksana was as tiny as a Chinese doll and as delicate as a lotus when I had left India to come here.'

'Nazim! Don't stop me this time, promise?'

'Don't stop you from what?'

'Wait here for me,' Prerna said, before bolting out of the lobby, crossing the dining area into the kitchen, where she vanished into the back office. She appeared in the lobby again, digging around for something in the depths of her knockoff Coach. 'Seeing the hope, the blessing of your daughter all grown up and about to be married has lifted my spirits. If you can't tell, I've been feeling really low since the morning. Almost in denial of the place closing.'

'And why wouldn't you be? You are not only closing a restaurant; you are closing a local legacy. That is not a small thing,' said Nazim.

'Perhaps,' said Prerna, pulling out four crisp fifty-dollar bills she had tightly rolled up and hidden in her purse.

The bright green of the bills immediately made Nazim turn away. 'Prerna, no! I can't accept this. Our friendship means a lot more than money. Our friendship is not gold, it's platinum.'

'Nazim, don't be ridiculous. Money is what makes the world go round. It's just one of life's necessities. I insist,' Prerna said, pointing the rolled-up bills at Nazim. 'Your daughter, and especially her fiancée, are both lucky to have found each other. And you and your wife, oh, heaven to goddess Lakshmi, what a beautiful daughter!'

Nazim cut Prerna off. 'I only wish Ruksana's mother was here to witness her engagement. She . . . My wife died right after my daughter was born, and I've been stuck here for twenty years. Thankfully, being "stuck" with the likes of you and The Curry Bowl has been like being stuck in honey.'

'Sorry about your wife. You never told me . . .'

'I try not to think about it. Her grandmother has been taking care of her all along. I do what I can, but that can be hard in a place like New York.'

'Understandable. Nazim, I want to support you in supporting your daughter and your new son-in-law, at least until you can afford to visit them in person after you get your green card. Now please accept the money,' she said.

Nazim glanced around, blushing at Prerna's generous gift. Prerna understood the power of money—something she had learnt the hard way.

'Nazim, don't be ridiculous. It's not that much money, but it will go far back home. Please? For me?'

'Okay,' said Nazim, holding up his palm. 'But please, just add this generous contribution to my final salary? Then I can send it along with the money I am wiring my daughter for her wedding expenses.'

'Deal!' Prerna said, shuffling and twisting the bills back into a roll before tucking them back in her purse.

Back in the dining area, Iqbal sprang out of the kitchen with a steel tray of dal and another tray filled with alabaster teacups.

'I better get back to work. Thank you again,' said Nazim.

'One more thing,' said Prerna.

'Yes?'

'I somehow feel the new lawyer you've hired will be the one to resolve your green card issue.'

'I hope so,' Nazim said, looking at his feet. 'I really hope so!'

Still in the lobby, Prerna cast one more glance at her father, sent up another prayer, this time for the newly engaged couple, and then stepped back into the dining room, grabbing pitchers in each hand to fill with water at the kitchen counter spigot. As she filled the pitchers, she took slow sips of her chai and finished it standing there.

Chapter 5

Last Lunch at The Curry Bowl

Prerna placed a tray of saag at the buffet table and hurried back through the kitchen into The Curry Bowl's cramped restroom. She turned on the tap, balanced the hot and cold to her liking, and placed her hands in the small steel sink. She squirted soap on her palms and furiously scrubbed her hands under the running water, before splashing her face again and again. Then she stopped, feeling blood course through her veins up to her temples, giving her a slight headache.

She looked into the mirror—she saw not herself, but a young, dark-skinned girl. Devi, her *sautelee dadi* (step-grandmother) of lighter complexion, stepped forward in the mirror, glowering at her. 'I'm trying,' the little girl sobbed, as she scrubbed her hands until they chafed and bled. 'I'm trying to make them lighter!' What Prerna didn't know then was that soap and scrubbing could not change the colour of one's skin.

The words, Devi's words, still made Prerna shudder even after so many decades. No words, no excuse could stop the glaring wrath of the aged 'goddess', which is what her name 'Devi' means. As the mean old woman shouted over her shoulder at her son, Karanjit stood concerned but silent in their kitchen. 'Keep scrubbing, Prerna, it will never help. I don't care how talented she is, Karanjit ji! I will never eat anything made by your orphan's black hands.'

The image, that voice, hadn't haunted Prerna for years. So why had it returned to her today—the day her small realm was shutting shop? Prerna stepped back and stared at herself: the child had grown, but her face, her cherubic face, had stayed almost the same; her eyes still sparkled with laughter and mischief, and her matted dark hair had given way to luxurious tresses. Prerna sighed, splashed water on her face again, then drew a calming breath and composed herself. She tore a paper towel from the roll spooled above the toilet, wiped down the mirror and sink, and then stepped out of the restroom as if nothing had happened, back into the world of The Curry Bowl.

'Iqbal!' she called out as she made her way to the counter.

Iqbal came running from the kitchen. 'Always keep an extra roll of paper towels on the washbasin counter,' she instructed.

'Certainly, ma'am,' Iqbal said, though his eyes betrayed his confusion.

'I know, I know. We close in ten hours, but our last day should be as great as our first!'

'Yes, I understand, ma'am,' Iqbal said, though that wasn't what he was thrown by—it was the haunted expression in Prerna's eyes.

The phone on the front desk rang again, but when Prerna went to answer it, Dilip had already beaten her to it. He had picked up the kitchen phone. 'The Curry Bowl, how can I help you?' asked Dilip.

Prerna watched as Dilip took down the order and handed it over to Iqbal.

'Right, let's get a move on. Service starts in twenty minutes,' she instructed.

Just as Prerna crossed over to the little temple to complete her prayers, the door flew open with a bang and Ruchi rushed in, juggling a backpack, purse and a sheaf of papers.

'Here comes the little princess,' said Dilip, glaring at Ruchi. 'Late again, but not too late to complete the tickets from the last few pickup orders.'

Ruchi picked up the ringing phone but forgot to say anything as her papers crashed down to the floor. She whispered a hurried 'sorry' to Prerna, begging for forgiveness, as she finally attended to the call.

Prerna recited her final prayers, the Ganpati mantra, praising Ganesha.

Vakratunda mahakaaya
Suryakoti samaprabha
Nirvighnam kuru me deva
Sarvakaaryesu sarvadaa
O Lord with the twisted trunk
with the effulgence (brilliance) of a billion suns
always remove all obstacles
in all my undertakings.

After Prerna finished her final prayers, she turned to find Ruchi organizing herself for work by the counter. She gave Ruchi a light, playful smack on her back for being late, then let her return to the first set of walk-in guests—usually, the lone wolf Wall Street traders or bike messengers, who were more about business than chit-chat. 'The lunch special today is a fish moilee lunch box with either rice for $7.95, or with roti or naan plus rice, for $8.95,' she intoned.

'I'll take it with naan; your naan is so good here, not as it is at Palace of Saffron—like white glue over on Wall Street.'

'Perfect, you will enjoy it then,' Ruchi said, grinning.

'Is it true it's your last day?'

Ruchi hesitated and looked over at Prerna. Prerna shrugged in the affirmative.

'Sadly, yes. It's been a good run.'

'Aww, darn! There's no place as good as this anywhere nearby.'

'It's true. Sir, please have a seat until your order is ready.'

'Sure.'

Ruchi ran the ticket back to Nazim, who was fighting for elbow room in The Curry Bowl's small kitchen, then ran back out to take more orders.

'Are your journalism submissions done?' asked Prerna when there was a lull in activity.

'Getting there.' Ruchi took a small bottle of liquid out of her jacket.

'What's that?'

'Artificial tears,' said Ruchi.

Prerna laughed, 'For what?'

'You are going to need them today!'

Prerna laughed again. 'Beti, as you know, my tears dried up years ago. I don't go in for this crying business.'

'Yes, that's why I brought the tears!'

'You didn't have to. The last day is just like the first day.'

'Ma'am! Everyone's favourite Indian restaurant is closing. Didn't you know?' asked Ruchi in mock horror.

'Enough, beta!'

Ruchi's eyes welled up as her voice suddenly cracked. 'It's a sad day, ma'am. We are like family here at The Curry Bowl.'

Prerna soothed her with a hug. 'Beta, I appreciate your sentiments but, what do the French say?'

'C'est la vie?'

'Yes. C'est la vie. Say la vie. Not so hard to say,' Prerna said. 'Tears aren't necessary for life to go on . . .' Prerna trailed off as she spotted the blank blackboard behind Ruchi. 'We forgot to put that outside,' she gasped, as she grabbed sticks of green and pink chalk to write the specials on it and placed it outside.

The phone rang again and Ruchi composed herself before answering it. 'The Curry Bowl, how can I help you?'

Out on the street, Prerna saw an impatient line of people, T-shirts and jeans interspersed between the white collars and dress shoes, stretched from The Curry Bowl's entrance out along Fulton. The Wall Street brokers stood shoulder to shoulder with Pace University students and working-class labourers who had no time to linger and eat, and so they loved The Curry Bowl's delicious, grab-and-go lunches.

Iqbal ran out with a stack of disposable plastic boxes, and small and large rubber tubs filled with fragrant dishes for takeout, shouting out orders.

Jim Golden, a prominent Wall Street broker, stepped forward to collect his order.

'Is it true this is The Curry Bowl's last day?'

'Sadly, yes,' said Iqbal. 'Sir, did you order the fish moilee special?'

'Yes, I did.'

Iqbal handed him his food.

'Gonna miss this place, especially the fish moilee. Best food around, and cheap.'

Iqbal ran another takeout order to a woman covered head to toe in tie-and-dyed yoga wear, wearing a Ganesh mandala, the elephant deity's trunk and tusks done up in gold.

'Miss!' Iqbal said to her. 'What did you order again?'

'Namaste. Hmm . . . I ordered the squash and okra.'

Iqbal juggled a few of the containers in his hands and produced the woman's order.

'Namaste!' she said, beaming. 'We are all going to miss this place. It's so warm, and, uh, human compared to other Indian restaurants. Eating the food here is like meditation.'

'Thank you. I will pass on your sentiments to the owner.'

'Hey! Where's my order?' A golden-turbaned Sikh taxi driver with a flourishing grey moustache and beard demanded. 'I just got off my shift; I want to make it home to my wife and family in Queens before the afternoon rush hour.'

'Sir, what did you order?' asked Iqbal.

'Bhindi masala and palak paneer with raita,' said the man, pulling out a small wad of cash.

'Right away,' said Iqbal.

After delivering the man's order into his hungry hands, Iqbal raced back inside The Curry Bowl to get more. 'Everybody is talking about our closing. I think we might get flooded with orders,' he said to everyone.

'That's fine, and we will meet the flood if that happens,' Prerna said with a satisfied smile, truly in her element. She turned back to her impatient customer, a boyish-looking man with tassels sprouting from his dress shoes, riveted to his Hermès watch. 'I'm in a rush,' he explained. 'Meetings. I only want two samosas, hot.'

'We have potato samosas today,' said Prerna. 'Very fresh. Two dollars each.'

The man handed Prerna a crisp twenty, who rang up the order and returned the man's change. She turned to Ruchi, whose ears were already buzzing from all the orders coming in.

'Ruchi,' Prerna said, 'can you rush this young man's order?' Prerna handed Ruchi the man's ticket.

'Sure,' Ruchi grabbed two samosas out of the glass food warmer behind her, bagged and handed them to the man, and turned towards the kitchen, where Dilip was cutting onions and tearing up.

'Dilip, stop crying and get another chicken tikka ready, please,' Ruchi said.

'It's not me, it's the onions. If the onions weren't making me cry, our closing certainly would,' said Dilip.

'So, your tears haven't dried up like ma'am's?'

'For this place, they won't ever dry up.'

Ruchi beamed. 'Dilip?'

'Yes, Ruchi?'

'And one cup of chai.'

'For the customer who ordered the chicken, or for yourself, so you can fall behind again?'

Ruchi rolled her eyes and faced the counter and phones again. The phone on the wall rang again and Ruchi picked it up. 'The Curry Bowl, how can I help you?'

'Is today really your last day? Don't say it's true,' said the woman on the phone.

'Thank you. Yes, it is,' said Ruchi.

'That's a shame! What happened?'

'Not sure I can answer that. Did you want to order something?'

'Of course. But I have a question. I am allergic to nuts, does your okra dish have any nuts in it?'

'Our crispy okra?'

'Exactly,' said the woman.

'Let me ask the chef,' Ruchi said, placing her hand over the mouthpiece and turning towards Prerna, who was hovering over the picture of her two children that she kept on the cash counter.

'Ma'am?'

Prerna only nodded.

'Sorry to interrupt but does our crispy okra contain nuts?' asked Ruchi. 'This customer has a nut allergy.'

Prerna just stared at the photo in her hands, seemingly too emotional to answer.

'Ma'am?' Ruchi pressed.

Prerna nodded again, before placing the photo back on the cash counter.

'Sorry. No. No nuts in our okra. The customer will be fine.'

'Thanks, ma'am,' said Ruchi, before completing the order and slipping the ticket into the kitchen.

Suddenly a bright-eyed young man of about twenty raced into the restaurant, locking eyes with Ruchi. 'Good afternoon! One mango lassi, please!'

'Look who's here for his daily dose of lassi!' smiled Prerna. She turned to Ruchi, whispering, 'Your Mango Lassi Man, right on time. We have a few in the refrigerator, beti. Do yourself a favour and get him the freshest one. He has eyes for you, and he's handsome.'

'Ma'am. Shh!' Ruchi said. She batted her eyes at the young man and went to the refrigerator, reaching into the back for the freshest mango lassi she could find. Prerna shifted out from between the two and Ruchi placed the lassi in the young man's waiting hands. 'Here you go, Paul, one mango lassi for our Mango Lassi Man,' Ruchi said, finding it impossible not to smile.

'Thanks!' The young man smiled in return before leaving.

'You already know his name?'

Ruchi screwed up her face. 'He comes in all the time. Why wouldn't I know his name?' she asked, trying unsuccessfully to cover her smile.

Prerna's raised eyebrows were interrupted by another customer, another regular, Dutch, the son of the local cobbler around the corner.

'My usual order please,' said Dutch.

'Of course, Dutch,' said Prerna. 'How many rotis?'

'Three, extra crispy.'

'Dilip!' Prerna called out. 'Tell Parminder to make three extra crispy rotis . . . And tell him to step on it.'

'How are your new shoe soles holding up?' asked Dutch.

'Well, I put a lot of mileage on them, but they're still holding up. I'll be back again, Dutch. Probably not for a while, but at some point in time.'

'Hope so; my dad and I consider you family.'

'That's sweet.'

The phones continued to ring off the hook and the takeout line now extended further down Fulton, bending itself down Nassau.

'Parminder!' shouted Dilip. 'Where are you? It's not the time for a smoke break yet. First, he comes in unshaven, and then moves as slow as an old cow on a Delhi byway.'

'Did you find him?' Prerna shouted back. 'Need that roti asap. It's for Dutch.'

'Right away, Didi,' said Dilip. His eyes found Parminder as he charged into the kitchen from the alley behind, and was now grumbling as he slammed some naan dough into the walls of the tandoor with one hand and picked at the scruff on his chin with the other.

'Parminder, three roti, extra crispy.'

'I can hear you, Dilip,' snapped Parminder, grabbing three roti dough balls and pounding his fists on to them to flatten them on the prep table. 'I am so fed up with this place. So much nagging all the time. I will never in my lifetime ever work under a female boss again. She finds fault with everything I do!'

'Relax, bhai,' said Dilip. 'Prerna has raised two children while working in this kitchen. She could hold them in one hand and cook with the other with her eyes closed, in her sleep. The day you understand all this, you will stop complaining.'

'Well, there will be no day of understanding for anyone here now, will there?' Parminder grimaced as he angrily flung a roti against the scorching inner walls of the tandoor. 'This is The Curry Bowl's last day. I'm happy about that.'

'Parminder, don't say that!'

'It's true. Prerna's been on me for months now, for some reason. If The Curry Bowl wasn't closing, I'd walk out,' said Parminder, placing the second and third rotis inside.

Back at the counter, another customer levelled his eyes at Prerna, who averted hers. 'Can I help you?'

'Three rotis, please,' said the man, who now stood waiting alongside Dutch. The man's slight frown indicated what was coming next. 'I am feeling so sad,' he said. 'This is the last day of The Curry Bowl!'

Prerna's gaze narrowed. 'Yes, it is. Dilip, tell Parminder three more rotis, regular.'

'Yes, ma'am. Parminder, three more regular.'

'I heard her,' said Parminder, attacking more dough.

The man spoke again. 'What happened?'

Prerna let out a deep sigh. 'Lease issues.'

'Yeah, after 9/11, there have been a lot of vultures coming around. People are getting greedy. Owners are getting greedy. They are forgetting what made downtown New York special. Places like this. Quality, family-style food, always delicious, at a good value you can get in a flash. You'll be missed. For a fact.'

'Thank you for your sentiment. I tried fighting, but there are some battles you can never win.'

'As I said, you'll be missed. I will especially miss your roti. It always gets me through my morning at the stock exchange. I'm an algorithm programmer, a quant . . . Not that you would know what that is. But algorithms could never create the flavours you come up with here.'

'Yes, you've been coming for years for our roti,' said Prerna, her eyes glowing with warmth.

'Orders up!' Dilip said from the kitchen, as he wrapped Dutch's rotis and then the other man's, first in foil to keep them hot and then in plastic to keep them moist. Ruchi appeared at the kitchen order window to place the rotis in their respective bags, topped them with napkins, neatly folded the bags, and marked one 'crispy' and one 'regular.'

'Sirs,' Ruchi said, beckoning the two roti hounds forward with the bags. 'Here are your rotis. Enjoy!'

Dutch reached over and grabbed his bag first. 'Thanks so much. I hope we all meet again somewhere.'

'Thank you,' said the other man, 'and your name is?'

Ruchi glanced at Prerna, who had been keeping her eye on Parminder's aggressive behaviour over the tandoor. Prerna sighed, then turned back towards Ruchi and the man. 'This is Ruchi,' she said.

'Ruchi, my name's Joseph. Joseph Warner.'

'Hello,' said Ruchi, smiling politely, though her mind was on Paul, the Mango Lassi Man.

'Ruchi, I hope you realize what a special place this is. For a fact. I don't know where I'll go now that The Curry Bowl is closing.'

'Nice to hear. I always tell ma'am here the same thing. Still, I can't get a tear out of her,' Ruchi giggled.

Prerna smiled. 'Ruchi, we talked about that.'

'I know, I know, just a business,' Ruchi said. She turned back to Joseph and smiled. 'Sir, enjoy your roti.' Ruchi handed him the bag.

'Call me Joseph, and I certainly will.' Joseph receded from the counter, passed through the dining area, which was still filling with takeout customers, exited through the lobby and bounded down the street with his roti. Ruchi's eyes caught both Dutch and Joseph, two strangers with a shared taste for The Curry Bowl's—Prerna's—rotis, already sneaking bites out of their bags. Most found it impossible not to.

Chapter 6

The Good Doctor Annu

Dr Dayama Annu, dressed in a white smock with her name and title embroidered across the chest, set aside the patient case she had been reading and craned her stethoscope-draped neck out of the window of her small clinic on the upper floor of an old, historic, gilded and bronzed building which, like her investment, The Curry Bowl, sat on Fulton, but further to the east, across Nassau. Foxy and in her late forties, Dr Annu might have passed off as Reema's twin—upper-middle class, stylish and always looking upward. She wore bifocals, but not the chic, expensive kind Reema would wear—plus, Reema wouldn't have been caught dead in bifocals. The bifocals made Dr Dayama Annu look slightly older than she was, but this was fine because it gave her more respect from her patients as she sized up both their health and their pocketbooks. With her gold necklace and hoop earrings, and streaks of grey and white in her otherwise side-swept charcoal river of hair, Dr Annu was not unattractive but had a quality that could remind one of a spider. Was it her spindly arms and legs, or her ability to weave some kind of a web, whether in her practice, in social settings . . . or in the food business?

Dr Annu pulled her head in from the window, where she had been observing the line of people forming, sighed, and then gazed at the black phone sitting on her desk. She then opened a lower drawer in her desk and counted some bills, before leaning back into her brown leather chair in frustration. She had been part of the most recent wave of Indian doctors who had first filtered into Canada and then into America to earn more lucrative pay for their years of underpaid service back in India. Internal medicine was easy, with not too much blood or other bodily fluids to worry about, unlike what those stressed-out surgeons had to deal with. Dr Annu had much of her training in India, and was technically considered an IMG, an international medical graduate. She was lucky to have been accepted into a medical programme at New York University. She wanted to switch disciplines to radiology or anaesthesiology; she hadn't decided which yet—to stare at people's bones or put them to sleep.

Setting up her Lower Manhattan office clinic hadn't been too hard because she knew the landlord, having rented her first office space in Jackson Heights from him too. As one of the only Indian internal medicine doctors running a cash clinic downtown, her small circle of patients from all five boroughs included both prominent Indians and other South Asians looking for a deal on their regular check-ups or discreet access to a doctor. The poorer, working or service-class people who worked in the area too came to her for treatment. All were served on a sliding-scale, cash-paying system; most of them poor, many of them illegal, some illiterate, but also some professionals, who only trusted their own. Currently, Dr Annu paid her bills as a volume physician, which she considered temporary, for her dream was to have a much more modern clinic that could thrive on the more lucrative insurance-system payments rather than cash (well, she might still accept cash under the table). That way, she could ply her trade and make a good living.

She also wanted to rise through the ranks. Things were more equalized in the United States, but Dr Annu didn't see it that way. It was still a bitter pill to swallow that in emigrating, she had been 'demoted' from her family's caste standing. Her goal was to make enough money between her medical practice and her patriotic retaining of her cuisine—if she missed anything, it was Indian food, especially from Punjab or Delhi—which would also give her more status among her peers. These two desires gave her the motivation to move both her office and her home, a rented high-rise apartment downtown, to be closer to the money-changing hands.

Those same investors, she thought, would easily open their pockets in exchange for quick, delicious and cheap lunches at the restaurant she would open, The Curry Bowl. The Curry Bowl would be the ticket to ride with them, while enjoying delicious food she would never have to pay for and elevating her standing, or so Dr Annu thought. Now it was going up in so much tandoor smoke, thanks to her thankless, perfectionist manager, Prerna Malhotra, the young woman she had saved from the clutches of harsh streets at Queens and a lazy husband.

Dr Annu didn't know all the details, and she tried to bite her tongue when the topic came up, but she knew Prerna's history. For that, she sometimes kicked herself. She had found Prerna through the woman's desperate husband, Manish, whom she had met in a few guises—as a taxi driver and then as a courier. In the hopes of increasing his living, Manish had gravitated to Lower Manhattan near Dr Annu's office—first dropping off documents and then very occasionally picking Dr Annu up after work to take her to a friend's uptown place or sometimes back to Jackson Heights in Queens, where a few of her relatives still lived. Though she preferred to stay downtown and build her culture around herself rather than having to travel elsewhere for it.

At first, Dr Annu held a natural sympathy for the man's wife. What kind of stability could a courier and taxi driver during those hard times offer an Indian woman from a lower caste, fresh off the one-way discount flight with a questionable marriage certificate? The good doctor had felt virtuous in helping the poor girl—who was basically an arranged wife whose husband had retrieved her from India—by sponsoring and expediting her green card by offering her a job.

Manish had kept pestering her about what a great cook Prerna was and what she would add to Dr Annu's life portfolio. It was all an accident of timing and need. And though she would never admit it, Dr Annu had tried to serve as Prerna's role model of what an Indian woman could accomplish in America, while keeping the woman as a sort of secret culinary status symbol under her upper caste thumb. That was simply the way it was, and everyone involved accepted it.

Hence Prerna, hence The Curry Bowl.

Her small clinic's proximity to The Curry Bowl, just down the street, also offered the advantage of surveillance. When she wasn't seeing patients, Dr Annu could push her chair to the window of her inner office, where she had a view of the sidewalk in front of the restaurant. It was a fine perch from which she could estimate the foot traffic going in and out of her restaurant. She could keep an eye on things: What time The Curry Bowl opened, what time it closed, how many customers were showing up, how many times Prerna's delivery guys were going out and coming back in. Sometimes she counted the number of people and estimated how much Prerna owed her for any particular month. And though she didn't hang around, she would sometimes surprise Prerna and her staff by showing up in the middle of the rush, throwing her owner weight around and sampling the food (which, she had to admit, was among the best she had ever tasted).

At first, her restaurant seemed like a good investment. But over the years, Prerna's receipts and the money she handed over for rent and her share of the profits started dwindling. Now, she always had to call Prerna and ask her—and sometimes demand—her share. Prerna had started refusing to move her bottom line or cut corners or fire extra staff, so she could continue to feed food of the best flavour and quality to those who—in Prerna's words—were 'everyday' people, a term Dr Annu always repeated with a tiny snarl. The woman she had given her first chance to, now insisted on feeding and pleasing patrons from every walk of life, as if she were running a langar at the Golden Temple. The nerve! That just wouldn't do! Dr Annu wanted her investment to give her class and status, while all Prerna wanted to do was to make the bare minimum and feed all kinds of people her delicious food.

Dr Annu retreated from her bitter thoughts, trying to distract herself by rifling through a few piles of patient records, before sighing again and pushing her chair back to the window to take another look at the line leading to The Curry Bowl, *her* Curry Bowl. The line still snaked across the street. She pulled her head back in, swivelled in her chair and stared at her phone, at first resisting the urge to call. She succumbed, however, and after failing to get through the constant busy signal, Dr Annu slammed the phone down, unable to bear the thought of what was happening at The Curry Bowl today.

Chapter 7

Captured Moments

Ruchi's ears were already buzzing from fielding calls, and dealing with customers waiting for their takeout orders, when a swaggering group of older white men wearing shades and dark suits—quite the definition of sharks in suits—overtook the lobby with their collective girth, blocking out any trace of the Golden Temple, her favourite Rumi passage on the wall, Ganesha himself and Prerna's most beloved picture of her father, Karanjit.

When Prerna dropped what she was doing and rushed out from behind the counter to greet them, her overly agreeable action sent Ruchi straight to the kitchen to stand by Dilip, where she munched on a cucumber. 'Trying to lose weight for the Mango Lassi Man?' teased Dilip.

'Not at all, Dilip ji,' Ruchi said. 'This is all I can eat without throwing up. Look, the new landlords are here—and look at how Prerna is fawning over them! Makes me sick.' Ruchi crunched loudly on her cucumber.

In the lobby now, Prerna gazed through the towering forest of men to the beacon that was her father's photo, as the men planted their heavy feet and measured out dimensions by waving their hands and stretching their arms out. A rapid-fire discussion broke out as they discussed numbers, square footage and rent figures, most of it Greek to her. What she loved was making delicious food for people. Numbers? What was that?

The tallest and most wide-shouldered of the men drew back one of the lobby's red-velvet curtains, revealing a brick wall covered with colourful, painted handprints of children. The man laughed. 'What's this? A kindie garden?' The other men laughed, too, until one of them corrected his colleague, 'Stu, it's kindergarten. Not "kindie garden". Where'd you grow up, in Minnesota?'

'New Jersey,' said Stu.

'Figures,' said the questioner. The other sharks laughed.

Prerna proudly chimed in. 'Gentlemen, there's a story behind that wall. Back in Delhi, new business owners often let children make similar handprints on one of their walls, for good luck. I did the same here at The Curry Bowl. I invited all the children from the working-class neighbourhood to place their handprints on the lobby wall in whatever colour they chose. I supplied all the paint and even fed them a puri lunch.

'What's puri?' asked Stu.

'Puri is an unleavened fried bread, often made from whole wheat flour, salt, water, potato, peas and squash,' said Prerna. 'You should try it.'

'Oh, yeah?' said Stu.

Warren cut Stu off, trying to be cordial. 'We'll take five orders before we leave.'

Prerna smirked as Stu turned back towards his group. 'Guys, whaddya think? Should we start demolishing this wall first?' Stu knocked his fist on the child's handprints as he spoke, as Prerna shrugged and gave up trying to charm the brutes with her stories.

In the kitchen, Dilip slashed at a half of chicken. 'Bloody predators! I wish Prerna would throw them out and refuse to feed them.'

'And now your Didi is just going to throw her smile at them and offer to feed them lunch specials with so much affection,' said Ruchi. Noticing Dilip's angry fervour, she added, 'Don't cut yourself, Dilip!'

'I won't . . . Been doing this for years; I could slice chicken with my eyes closed. These landlords make me angry. Look at how she still talks to them.'

'Maybe she's got some forward plan?'

'Doubt it,' said Dilip. 'Prerna's all about maintaining the status quo.'

'Well, her status quo is very good.'

'Well, the status quo is not always profitable!'

'Let's not argue about it again, Dilip.'

Ruchi snuck a glance across the dining area into the lobby, where Prerna was still smiling and chatting up the suited developers.

'How can she even tolerate standing with them?' Ruchi asked quietly.

'Beats me, *chhoti behen* (younger sister),' shrugged Dilip.

As if she was hearing their thoughts from the lobby, Prerna caught Dilip's eye and made her usual head movement, indicating she needed something special, and fast.

Dilip slathered on a fake smile. 'Yes, ma'am?'

Prerna shouted across the dining area, which was now filling with more takeout customers. Word seemed to have spread. 'Five puris, two rotis, gluten-free. No flour for rolling, and don't use any ghee, got it? That's in addition to the three samosas, chicken tikka, the dal, channa masala, and saag paneer. It's for the developers. Got it?'

'Right away, ma'am,' said Dilip, slamming a ball of roti dough on to the kneading table.

'And Dilip?'

'Yes, ma'am?'

'Where's Ruchi?'

Ruchi had sunk into a chair near the prep table, as though burdened by the weight of the depressing scene occurring in the lobby. These men were out to destroy beautiful small business owners like Prerna. She couldn't believe she was even giving them any time of her day—not to mention a large order of food—as they discussed smashing down The Curry Bowl's walls, their most-beloved wall no less. The nerve!

'Psst, Ruchi,' Dilip hissed as he flattened the dough, careful not to let any flour touch it, before placing it in the tandoor. 'Where's Parminder? We need him! The sharks need to be fed.'

Nazim appeared at the prep table next to Dilip. 'He's in the back alley on one of his chronic smoke breaks,' he snorted.

'Well, tell him we have a big order to complete,' said Dilip.

'Right away,' said Nazim. He headed out to fetch Parminder.

'I'm sunk,' Ruchi said, groaning and staring at her sneakers. 'How can she talk to her destroyers . . . So friendly, like they were her best friends?'

Dilip sighed. 'That's life in the big city. I guess Didi is jaded, her skin and heart have become as thick as a jackfruit.'

'Dilip!' Prerna shouted again. 'Where's Ruchi? I need that order for these gentlemen asap!'

Gentlemen? Ruchi popped up from her chair, doing her best to slather on a smile. She wiped her hands on her apron. 'Sorry, ma'am, just cleaning up a little spill,' she lied blithely.

Dilip slipped the roti out of the tandoor, letting it cool on the cutting board.

'Ruchi, the roti first, please. And get the rest of the order ready for takeout. Ring it up as only five basic box lunches,' Prerna instructed, as she led the circling suits into the dining area.

'Dilip, now she's letting the sharks come into the dining area,' gasped Ruchi, flabbergasted as she grabbed the roti and started to wrap it.

'Life in the big city,' shrugged Dilip.

In the kitchen, Parminder began to throw together the ingredients for the sharks' food, while Ruchi slipped behind the checkout counter just as Warren, the politer of the sharks, did. Beaming, he handed her a crisp 100-dollar bill. 'Break a Benjamin, young lady?'

Ruchi could have punched the blowhard's face, but instead, she let her smile grow so sharp it could have cut into the tension.

'You have anything smaller?' she asked, her legs planted down stubbornly, her hands gripping the till.

'It's all I carry,' said Warren, 'Benjamins.' He grinned wider and held the bill out across the counter. 'And, to be honest, I really don't like Indian food. Well, I like it, but my stomach can only handle Indian breads. I'm sensitive to spice. And I have a gluten allergy, and I haven't been able to handle any milk products for a long time either. Lactose intolerance. No spice, no glutens, no lactose. My partners love Indian food, though, especially the way your mom makes it.'

'She's very caring, but she's not my mom. Thanks anyway.'

'I'm a red-meat guy. Prime steaks from steakhouses are my thing. Name's Warren, by the way. We'll be redeveloping The Curry Bowl soon. My partners and I haven't decided yet, but to me, it's going to make a fine, high-end French or nouveau American restaurant. You know, high-end fine dining, rather than low-end takeout.'

Ruchi dearly wanted to flip him off but knew Prerna would have none of it. Instead, she held back and contented herself with a pronounced glare that was hard to miss.

'You sure the Indian bread's not too spicy?' he pressed on.

'Roti, sir, it's called a "roti". It's mild, no ghee—clarified butter—it is gluten-free, and is the perfect Indian food for a weak . . . uh . . . sensitive stomach,' said Ruchi, glancing down at the man's belly, which was straining the buttons of his dress shirt. *He could certainly do with more vegetarian, healthy food,* she thought to herself spitefully, just as Prerna's voice cut through.

'Ruchi, please get Warren his change.'

'Right away, ma'am. Sorry, Warren,' Ruchi said. 'Iqbal!'

Iqbal ran over from the buffet table, where he had been refilling the tray of saag paneer and was wiping a green trace of spinach from his hands.

'Yes, behen?' said Iqbal, washing his hands at the small sink behind the counter.

'I'm out of change. This gentleman only has a "Benjamin",' said Ruchi, smirking.

'A what?' Iqbal mouthed, no words coming out as his face twisted with confusion.

'You know, a "C-note", a "yard".' Ruchi had to laugh now or she would either cry or lose her cool.

'Huh?'

'A hundred-dollar bill. I can't make change for it. I'm out already.'

Iqbal finished drying his hands and straightened out his apron, as Ruchi drew a counterfeit-detecting pen across the crisp bill. The Benjamin was indeed real.

'Hey, young lady, you think I'd try to pass off a fake Benjamin?' Warren asked, grimacing. 'This isn't Canal Street.'

'We check every, uh, "Benjamin" and above, sir, don't take offence.'

'Fine. Is it true that most Indians don't eat beef or cows?' he switched tracks suddenly.

'Yes, they are sacred. Traditional Hindus look at the cow as a motherly, giving animal. Hence, out of respect, people don't eat it.'

Warren's nose wrinkled in confusion. 'Okay. Interesting. I'll try not to remember that when I'm at the steakhouse.'

Iqbal reached out to snatch the hundred from Ruchi's hand. 'Be right back, behen.' Iqbal raced out of the lobby door and darted left to race to the bank to get change.

Ruchi handed Warren a single bagged roti. 'A little advance for your sensitive stomach, sir. We'll have your change and the rest of your group's order in a moment.'

'That's kind of you,' Warren said, sneaking a bite of his roti behind his hand so the others couldn't see.

Another group of five, Steve Nesmith and Kerry Assante, an old-school, interracial married couple, bespectacled human rights lawyers, and their three kids who ranged from olive to brown, with blonde hair and dark hair, waded through the crowd. Steve gently put his hand on Prerna's shoulder and coaxed her away from the suited developers. 'Excuse me, gentlemen, I have to speak to this very special lady for a minute,' Steve said.

Prerna wheeled around on her heels to greet the couple and smiled. 'Steve and Kerry! Great to see you. Who's this?' Prerna said when she saw their kids. 'I didn't know you had such a lovely family.' She quickly instructed Ruchi to take care of the developers, as she stepped away with the family.

'Prerna, we are all going to miss you and The Curry Bowl,' cried out Kerry. 'You made the best Indian food in the neighbourhood. Probably the best in New York. We usually ate Thai or Ethiopian, but I have to say, you were the reason we started eating Indian cuisine more often. I mean, those flavours, and at such a value.'

Prerna almost blushed.

'She's not exaggerating!' said Steve.

'Not at all,' said Kerry. 'In fact, around our co-op, we didn't say, "Let's have Indian food tonight", or even, "Let's order from The Curry Bowl tonight"; we said, "Let's eat Prerna's food tonight." And the kids just love it.'

Their kids smiled and nodded politely.

'I'm blessed to have known you,' she told Prerna as she was about to break down. She had been complimented before, but seldom were the words so sincere. She always thought the reviews The Curry Bowl had raked up were too flashy and self-serving. She lived for simple and earnest compliments like this. Prerna thought of the one very bad review—certainly a fake, it was so mean and badly written. She had received it from someone who was most certainly a jealous competitor, probably the son of the owner of Wala Masala, a 'higher-end' Indian cafe further uptown on Broadway (Prerna knew for a fact they didn't use fresh ingredients). She closed her eyes and sent up a small prayer: That Karanjit, wherever he was, would never get wind of any harsh criticism directed towards her.

'I don't know what to say, Steve and Kerry,' Prerna said. 'I only do what is expected of me as a cook. Nothing more, nothing less.' She resisted the urge to throw her hands around the entire family and draw them into a bear hug.

'*Dhanyavaad*,' she said with a little bow of her head.

'Huh?' Steve asked, staring around at his wife and children.

Prerna placed her palm across her chest. 'I'm sorry, I spoke in Hindi,' she said. 'Thank you for your compliment. It was always and still is my pleasure to share with you and your family what I love best in life.'

'You're too humble. We'll miss you.' Steve threw his arms around Prerna, and she blushed and stiffened as Kerry and their kids proceeded to draw her into the first group hug of her life. And to think she had said thank you in her native tongue! And despite the busy lunch, no pain had yet appeared in Prerna's wrist. The family released Prerna, and she stepped back to see the developers looking at her with some amount of confusion—they didn't seem to know how well-loved she was.

'Order up!' rang Iqbal's voice from the kitchen. 'Three samosas, chicken tikka, dal, channa masala, and the saag paneer, five roti, five puris.'

'That's us,' said Warren, stepping to the counter and receiving the developers' large group order from Ruchi, who without even a glance, placed his change in his hand.

'Thanks, Richi,'

'It's Ruchi.'

'Sorry. Hey! Stu! Give me a hand.' Stu stepped up and the two developers led their group through the busy dining area and out the rich red lobby they were so hungry to renovate. The lunch they had prepared for them was a meal Ruchi and Prerna hoped they would never forget.

Steve stepped back and took out his smartphone. 'Prerna, can we take a quick picture with you? Please?'

'Absolutely not! I don't like having my picture taken,' said Prerna firmly.

'Prerna, don't be so humble. Please?' Kerry pleaded.

'Okay, you win,' Prerna said, stepping back into the embrace of the family, who now flanked her on either side. Prerna smiled shyly; she never liked to reveal her teeth.

'Sir?' Steve asked a seated, maroon-turban-wearing Sikh. 'Would you mind?'

'Not at all,' said the man, another no-nonsense taxi driver who came to The Curry Bowl during his breaks. He always ordered the same thing—chicken tikka masala with white basmati rice. He stood up and received Steve's smartphone, taking his time to compose a balanced picture, with Prerna in the centre. 'Everyone say, "Ghee!"' he called out.

Smiles surrounded Prerna as she slightly lifted her chin with pride. Ruchi couldn't stand it any longer and ran over with her own smartphone to capture this incredibly warm moment.

Ruchi convinced the Sikh to join Prerna and the Nesmith-Assantes, so she could compose her own picture. It took everything she had to not burst into tears at that moment. Her heroine stood proudly in the middle, barely smiling, but with a new elevation to her shoulders and her chin, and eyes that sparkled like Ruchi had never seen before, like two chandeliers. The family, including their new turbaned member, suddenly swallowed Prerna whole in an embrace, probably the second group hug of her life. It was a captured moment Ruchi would treasure forever.

After the photoshoot, Steve leaned down to gently touch his cheek to the top of Prerna's head. 'Everything will be okay,' Steve whispered.

Would it really be though? thought Prerna as she smiled a sad smile.

Chapter 8

The Last Message

The last lunch at The Curry Bowl had concluded, with every past and present customer who had taken the time to show up served and satisfied. It was as if the place hadn't lost its lease, but had signed a new one. The sun falling over the shores of New Jersey and Staten Island became an intense amber, then pink. A cool breeze picked up outside, awaiting the hotter onset of rush hour, which would bring people into the streets on their way home on the ferry or subway, or to do some last-minute shopping or grab a takeout at one of the few shops that remained along Fulton before their commutes. Prerna's life's work would no longer be an option for them.

Inside The Curry Bowl, the onset of evening saw Prerna and her loyal staff sitting down together in their own dining room for a last meal and conversation. Prerna had made her signature dishes for the staff—from khoba roti to Dilip's favourite chicken curry. The hobs inside The Curry Bowl had been turned off, and the tandoor left to cool. Iqbal, Nazim, Dilip and even Parminder, all of Prerna's 'boys', sat at the simple wooden tables and chairs, which had held thousands of customers for over two decades. Ruchi had curated a playlist of their favourite A.R. Rahman tracks, though she herself was missing, sorting through all of Prerna's bills. The dining room grew warm with their conversation.

'Twenty years have gone by just like that since I was just a bike delivery guy and Didi was like Ruchi,' said Dilip, sighing and clasping his fingers together on the table. 'Except Didi always showed up on time and worked very hard.'

Everyone laughed.

'I think I hear my name,' called out Ruchi from the office. 'Dilip, shut your mouth!'

Dilip threw his hand over his mouth but failed to cover his laughter.

'Ruchi, beta, don't pay Dilip any heed. He's just teasing you,' Prerna said. 'Stop fuming over all my bills, come over and join us. And bring that khoba roti I made for everyone on your way out. I made it for this occasion last night, especially for all of you.'

'Twenty years!' sighed Dilip again.

'Has it been that long now?' said Prerna. 'Time surely flies. Much faster here than in Delhi. As the saying goes, "In a New York minute".'

'I still don't know how you went from delivering documents on a bike to getting caught up in this Curry Bowl mess with me,' Prerna said to Dilip fondly, finally showing her teeth as she smiled—which were not as yellow or crooked as she believed them to be.

Iqbal smiled. 'It amazes me that you can smile on a day like this, ma'am.'

'Prerna,' Dilip said, becoming wistful again, 'I had no choice. The bike delivery business downtown plummeted after 9/11. Either I starved to death or found work in an Indian restaurant. Then I could at least fill my stomach. At that point, I would have worked for naan alone.'

Prerna smiled.

'Luckily, you paid me, and I've got to enjoy the best of the best Indian food for so many years.'

Prerna nestled into her sari, 'Ah, Dilip, what is it I always hear New Yorkers say, "Those were the days"? That was around the time Dr Annu handed The Curry Bowl over to me.'

'She did indeed. Handed the restaurant over based on a trick and an unfair twenty-year contract,' Dilip said, easing back into his chair until the front legs rose off the floor.

'Let's not discuss these negative things on our last day. We had a great last lunch, right?'

All the staff agreed, nodding and throwing their towels on the table. 'Hear, hear!' said Nazim.

'We should be celebrating that we survived this long and the fact that we did it like a family. Not to mention that we pleased so many customers.'

'Apologies, Didi. You are right,' said Dilip.

The phone, which had finally stopped ringing during their meal, suddenly rang again. Prerna's eyes flitted back towards the front desk, where Ruchi now stood, organizing another pile of tickets and bills. 'Ma'am, should I answer?'

'Sure,' Prerna said. 'Why not? Take the call, then please join us.'

'Yes, ma'am, one second.' Ruchi picked up the phone. 'Hello, The Curry Bowl . . . Oh! Hi, Mr Richards. Give me a minute.' She covered the mouthpiece with her hand. 'Ma'am, it's the meat supplier from Richards' Meat Emporium. He says he wants his payment by the end of the day.'

'Politely tell Mr Richards that he can wait. He will get his money, not to worry.'

'Will do, ma'am.' Ruchi delivered the news and hung up.

'Ruchi, beta, the khoba will get stale; heat it up and bring it with you. You can settle the accounts later,' instructed Prerna.

'I will give you all the necessary cheques later. Now it's time to relax with me and the guys, as we are forced to reminisce. I need your support with these sentimental boys!'

The table laughed. 'Where's Parminder?' Iqbal asked, noticing the suddenly empty chair.

'Where do you think he is?' asked Dilip. 'On one of his smoke breaks.'

'That desk phone has become both a third hand and third ear and second mouth to everyone,' continued Dilip, who would not be stopped. 'Twenty years we've abused that thing. That brick with a bell inside is shamefully outdated now.' Prerna had rarely considered The Curry Bowl's main tool—the dented, stained, chipped desk phone. She had replaced the even more outdated phone Dr Annu had originally purchased for the place, which had only one line and was relatively the size of a construction brick. The current phone is still as trustworthy as her father's Maruti.'

Prerna looked around the table, and at the relatively flimsy-looking phone.

'Times have changed. In tech and in the Indian restaurant business,' said Prerna. 'I can't keep up.' She called out to Ruchi again. 'Ruchi, stop! Now come sit with us.'

Ruchi stopped her organizing, grabbed the khoba out of the microwave and found a chair closest to Prerna.

'I want to express a few things,' Prerna said, growing serious. 'Without tears!'

'You can borrow mine,' said Ruchi.

'Don't be depressed that The Curry Bowl is closing. The end of one thing can be the beginning of another, like the seasons. As my father taught me . . . You can all be the seeds of your future. And I hope your future brings you all work in Michelin-starred restaurants.'

Prerna's staff, her family really, shifted in their chairs, threatening to applaud.

She continued, 'Ruchi, I appreciate the work you've put in here. I know the restaurant business is not your life's work. So, I wish you luck in your journalism career . . . Your future with Mango Lassi Man, Paul.'

Ruchi blushed, throwing her hands across her face to hide any tears, as the others laughed. 'Ma'am! Thank you!'

'You've been The Curry Bowl's ray of light. In Hindi, we call that *noor*. I will always think of you as the noor of The Curry Bowl.'

'I'm honoured . . . Blessed,' said Ruchi, openly crying now. 'Thank you. You are our inspiration!'

'Ma'am's late-arriving light,' sniggered Dilip.

'Dilip, enough. You know, my father always said, "One cooks with their heart, not with their hands." That's true. And my feeling is we have all done that. Even Parminder . . . when he wasn't grumbling.'

Everyone cackled just as Parminder finally arrived and took a seat.

'What's so funny?' he demanded.

'Nothing, Parminder,' said Nazim. 'Nothing. Relax and listen, and enjoy some khoba.'

Prerna continued, 'I remember one of my first days here, I added salt instead of sugar into the kheer dessert.'

Ruchi's eyes opened wide, as Iqbal nearly fell apart laughing.

'And we still sent the order out!' Prerna slapped her knee as she laughed. 'We had to! We couldn't afford not to! And to think The Curry Bowl has so many good reviews now. No one knows the beginnings of things, the struggles, and the silly mistakes that get made in the process.'

Nazim smiled, then stared at the jagged tips of his fingernails. 'It wasn't your fault . . . In America, salt and sugar look the same! You had just arrived and didn't speak English!'

The main phone rang again, all three lines lighting up, causing the staff to stir in their seats, though their last day's work was done. Prerna closed her eyes, hoping she could somehow stop the phone from ringing so she could enjoy some peace with her surrogate family.

'Ma'am? Shouldn't we answer?' asked Ruchi at last. 'At least that will stop the old beast from ringing.'

Prerna sighed. 'Okay, fine. But if it's Dr Annu, I'm busy . . . In fact, I'm not here at all.'

Ruchi stood up and grabbed the phone. 'The Curry Bowl,' she said.

'Ruchi, it's Reema,' said the caller. 'I couldn't get through on my sister's cell.'

'It's been a busy day, Reema Didi. We are all taking our last meal together now. By the way, how is Kris?'

'He's fine. I'm in the car, Ruchi,' Reema said. Reema had just specially imported an Audi S3 Saloon from England, and could not resist bringing it up in conversations.

Ruchi covered the mouthpiece and beckoned Prerna. 'Ma'am, it's your sister, Reema,' she whispered.

Prerna froze in her chair. 'Give me a minute,' she finally said.

'Ruchi, Kris is so sad today,' continued Reema. 'He's still convinced he works at The Curry Bowl. He can't stop watching all those videos that he and Sarah took of his "career" there before he had to start school. He'll probably never stop watching them.'

'Funny,' said Ruchi.

'So how are you, Ruchi? Did you submit your last paper?'

'I did! It was due today, hence I was late for work again. Would you like to speak to your sister? She's sitting right next to me,' Ruchi fibbed.

'Would love to . . . Sure!' said Reema. 'But I'll call her cell. Please tell her to watch for my call.'

Ruchi hung up and walked back to her chair next to Prerna. 'Ma'am, your sister's going to call your cell.'

Prerna slipped her phone out of her sari pouch and stared at it: there were 12 missed calls. Three from her sister, two from her nephew, Kris, one from her daughter, Sarah, four from Manish, one from Dr Annu, and one from a private number.

Just then, her screen lit up again and she answered. 'Hi, Reema,' she said, injecting as much bravado as she could in her voice.

Ruchi slunk away to complete The Curry Bowl's bookkeeping and bill organizing.

'Prerna, I've been calling for an hour,' said Reema. 'I'm in the car. Where have you been?'

'Where do you think I've been? It's our last day. I was so busy!' said Prerna.

'Work? It's your last day. What work is there to do?'

'Reema, you don't know what it takes to actually run a business.'

'Let's not discuss it,' said Reema, glancing down at her nails. 'I need to get my nails done again, then take my car in for some maintenance, then get my Gucci handbag repaired. A thread came out, can you believe it!'

'We just finished the lunch service . . . It was busier than usual today,' said Prerna, ignoring Reema's asides.

'Probably because it's your last day. Prerna, listen, Manish has been calling nonstop,' Reema said. 'He's been looking for you. He said that he called your cell a hundred times, but you didn't answer.'

'He knows I don't answer my cell at work,' said Prerna.

'At any rate, please call your beloved husband, so he will stop calling me.'

Prerna rolled her eyes. 'I'll call him from the ferry on the way home.'

'Please call him now. I don't have time to play receptionist.'

'Yes, Reema. I'll check my cell and call him asap. Hugs to Kris!' Prerna said.

She grabbed the last piece of khoba and stepped out to call Manish.

At their home in Staten Island, he was sitting on their couch, watching cricket, when the phone buzzed in his hand. 'Hello?' he said, springing to his bare feet.

'Manish,' said Prerna. 'Did you—'

'Yes, I called! Why don't you pick up your cell? Where have you been?' asked Manish.

'Manish, dear, you know I rarely answer my cell when I'm at work, and it's The Curry Bowl's last day, in case you've forgotten. I've only been working here for twenty years,' said Prerna gently.

'The restaurant's phone is also busy all day long,' complained Manish.

'I already explained! It's our last day, so of course, I've been here.'

Manish slumped back on the couch, kicking his bare feet on to the arm of the couch. He began to rub his eyes.

'So, how did the judgment go?'

'Not good,' said Manish.

'How so?'

'The judge thought it was an insurance scam.'

'Hare Krishna, why?'

'The judge was a bully. In this country, there are different rules for everyone based on one's skin colour. Terrible system! I have already decided to appeal the judgment. I spoke to Reema and David and they agree.'

'Dear, don't worry, whatever is meant to happen will happen. I put your dinner in the refrigerator. You can warm it in the microwave.'

Holding the phone to his ear, Manish stood up and marched into the kitchen. He found the container in the fridge and shoved it into the microwave. 'When are you coming home, Prerna?'

'I'll try to make the 8 p.m. ferry.'

'Try?'

'Manish! It's The Curry Bowl's last day! There are ends to tie up, and people to say goodbye to!'

'Okay,' Manish grumbled, as he yanked the microwave's door open and went straight at the food with his hands.

'Don't be so upset,' said Prerna.

'I will be what I need to be, especially after the bully judge's judgment. I was planning to wear my millionaire jacket by now.'

'In time,' said Prerna. 'In time. Bye.'

'Bye,' said Manish, and went back to the couch and his cricket match with his plate of food.

Prerna clicked off her cell and slipped it back into her pouch.

She took her place back at the table, causing Ruchi to scamper back.

'All these months I tried to save The Curry Bowl from closing down,' said Prerna, picking up from where she'd left off. 'However small, it was ours. If I've been harsh with any of you in any way, I apologize. Running a small restaurant while maintaining quality causes a lot of stress, especially if you are a woman in a man's world. Thank you all! I just wanted to glorify Indian cuisine. I hope and pray that all of you do very well in life.'

One by one, Prerna's boys rose from the table—Iqbal, Dilip, then Nazim—and each bowed to the floor to touch Prerna's feet. 'We thank you for your kindness,' they said, almost in unison. Except for Parminder, who strutted past, pulling at the hair of his scruffy beard, which seemed to have grown an inch since the morning. He offered Prerna a handshake, as he stuck a cigarette in the corner of his mouth. Parminder's lack of emotion made

Prerna a little sad, but what could she do? She watched as they grabbed their things and left.

Ruchi appeared from the back with a stack of order blanks and receipts, and The Curry Bowl's very thick, dishevelled and dog-eared ledger. 'Ma'am, here's the full account. What's in the bank and what is owed to the vendors,' she said.

'Thank you, beta,' Prerna said, placing her hand atop Ruchi's head for a fleeting moment.

'I . . .' Ruchi's eyes began to spill tears again, as she struggled to speak. 'The guys already cleaned the kitchen and put the excess oil in containers. I have put all the unused soda cans in a container for pickup. And I have turned off the refrigerator.'

'Beta! No! No tears. As I said before, you have so many opportunities ahead of you. Opportunities I never had. You should be happy to be free of The Curry Bowl,' said Prerna. 'Chin up! Help me take the decorations off the walls.'

Ruchi wiped her cheeks and untied her hair, revealing long, flowing auburn hair she never revealed at work. 'Paul will be a lucky man someday,' smiled Prerna.

'Stop,' said Ruchi, running her fingers through her hair to freshen it up, as Prerna pushed the tables into a tighter huddle and then stacked all the chairs.

* * *

The two women stood before all the pictures of India that Prerna had, sometimes in a haste, placed across The Curry Bowl's walls over the last two decades. Especially striking was the Golden Temple—her father had learnt of grace and the karma created by feeding thousands in the act of langar over here. And Prerna had tried recreating that in her little corner. All of it would soon be gone from the wall and stuffed into her bag, destined for a place she was too hesitant to name, even in her mind: her basement storage. That picture of benevolent grandeur collecting dust in the depths of her Staten Island home.

Prerna went to the counter and came back with an oversized canvas bag. One by one, she took down the pictures and placed them in the bag, appearing just a little wearier as each went in. She glanced towards the lobby, where Ruchi stood before the idol of Ganesha. Ruchi had learnt about the *modak* the idol held in his hand from Prerna (and ate too much of it whenever it was offered).

She walked up to Prerna quietly and stood beside her. Prerna's eyes blurred as she took in the little mandir she loved so dearly, with her father's photo smiling down on them benevolently.

'You like Lord Ganesha?' she asked.

Ruchi jumped. 'You scared me, ma'am. I love this idol of Lord Ganesha in particular. Even when I arrive late, I always stopped to admire the mandir.'

'Ruchi beti,' Prerna said, gently lifting the murti from the mandir. 'You can have it. My little Lord Ganesha is now your little Lord Ganesha.'

Ruchi held the idol in her arms like a baby. 'Ma'am, I couldn't! This must mean so much to you.'

'Beti, I insist,' said Prerna. 'Ganesha is the god of new beginnings. One of the few gods I worship. To me, The Curry Bowl closing is just a new beginning. That is why I shed no tears. I suggest you do the same. See our closing as your own new beginning.' Prerna reached down to touch Ganesha's trunk as it seemed to come alive in Ruchi's arms. 'Ganesha would want it that way.'

The two shared warm smiles under the image of Prerna's father and inhaled the last scent of nag champa, the fragrant but subtle magnolia and sandalwood incense Prerna always burnt in the lobby.

'Ma'am . . . Where did you learn to cook such delicious and diverse food?' asked Ruchi.

'From my father, strangely.' Prerna smiled at the photo.

'What was your father's name?'

'Karanjit.'

'Was he a restaurateur too?'

'Not at all! He just loved cooking and was a natural chef in addition to being the most curious man I have ever known,' said Prerna. 'His curiosity is what compelled his excellence. He never made one rupee as a chef or even a cook, but he knew how to put his love into food. So it always tasted fantastic. I am not only his daughter—I am his vessel. That's the way I feel about it. I paid tribute for twenty years, and I feel good about that. Whatever I know about food, I learnt from my Pita ji. And like him, I love cooking. And I like serving people even more.'

Ruchi tightened her grip on the idol. 'Ma'am?'

'Yes?'

'I think this is another new beginning for you. You've convinced me!'

'What do you mean?'

'I don't know why, but now I feel this is not the end for you. There are so many other opportunities for someone with so much talent.'

Prerna took a deep breath of the nag champa and sighed. Finally, she stiffly reached for the picture of her father, the last trace of Prerna's presence on The Curry Bowl's walls. Ruchi stopped her. 'Ma'am. I know I'm young and was often late . . .'

'Ruchi, don't listen to my guys.'

'It's okay, I know I was. Ma'am, listen, I don't want you to stop. You can continue to cook and share all the things your father did with you, on the Internet, on YouTube or Instagram, or Twitter, or even write a cookbook to seal your legacy. I am sure thousands, if not millions, would buy it and learn what The Curry Bowl really meant to people in Lower Manhattan during difficult times.'

'I don't know, beti, I have always had simple aspirations. Reviews and awards are nice, but I'm Indian, and worse, I am an Indian woman. I'm not one of those fancy French chefs, so I've always kept my food aspirations realistic—down to earth, of the streets, for everyone. I don't make food expecting awards or accolades—'

Ruchi cut Prerna off, 'But you deserve all of them!'

'Beti! Shush,' said Prerna. 'Let me tell you a secret. My son, Karan, promised me something similar. He swore to me that I'd be appreciated in the future if it was the last thing he'd do. I've always wondered if The Curry Bowl fulfilled that promise or if there was some other new beginning he had planned for me. Well . . .'

Prerna fell silent, and Ruchi understood.

'Your son was right. We are standing in the lobby of some new beginning. Ganesha wouldn't have it any other way.'

'Hmm,' said Prerna thoughtfully. 'Not sure I can do all that. Ruchi?'

'No?'

'No—hey, since we are talking about new beginnings, what about your Mango Lassi Man?'

'What about him?'

'His eyes are just like my Karan's! And I don't think he came in such a rush for two years just to get his lassi. I think *you* might be his mango lassi.'

Ruchi giggled and covered her mouth. 'Maybe so, but I'm not interested. Yet. My career comes first.'

Prerna ran a finger along the edge of her father's picture frame, staring into Karanjit's laughing eyes and mischievous smile, before holding it close to her chest and letting her eyes wander across the now barren landscape that just hours ago was the warmest Indian restaurant for miles around.

'Ruchi, beti, would you mind switching off the lights?'

'Ma'am, no. That should be your honour. You brought light into this place; it should be you to take the light out of it.'

'So sentimental. Don't be silly,' laughed Prerna. 'Remember what I said about you being noor.'

'Ma'am—'

'Beti. Please call me Prerna from now on. I, the light bringer, Surya, give you permission to turn off The Curry Bowl's lights,' said Prerna, hoping Ruchi wouldn't see how hesitant she was to do it herself.

Her hands were trembling so badly, she hid them under her sari's pallu. 'I have to make it to the 8 p.m. ferry, so turn off the lights.'

Before reaching over to flick the main lights off, Ruchi collected her things from behind the counter and then bent down to touch Prerna's feet. She headed for the door with her backpack and purse, the Ganesha still in her arms. When she got to the street, she turned around. 'Ma'am, aren't you coming?'

'Ruchi, you go before it gets dark. I want to collect my thoughts first. Spend some time in the place. I'll be fine. Oh, wait!'

'What?'

'Can you write up a final message for the chalkboard? I forgot, and my handwriting is so bad.' Ruchi set down her things and dragged the chalkboard into the lobby, quickly scrawling a final message on it. 'There,' she said. 'I'll leave it out front.'

'Thank you,' said Prerna, pinching at her wrist, which had begun to throb. 'I can barely use chalk with this wrist of mine.'

'Till we meet again.' Ruchi grabbed her things and left, leaving Prerna standing alone in the middle of what used to be The Curry Bowl.

Chapter 9

Karan's Court

Karan—to Prerna, it seemed like a whole other lifetime when he was around. People rarely uttered her firstborn's name any more, especially in front of her. She, too, didn't like speaking about him, except to those she was closest to. His memory constantly tugged at her, sometimes surprised her, sometimes attacked her, but it was always there with her, no matter where she was or what she was doing—on the ferry, the subway, in the car, at The Curry Bowl, but especially at home, when she had a moment to sit down, a silent moment by herself. This was the time that Prerna dreaded most, and now she would have too much of it. There was nothing she could do to bring him back, but he inspired her every action at work and in life. This made The Curry Bowl's closing bittersweet.

Karan was no average boy. Despite his mother working all the time and his father glued to the TV, his cricket matches and his schemes to make a quick buck, the awkward and sensitive child preferred to spend his time alone—time spent thinking and walking alone, finding ways to entertain himself. But sometimes, he wanted to get involved with other kids in school. There were white kids, Black kids, Hispanic kids, Asian kids, and yes, other Indian kids, but somehow Karan still felt as if he didn't fit in with anyone. For some reason, no one embraced him as one of theirs, who or what he was or how he fit in.

Many of the kids would hang around after school at the local basketball court in a park that he'd pass on his way home from school. He would go there before taking the bus home. Karan always admired the skill it took to dribble a ball and shoot it into the hoop. He had started watching classic NBA; his favourite team was the Chicago Bulls—Pippen, Rodman, Jordan. He would never tell anyone, but he knew their names, jersey numbers and their stats. He was in awe of them. But he had no skills, only desire.

One day, he really wanted to prove himself on the court. On his way home, Karan saw a kid from his math class, Lenny, a tall, knobby-kneed, sharp-elbowed Black kid, playing hoops with some other kids, in a game of three on three. One of the kids had to go home because his mother had shown up screaming at him, and dragged him by the wrist off the court and into her car. The kids looked around for a replacement and there was Karan, standing and staring enviously at them from the other side of the park fence.

'Hey, Karan the math whiz! Is that you?' Lenny called out.

'Hey, Lenny!' Karan waved weakly. He shrunk inside himself, knowing what Lenny was going to say next, but he wanted to try.

'Tim's mom came to get him. Can you play hoops? We need another guy.'

'I can try,' Karan said.

'Okay, get your Hadji ass over here and let's get down.' Karan wasn't Muslim, so he wouldn't have attended the Hajj anyway. He heard some form of abuse nearly every day, but it still ate at him.

Lenny, meanwhile, had turned to the other guys. 'Okay if Karan fills in? Not sure if he's any good at buckets, but he aces all his math tests . . .'

It wasn't particularly true, but Karan could play the role of the brainy Indian kid if it gave him the additional cred to play.

'Let's see what skills this towel head brings to the court,' said one of the other kids from the opposing team—Liam, bigger and brawnier than most seniors at their school. Karan sometimes saw Liam shaking other kids down for their lunch money. He wore a green Celtics jersey. 'Celtics?' Karan thought. 'Bulls!'

The game began, and every kid, except Lenny, proceeded to break his balls.

'Basketball's probably not your thing. It's an American thing. We don't have sticky wickets!' sniggered a kid from the opposing team.

'Algebra won't help you make three-pointers!' snorted Liam.

Everyone laughed, and the more they laughed at him, the more they laughed among themselves. At least Lenny kept his mouth shut.

'No cricket here. What the hell is cricket anyway? It's an insect. A black insect!'

'Curry muncher.'

'Brownie.'

'Raghead.'

The kids went on at their game, dribbling around, passing the ball to each other, making feints, shooting, and taking every chance they got to elbow Karan or steal the ball from him or block him—hard.

'This curry muncher can't play. Show me a layup,' smirked Liam.

Karan double-dribbled the ball and went in for an awkward shot.

'Double dribble! Our ball,' said one of the kids.

Karan's 'shot' hit the bottom of the steel rim and rebounded into his glasses, knocking them off. Now, he was blind besides being winded. However, he still wanted to suffer through it all just to fit in with the other kids.

'Oh, man! That was the worst layup ever. You suck. But that's okay.'

Karan's side drove down the court into the other side's basket, and Karan received a pass he wasn't ready for. He dribbled it with both hands again.

'Hadji! I told you not to dribble with both hands. That's double dribbling. Like a sticky wicket.'

Karan aggressively pulled the ball to his chest and turned to face Liam. 'Don't call me Hadji!'

'Whoa! Hadji's getting pissed!'

'Lay off, Liam. His name's Karan,' said Lenny. 'He's a good kid.'

'What kind of a name is Karen anyway? You have a bitch's name! Who named you like a girl?'

'It's Ka-Ran, with two a's,' said Karan, thinking he could just as easily think of insulting names for 'Liam', such as 'Lamb', or better, 'Lame'. Prerna had at least taught him when and how to hold his tongue, so he did.

Frustrated, Karan picked up the ball and threw it underhand, like a bucket of water on a fire, up towards the hoop. It bounced off the rim again, when Liam stole the ball out of his hands, elbowed Karan's ribs hard and dribbled down the entire court for a slam dunk into the lower-than-usual rim. 'Slam! Dunk!' exclaimed Liam, as the bully raced a victory lap. Karan's team shook their heads as Liam's team whooped and high-fived. 'Why'd you give us this Hadji? Indian kids can't play basketball!' said one of Karan's own team, trying to suck up to Liam.

The kids grabbed the ball and started bouncing it towards him, getting closer and closer until finally, Liam bounced it so hard off his chest that it knocked the breath out of Karan's lungs.

'Go home, Hadji. This isn't your sport.' And Lenny didn't even defend him this time.

Karan was so angry and scared he fled the court, skipped the bus and ran all the way home.

He finally came home much later than he was wont to—to Manish's wrath and his mother's worry. He walked right past them and marched up to his room, threw himself on to his bed and soaked his pillows with tears. He heard his mother and father yelling at each other downstairs, over him and his whereabouts. He heard heavy footsteps up the staircase, and then a warm hand on his back and head, and his mother's soothing voice.

'*Pasandeeda*,' Prerna said.

'Talk to me in English,' Karan said, without lifting his face from the pillow.

'Karan, darling, what happened?'

'I was walking home, and I saw some kids from school playing buckets.'

'Buckets? What's buckets? They have kids washing dishes after school?'

'Maan! No! Buckets is basketball! The kids finally let me play and then started bullying me. What's wrong with them? What's wrong with me?'

'Karan, it's not your fault!'

'Can't you or Dad do something about it? Call my school or something.'

'I'll talk to your father, I promise. We'll take care of it for you. Don't worry. Your father and I will do something special for you. Give us a few days.'

* * *

A few days later, Karan came home to a small portable basketball court—complete with hoop, net, backboard and court markings—Prerna had situated it near the cinderblock wall to the side of the small garden she had tilled. Prerna's backyard was small, but it was hers. A patch of green in an otherwise bleak suburb.

Karan strode into his new court, speechless. Prerna appeared behind him, holding something behind her back. A smaller-sized, junior basketball.

'You like it?' Prerna asked.

'Love it, Ma. Love it!'

Prerna pulled Karan across the court and the two wrote 'Karan's Court' on it, as though he were not only a budding basketball player but a king. He could practice and feel more confident playing with the gang of kids after school, even Liam, whom Karan vowed he would impress enough so he and his cronies would stop calling him names. He would no longer have to beg to play or be chosen last.

Karan tossed his new ball to Prerna, who shocked him by double dribbling, but then *swish*! She sunk her first shot, which she had taken 'granny-style' from between her legs.

'Good shot, Ma!'

'What do they say? "Beginner's luck"?' Prerna laughed, more at herself than anything else. 'Karan, I can't play much longer. My wrist.'

Karan understood, and eventually, he started teaming up with Sarah to convince Manish to unglue himself from the TV long enough to take a shot or two. One time, they played a half-game of 'HORSE', and by the time Manish gave up, Karan was ahead H.O.R.S. When Sarah was home, she'd always find time to play with him, despite her brother mopping up the lawn with her—Sarah had only scored one point against him ever. His mother's gift had really improved his game—now he could not only swish his shots but dribble between his legs and pass from behind his back. Karan started inviting Lenny and a few other kids to play at Karan's Court and have leftover Indian food afterwards. And now that Prerna's delicious food was part of the deal, more kids started coming home. Like mother, like son.

Chapter 10

Return to Staten Island

Alone inside the restaurant, Prerna retreated to its very belly—The Curry Bowl's kitchen—its stainless steel, tile, clay implements and appliances gleaming, but quelled of its flames and gutted of its vibrancy, scents, taste, foods and her 'family' of staff. She already missed all of them, even Parminder and his grumbling. It took all of Prerna's energy just to stand up and take it all in, this new silence. She pulled out a pin from behind her head and let her lush hair fall to her waist. Prerna stood meditatively, taking in the space and all the memories of two decades of work in it. And that's when the phone rang again, as if it was waiting to pounce on her when she was alone.

Prerna leaned against the tandoor staring at the ringing phone, letting the last pulses of the tandoor's warmth soothe her. She picked it up. 'Hello? The Curry B—' she stopped herself from saying it. 'Hello, this is Prerna,' she said instead.

'Prerna, it's Dr Annu,' said a voice on the other end.

'I recognized your voice. How are you?'

'The question is, how are you? You've closed The Curry Bowl.'

'I had no choice. You know that.'

'I didn't sponsor you so you could close down our money-maker. We have to work something out.'

'What?'

'When you came around looking for work so many years ago, you said you wanted to feed your kids and make people happy . . . Our people. Remember? Now, what am I going to tell everyone in the community? That my one-time receptionist whom I built into a real chef ran The Curry Bowl to the ground?'

'I didn't run it to the ground. I put love into the food, my father's love into every last meal for every last customer, so they remember us.'

'But there's been no money coming in!'

'I'm sorry about that.'

It didn't help that Dr Annu interfered with Prerna's operation at every turn. She never complained, but Prerna had to bear the burden of all the responsibility and received very little of the profits.

Dr Annu continued, 'It's a business to supplement my physician practice. Part of my portfolio, and now you, a girl from the streets, who, if you recall, I hired as a phone girl out of pity for her being a struggling mother with a deadbeat husband. I'm not pleased, Prerna. We have to save face in front of our community. It looks very bad to have The Curry Bowl close under these circumstances, especially by my own manager.'

'I'm not your manager.'

'I sponsored you, you are what I say you are. You aren't some rainmaker, you are a low-caste girl . . . One whom I took pity on.'

'Dr Annu—'

'Believe what you want, but I know who you really are,' said Dr Annu, before hanging up.

The call rattled Prerna, as if a snake had slithered across her feet. She exited the kitchen and re-entered the now-empty lobby. She pulled back a curtain and opened the circuit breaker, clicking off each row one by one. After exiting, she found her keys in her bag and, for the last time, locked The Curry Bowl's door and pulled its heavy steel grate down, fixing it to its frame with a heavy padlock. She had opened these doors thousands of times, juggling her bags of produce, excited at the prospect of a new day and new customers to please. Excited at the thought of working with her boys. Now, all she felt was a dull pain in her shoulders and back. 'I'm getting older,' Prerna thought. 'Older is okay.'

She stood alone on Fulton Street, staring at the chalkboard propped up on the cracked sidewalk, with the message that Ruchi had written:

'Thank you, New York City, for letting us cook for you for almost two decades. We are humbled and we are very thankful for your patronage. We will cherish these memories. Hope you will too. Much love, The Curry Bowl team.'

She looked at the entrance once more, which she'd designed to look like a mini version of the entrance to the Golden Temple. The funny thing was she had actually never seen the temple. But she'd seen so many pictures of it and heard so much about it, she felt like she was a regular there. What would the developers do with it? She only hoped they'd keep the wall bearing the children's hand prints as some sort of rune for the next business that opened there.

A light wind coming off the East River eased Prerna's stride along the colonnade of locust trees and maples planted along Fulton Street leading to Broadway, as she retraced the path she had taken every day for two decades. She had worn out at least three pairs of sandals and five pairs of sneakers in doing so (and she had secretly kept all of them, thinking she might someday use their worn soles to teach Karan a lesson about hard work).

A rush of autumn leaves swirled past Prerna, scraping against the earth as she made her way down Broadway towards Battery Park and the ferry. Music filtered in from somewhere. Up ahead, she spied a lone harmonicist playing, keeping a beat with his foot. One thing Prerna loved about her adopted city was its ever-present music, so she didn't hesitate to place a dollar and some change in the overturned hat in front of him.

When she reached Battery Park, Prerna lingered among the plane trees and considered sitting on a bench to enjoy the brackish mist coming off the waters at the tip of Manhattan. But then the deep horn of the Staten Island Ferry sounded. It was time to get on the boat and meet Manish. Prerna felt a droplet near her eye. Whether mist or a tear, both tasted of salt.

Caught in the tide of commuters, Prerna carried her bags of memorabilia into the terminal, up the escalator, towards the massive glass gates.

'Miss, don't drop your bags,' said a man in a suit, who came up from behind. 'You're carrying quite a load.'

Prerna smiled at him and hoisted the stuffed canvas bags up her shoulders. The weight of the bags made her wince in pain.

She wove through the crowd and up the stairs to settle in her usual seat, which gave her the best view of the Statue of Liberty. She watched as Manhattan receded into the distance as the ferry set off towards Staten Island.

She settled her bags around her to ensure no one came too close—at the end of a long day, she preferred keeping her distance.

'Excuse me?'

Prerna looked up, startled. 'Yes?' she said cautiously, to the man who spoke to her.

'Are you the owner of The Curry Bowl? Or do you just work there?'

Prerna laughed. Did she just work there? 'The nerve,' she thought, but she had adapted to this sort of condescension reserved for her lot. Prerna adjusted her bags and smiled. 'You could say that,' she said. 'I ran the place for twenty years.'

'Is it true the place is closing?'

'It's true. It was our last day today.'

'Ahh. Thought so. A real shame. I've been ordering from your place for the last three years. I saw the sign out front.'

'What did you usually order?'

'Palak paneer with brown rice.'

'You have good taste, sir. That's one of my specialities. It's an acquired taste—many Americans don't like green-looking dishes—but it's really my favourite to cook. It came directly from my father back in India.'

'Yeah? Not asking for a trade secret, but what's in it?'

'Don't be silly. I closed my restaurant anyway. It's puréed spinach with ginger, garlic, garam masala and other spices. Garam masala gives it that zing.'

'Ah, it was the zing that caught my attention,' said the man.

The two felt a bump that almost sent Prerna's pictures spilling out of her bag. The ferry had docked into its slip at St George.

'Need help disembarking?'

'Thank you, but I'm okay,' said Prerna, collecting her various bags. The man stood up and extended his hand. Prerna took his hand in hers and gave it a firm shake.

'Thank you for making daily lunch so special for so long. I can only imagine how all your customers feel about you not being there any more.'

'One can only imagine.'

'In this day and age, you can always see your legacy online.'

'If I ever look online for my legacy,' Prerna giggled as she considered what Ruchi's opinion about this conversation would be. 'Normally, I rely on others to check my reviews. I can't bear to see the bad ones.'

'From what I've read, The Curry Bowl had great reviews. I remember only one bad one, about bread being like glue or something. It was obviously written by a competitor. I wouldn't pay attention . . . Well, my wife's waiting for me,' said the man, turning to leave. 'Bye.'

'Goodbye, sir, and thank you for the compliments,' said Prerna. As most rushed to disembark, Prerna hung back, a new sensation for her. After the main throng thinned out, she finally made her way down. Prerna strode past the stragglers, casting their lengthening shadows across the terminal's exit. When she reached the cowled and graffitied St George bus stop, she heard a familiar honk—three sharp blasts. She spotted Manish parked on the other side, waving at her from within the car.

Prerna crossed the road and climbed into the passenger side.

Without looking up from his phone, Manish said, 'Today is the start of a long holiday for you.'

'Yes,' said Prerna, fussing with her bags in the passenger seat and strapping herself in.

He tossed his phone on to the dash, did a U-turn and accelerated.

When the Malhotras reached home, Manish parked at the curb, got out, slammed the door and headed straight in, leaving Prerna to struggle with her bags alone. 'I want to catch the last innings of the match,' was his excuse.

Once inside, Prerna's eyes adjusted to the wasteland she had never noticed before, despite living there. How had her husband always kept their kitchen—a well-appointed, blue-and-yellow tiled affair with copper counters and pots—and living room so rank and slovenly? Dishes with fresh or old food crusted on them sat in the sink, food-stained takeout containers and a collection of bottles and cans littered the floor—all emitting smells she couldn't decipher. Her hygiene had been trained by the New York City health department—thank Ganesha they didn't dole out health grades at home. Theirs would receive a certain 'F'.

Manish flicked on the cricket match and spread himself across the sofa. Prerna sighed as she set her bags down and began to clean the mess.

A pained yelp sounded from the living room. 'Triumph Knights Mumbai lost again!' Manish appeared from the living room to stand over Prerna as she laboured on. 'Did you settle all the payments?' he asked, leaning against the edge of the kitchen counter.

'Yes, I have paid cash to the staff and handed Ruchi the cheques to mail. Manish, can I make you some tea?'

Manish still had his mind on cricket and went back to the sofa without saying anything.

'I guess that's a yes,' Prerna mumbled.

The ring of the phone pierced through the silence and Prerna picked it up. 'Hello, The Curry B—' Prerna rolled her eyes as she caught herself. 'I mean, Malhotra residence.'

'Mom! How are you feeling after your last day?'

'I feel fine, beti.'

'Twenty years running a business in New York is a big deal, and closing it must be an even bigger deal,' squealed Sarah, her daughter. 'Congratulations!'

'Beti! Don't make me sentimental.'

Sarah sighed, 'Oh, mother, okay. You win. I know you're not one to cry over spilt saffron milk or the closing of a highly reviewed but humble restaurant, for that matter. By the way, my roommates loved the food you sent me last weekend.'

'Thank you, and I hope you managed to eat some too.'

'And Pita ji must be glad to have you back,' continued Sarah.

Prerna turned to see Manish, lavishly sprawled on the sofa, cursing at the television.

'He's jumping for joy. Look, beti, speaking of your father, I need to make him some chai.'

'Okay. Talk soon . . . And welcome home.'

Prerna hung up and brought some water to a boil.

Chapter 11

Waking up to Nothing

Sunlight dappled Prerna's cheeks for the first time in years as she thrashed around in bed, still in her clothes from the day before. She muttered in her sleep, eyes racing under her closed lids. Dilip was calling her up, 'Ma'am! We have trouble. Where are you? You never arrived today. The health department is here poking around with their flashlights for cockroaches and asking about our health certificate. It doesn't make any sense, because we have always maintained an 'A'! We don't want to lose it! It's The Curry Bowl's gold! Oh no, Ma'am! I wish you would pick up the phone, I smell smoke . . . The tandoor is on fire! Parminder! I knew you shouldn't have trusted the bloody bastard! He's probably the one that wrote that naan-like-glue review! You should have fired him a long time ago!'

For twenty years, Prerna barely had time for nightmares. Now that The Curry Bowl had shut down, it was only a matter of time. Now, voices invaded her head every single night—spelling out her worst fears, drawing out her worst memories.

Prerna thrashed about in her sleep again. 'Karan. *Sundar ladka* (beautiful boy),' she whispered in her sleep. She heard a scream, then an unbelievably sick thud. 'God no!' gasped Prerna, throwing her arms across her face to block the stronger rays of the sun now flooding the room.

A voice. Cardamom-smooth, honey-sweet, as enticing as saffron strands, suddenly curdled—sour as yogurt. 'Ma? Today all the other kids, some of the teachers and monitors complained about my Indian lunch. They said it stinks and called me a piece of brown shit. Why can't I just eat mac-and-cheese or a burger at lunch like everyone else? I'm never going to school again!' screamed her distraught boy.

The dream wouldn't let her go, as Karan burst into tears and tugged at the sleeve of her blouse. Prerna stroked her boy's head. 'Karan, you are a big boy now, almost a teenager. Don't complain; your friends will grow out of it,' muttered Prerna.

'No! Do something about it. Stop them from teasing me, Mom!'

Manish, still dressed in his pyjamas, shaking off his own nightmares of his last foiled insurance scheme, shook his wife gently by her shoulders. 'Prerna, wake up! You fell asleep in your clothes again. You always have nightmares when you fall asleep that way.'

'Karan!' Prerna shrieked, her eyes slowly opening as she oriented herself back into waking life. She threw her arms around her husband's neck. 'Manish, I was having a nightmare about—'

Manish cut her off. 'Yes, I know. Anyway, I've been meaning to tell you this. Now that your work is done, you can finally put your efforts back where they belong—towards our house. It's such a mess downstairs.'

Prerna eased back on to the bed and yawned.

'Maybe you can start by making me my morning chai?' Manish continued. 'Are you finally going to cook me a proper Indian breakfast, or do I have to have cup noodles or a microwaved egg muffin for the thousandth time?'

Prerna blinked away Manish's scowls with her bleary eyes. 'Give me a few minutes and I'll be right down.'

Manish strode out of the room. As his steps receded down the stairs, Prerna went to the window. The sun warmed her face as she stared down the street. Some stubborn droplets of morning dew still clung to the tree branches closest to her bedroom window.

Prerna found her phone tangled up in the sheets of her bed, and began scrolling through her messages. Sarah had called and left a message. Prerna hit play. 'Hi, Mom, I wanted to check on you. Must be a strange feeling, but at least you can finally relax. Call me when you have a chance. I love you.'

Relax? It was a term Prerna understood only in theory.

She went downstairs and set water to boil, and then took a glass of warm water to her small backyard. In the garden grew the basil, mint, lemongrass and her ajwain plant's offspring, carom seeds that Prerna used in her cooking. She laughed to herself. In the beginning, she used to use the peppermint she grew in her garden for dishes at The Curry Bowl, not realizing at the time the proper mint for cooking was a different strain with a completely different taste!

Just off the garden, in one corner of the Malhotra backyard, stood a wooden birdhouse and feeder where birds—robins, sparrows and the rare blue jay or cardinal, thank Ganesha, no pigeons!—used to pay regular visits, a small delight to behold. The birds were all gone now as Prerna no longer left seed or suet for them. She had neglected her lime tree, which no longer produced fruits because the blossoms would always wither away. Then there were her tomatoes, which she had persevered over, but were known to vanish off the vine prematurely—no doubt taken away by an inquisitive neighbour's child.

The backyard also contained Karan's Court. She glanced at it, and could almost hear Karan laughing as he dribbled a ball.

As if electricity had struck the steel cup Prerna held, it jumped from her hands and rattled loudly on the floor.

She swallowed and rubbed away the pain that had appeared in her wrist. She turned back to her kitchen to make poha for Manish.

'Going to the city later, Manish?' she asked as he came into the kitchen.

'Why?'

'I wanted to come with you,' Prerna said, turning off the stove's flame. She placed the poha on a plate for him. 'Just to meet up with Ruchi and Sarah. Haven't seen either of them in weeks.'

'You don't need to meet them today itself,' Manish said. He spooned the poha Prerna had made into his mouth as he continued reading.

'Manish . . .'

Manish ate the last of his poha and got up to leave. 'Listen, Prerna, you have been ignoring this house for twenty years under the pretext of being busy and tired. Look at the condition of the house; just check out the storage. I think it's time for you to focus on this first.'

Prerna picked up his plate and placed it in the sink, sighing as she heard the Nissan's tyres squeal.

What if Manish had married Reema?

She remembered the day back in Delhi, when her handsome future husband, who had been introduced to Karanjit through friends of the family, had come home. The 'entrepreneur' from New York with his own taxi medallion, worth 'hundreds of thousands'. It had been exciting news that he was coming to formally meet her in their home, especially to Reema, who was younger and less sceptical and more prone to have her head spun by distant stars. In the end, Reema remained fickle. Devi had ensured Prerna wore her cleanest, though not her prettiest, clothes. But she had taken great pains to ensure Reema was the one most dolled up for the day.

Prerna had actually been impressed with the handsome young man who had come all the way to Delhi from New York to find a wife suitable enough to return with. A blissful occasion was finally transpiring in the living room in which conflict usually occurred.

Back then, Manish was a spitting image of her father, with his eager grin and thick moustache. She remembered sitting up as straight as possible, trying to flutter her eyes at Manish, while Reema concerned herself with her nails and scent, and a hand mirror she kept pressed to her face. Manish's eyes had immediately focused on Reema; yet, when he tried to speak to her politely or coax her into accepting his look and suitability, she went rigid and cold. When Manish's eyes found Prerna's, their glaze dissipated. He saw the reality of her almond-shaped eyes that rarely blinked and the lids that seemed to float in the air like moths. Over the next minutes, Prerna's natural depth, presence and flashes of energy transcended the more superficial delights of her sister.

While the families continued their conversation, carrying on small talk, Manish and Prerna moved to another, quieter corner of the living room to speak alone. Prerna had expected to be bombarded with questions, she hoped about her loyalty or cooking ability, but all she received were occasional darting glances from Manish, who kept throwing glances over his shoulder to admire Reema, who still wouldn't give him the time of day.

It ended up being a one-sided conversation, with Prerna asking the most questions, mostly about what New York was like and what foods Manish preferred. In between all the blushing, shyness and silence, Prerna's enticing talk was what sealed the young suitor's affection, and the two decided to get engaged and marry. Devi's blessing never came her way.

Karanjit had sold Manish and his family on Prerna's obviously superior qualities. Namely, her loyalty, her frugality (she certainly wouldn't be running around spending all the entrepreneur's money on the latest fashions), and best of all, if a man desired a wife who was an excellent cook, well, a man could find no better than his daughter Prerna.

Prerna accepted the imperfect circumstances under which she got married. She appreciated the chance to go to New York while appeasing Karanjit's wish that she would have a better life. It wasn't a mistake, and it wasn't not a mistake either. It just was.

While The Curry Bowl was open, Prerna only focused on practical matters, the challenge and pleasure of feeding customers and creating a small community around her little restaurant. But now that she had 'retired,' she couldn't help but consider the origin and prospects of her marriage, and that meant considering the memory of her son.

Chapter 12

The Strongest Seeds

Prerna spent the morning cleaning all the bedrooms. She made and remade her bed, then did the same with Sarah's. Without pausing to think, she put fresh sheets on Karan's bed too. Then, on an impulse, she headed down to the basement. She found the basket she was looking for. It was a laundry basket but stuffed with toys and trinkets. She dragged it upstairs and placed it at the foot of the sofa, knelt down and gingerly removed all the objects from inside it. 'I Love You Mom', read one in colourful block letters. Karan had written the note on a scrap of paper, which Prerna now pressed to her cheek. She found the plastic amulet of the Golden Temple her father had hung from the rearview mirror of his trusty Maruti. This she touched to her forehead. She heard Karan's voice, 'Don't lose the gift card me and Kris and Sarah got you. This is so you learn how to drive!' She dove into the basket, and there it was, collecting lint. She kept it aside safely. Prerna and driving! Her eternal sore spot!

Then Prerna stumbled upon a small, battery-operated fan sprinkler—the kind people use to cool themselves off on the hottest days. She held it close to her chest.

'Close your eyes, Mommy,' said Karan from near her. 'Let me make it rain for you.'

Prerna felt a mist spray across her face and closed her eyes. 'It's raining, Mommy. Look!'

Her wrist throbbed. 'Why?' she cried out.

She brought the fan to her lips and gently kissed it, before pulling a hand towel from the basket and gently dabbing her face until it felt dry again. Prerna stood up and arranged the remaining objects on to a small shelf behind the sofa.

She then walked over to a corner of her small garden, where a ramshackle shed with garden tools and bags of seeds and bulbs stood.

Prerna grabbed a trio of lily bulbs, one for each of her three children—Karan, Sarah and Kris (though Kris was more Prerna's spiritual child). The bulbs looked a bit like malformed shallots that Prerna immediately imagined would make a great sambhar. But she wasn't in the garden to make lunch; she was here to plant flowers to bloom bright and yellow in the spring. She pulled her sari up over her knees and sat on her haunches, digging into the earth just as her father had taught her. After pressing three deep holes with her thumbs, Prerna dropped in the bulbs, then covered and packed them with earth.

After planting the bulbs, she stood up and stared at her hands, now completely blackened with soil. Her eyes hurt. She brushed the crumbs of dirt from her hands and went back into the house, heading immediately to the kitchen sink. She grabbed a dish brush and a bottle of soap. She sprayed dish soap all over her hands, turned on the hot water and drenched her hands, going furiously at them with the brush. She scrubbed until all the dirt was off, and the natural pigment of her hands appeared again, lighter than earth, darker than basmati rice. She had scrubbed her hands red and they had almost blistered. That was okay, she would rub them with aloe or honey and turmeric. It wasn't as though it was the first time she'd washed them so furiously. No one, not Manish, not Sarah, nor Karan, knew how hard Prerna scrubbed her hands any time they got soiled. It was better that they didn't.

Then she dried her hands with a dish towel and thrust her hand into her sari pouch to find the eyedrops Ruchi had given her at The Curry Bowl. She tilted her head back and squirted the soothing drops into her dry, red eyes.

It was late in the afternoon, with the sun beating down on them. Prerna didn't want a moment of silence just yet. She didn't want to hear Karan's last words, and she didn't want to think about what she'd be doing at The Curry Bowl at this moment. She decided to call her daughter. Her call went straight to Sarah's voicemail.

'Hi! This is Sarah! Leave a message!'

'Sweetheart, it's your mother. Nothing urgent, but call me when you get a chance.'

Then Prerna called Ruchi up on the number she'd given her of the office she was interning at. 'Ma'am! So excited to hear from you!' Ruchi had picked up the call almost at once.

'Shouldn't you answer more professionally? Try it again.'

Ruchi cleared her throat. 'MacMillan Associates. This is Ruchi . . . Better?' Ruchi laughed.

'Much better. How's the new job?'

'It's going great so far, ma'am.'

'Ruchi! Call me Prerna! I insist.'

'Ms Prerna.'

Prerna rolled her eyes and reached into the cupboard to pull out a glass.

'Prerna, can I call you back in a few minutes? I'm on a deadline.'

'Not necessary. I just wanted to see how the new job was going.'

'Going great. Speak later?'

'Sure.' Prerna hung up and filled the glass with water, drinking every drop.

It was in another backyard, Prerna recollected as she stared into the cup, that Karanjit finally escaped from the wrath of his mother's relentless tongue. He strode out, finally smiling again, to walk his eldest daughter into the family garden where he cultivated both a neem tree and a lime tree that hadn't produced a tart green fruit in years. At least his two trees gave birds a place to build their nests. In his garden, Karanjit would grow lentils and various beans that would end up in his most magical dishes. Soon he was guiding his daughter's hands in sowing seeds for vegetables, and for herbs and spices.

Under her father's guidance, Prerna sowed cumin seeds. 'Pita ji, why doesn't Dadi ma like me?'

'Don't pay her any attention, beti. She's old and judgemental. Just pay attention to the seeds.'

Prerna did just that, poking cumin into the earth one after the other with more and more enthusiasm, until she seemed almost elated by her seed-sowing. She didn't care how dirty she got!

Karanjit laughed. 'Very good, Prerna, I can see you like sowing seeds.'

'Yes, but how many seeds do we have to sow?'

'Only a few more. Are you bored of it?'

'Not at all,' Prerna said, opening her fist. 'But I am running out—and I am afraid to stop.'

'Why?'

'Because then I have to go inside and see Dadi ma's wretched face again,' said Prerna, stifling a giggle.

His daughter's sharp remark caused Karanjit to throw his head back and laugh. He sat on his knees, soiled fists on his hips, beaming proudly at his industrious daughter as she finished sowing the last of the cumin.

'Prerna,' said Karanjit.

'Yes, pita ji?' said Prerna.

'The seeds you are sowing are very lucky. Do you know why?

'No.'

'Seeds possess everything required to sprout and grow into plants,' continued Karanjit. 'Any seed can grow if the conditions are favourable, if there is enough sun, enough water, or enough praise, prayer and belief. But it's the seed that must grow against the odds, without all of those favourable conditions, which can break through any rock to become the tallest, sturdiest, most fruitful plant. Understand, beti?'

'No,' Prerna laughed.

'Someday you will,' said Karanjit. 'The seed that sprouts and grows against the odds is the one that never loses hope.'

Chapter 13

Road to Freedom

A month later, Prerna sat on a park bench overlooking the amber-lit Manhattan skyline, staring into her smartphone, swinging her sneakered feet back and forth. The view of Manhattan from Hamilton Park was gorgeous and well worth the metro and bus ride north into New Jersey. Almost like a mini vacation. A few wrinkles threatened the corners of Prerna's soft eyes and mouth; a new glow of relaxation smoothed her complexion, made her smile more easily, and eased what, on occasion, might have been a frantic gaze. Even her wrist hurt less. She resembled the hopeful girl she was in her youth more than ever.

'Siri,' Prerna said, trying to control a wistful smile. *Was she becoming like Ruchi? A millennial always glued to their phone.* If so, she didn't care. 'What was the address of The Curry Bowl restaurant?'

Siri's soothing voice returned what Prerna expected. 'The Curry Bowl restaurant. The Curry Bowl restaurant was located at 141 Fulton Street. In New York City.'

Prerna laughed out loud. She was alone with her smartphone before a flowing river and the stunning Manhattan skyline, close enough to catch a glimpse of Lady Liberty's stoic expression and the golden hues of her torch. But it was still no match for the Golden Temple in Amritsar, she was sure of it.

Prerna muffled her laughter with her sari pallu. 'Siri . . .' Prerna said again into her phone, as the booming horn of the crossing Staten Island Ferry sounded, and she watched its churning wake dissolve into the dark blue horizon. 'What was The Curry Bowl's overall rating?'

'The user rating for this restaurant was 4.3 stars,' intoned Siri. The report only pursed Prerna's lips, but inside she welled with pride and sat up straighter on the bench. What she would do for the rest of her life, she wasn't sure, but she would always relish her memories. Prerna sighed, folded her arms and stopped kicking her legs. 'Thank you, Siri. Bye-bye.' There were other questions she wanted to ask, but now was not the time.

Prerna breathed in the fresh Hudson River air and watched a moving distant ferry, like a pinch of turmeric and chilli on the horizon, bump into its slip at the point of Manhattan.

The next morning, a little tired from her mini New Jersey vacation, Prerna sat in her now clean and shiny living room, sipping on a hot cup of chai, when she first heard from Ruchi again. It was a voice message left on her cell, which Prerna now admittedly wished would ring more, if the high frequency of her eyes staring at the screen was any indication.

'Hello, Ms—uh, Prerna!' said Ruchi brightly, making Prerna smile. Ruchi's voice lowered almost to a whisper. 'Sorry for not calling you back before. I'm on another deadline. My new boss is sitting right next to me. Call me back when you can . . . Miss you lots.'

Prerna called Ruchi back, smiling broadly—if Manish had stepped in now, he would think she had drunk bhang.

Ruchi answered right away. 'Prerna!'

'Morning, Ruchi, I had gone off to sleep earlier, so couldn't answer your call,' said Prerna. 'How's the job? Show me your office.'

'Let me switch to video,' Ruchi said, appearing on the screen of Prerna's smartphone, dressed more smartly than she ever did at The Curry Bowl.

'Wow. You've really grown up! A smart young professional woman.' Ruchi sat like new royalty in a swanky black leather chair before an iMac amid stacks of books, manuscripts and the idol of Ganesha that Prerna had bequeathed to her months ago.

'Look how messy it is but that's the publishing business for you,' said Ruchi.

'Okay, now show me your lovely face,' Prerna playfully demanded. Ruchi turned the camera back around to her face, revealing sharper cheekbones and sweeping bangs contrasting with slightly sunken eyes.

Prerna put her hands to her own full cheeks, 'My god, Ruchi, you've lost so much weight! What happened?'

'What do you expect? No more Curry Bowl to feed me. Reading manuscripts certainly doesn't fill my stomach—and I'm drinking coffee now!'

'Girl! Watch your health. Whatever happened to your Mango Lassi Man? Doesn't he take care of you?'

'Paul tries his best between trying to finish school and batting his eyes and worshipping me. EMT school's putting a lot of pressure on him right now. He wants to be a paramedic.'

'That's a good, honourable profession, but you think he'll still have time for you? Stressful job.'

'We're not thinking too far ahead right now,' laughed Ruchi.

'That's good.'

'You were right about Paul. He always had eyes for me,' Ruchi said, blushing.

'When is that crazy boy going to get smart and ask you to marry him?'

'Well . . .'

'Huh?! Well, what?'

'He kind of did. And I almost fainted. We're living together now, to begin with. Getting along very well. And you know what he did? He surprised me with dinner, a bottle of wine and something else.'

'What?'

'An engagement ring!'

'You're not pregnant, are you?'

'Not even close.'

'Ruchi! I'm happy for you. You were the lassi he came in for every day. What do they say here, "love at first sight."'

'Maybe. I was too busy taking orders to notice, I guess, especially just before we closed. I miss your place and everyone who worked there.'

'Don't be ridiculous, Ruchi, it was *our* place. So, Mango Lassi Man—Paul—Paul what? What's his last name?'

'Kumar. Paul Kumar.'

'Ruchi Kumar, I like it.'

'Prerna, stop! We're just engaged. And I might keep my last name.'

'Well, the name has a nice ring to it. Like an old Bollywood pop song.'

'But we won't have a traditional wedding. We'll have more of a hipster wedding. Shotgun style.'

'Shotgun style?' Prerna laughed. 'Sounds more like you are going to kill each other.'

'No, like a quick, low-key civil wedding ceremony at City Hall—not far from The Curry Bowl, as a matter of fact. With a party and dinner after. You'll be the guest of honour, of course.'

'Very sweet. It will be my great honour to cook for the newlyweds if the bride will allow me the pleasure and my wrist isn't hurting me too much.'

'So exciting! When it actually happens.'

'What do you mean?'

'Paul and I are getting along great, but we'll probably wait until he lands a job. He doesn't want me to have to support him forever.'

Prerna cleared her throat and pulled a small piece of paper, a card, from her pocket.

'You okay, Prerna?'

'I'm fine. Just thinking about something. I need a small favour from you.'

'Anything you want.'

'I'm a little scared, but Sarah and Kris got together and got me a gift certificate for driving lessons. Gotham Driving School, near my sister's place near Columbus Circle. I'm too nervous to even sign up. Will you make the call for me? Then, I will have to do it. I don't want to disappoint those two, but I do want to learn how to drive finally.'

'Sure. Text me the number, and I'll ring them up for you and make sure they get you signed up.'

'Will do. You're too sweet, Ruchi,' Prerna said. 'You better get back to work . . . And Ruchi?'

'Yes?'

'Please don't tell anyone I'm taking driving lessons or getting my licence. I want to surprise Manish and the rest of my family.'

'Of course,' Ruchi said.

Chapter 14

Test Drive

Weeks Later

Snow hadn't blanketed Staten Island white yet, though most of the trees lining the streets or huddling in the yards of the Malhotras' neighbourhood now stood skinny, black and naked as skeletons, having lost most of their leaves to the oncoming cold. Manish sat fidgeting in a thick warm robe at the Malhotra kitchen table, staring at the headline of that day's *New York Post*—there was another pauper-to-king story about a lottery winner. He folded the paper up and smacked it on the table. 'Prerna!'

'Yes, dear,' Prerna said, entering the kitchen still fitting her purse around her shoulder.

'What's for breakfast?'

'I made you upma today,' Prerna said. 'It's in the refrigerator. You can warm it in the microwave along with your chai.'

Manish fixated on Prerna's checking and rechecking herself out in the kitchen mirror. 'Where are you going?'

'To the city,' Prerna said, pulling a puffy down jacket on.

'I don't understand. The Curry Bowl closed, and you are still going to the city all the time,' Manish said. 'It's become your daily commute again.'

Prerna sighed. 'I had forgotten what it's like to run errands for myself. I'm catching up on normal life.' She threw her arms around her husband's neck and pecked him on each cheek. 'At least we have a clean house to live in, and I can make you better food to eat while you look for work.'

Manish kissed Prerna and went back to reading his paper.

'See you later, not too late!' He called out to her retreating form.

An hour later, Prerna stood waiting for her driving instructor outside Gotham Driving School, too close for comfort to Reema and her husband David's high-rise. Prerna behind the wheel of a car? Reema would fall over laughing. Driving lessons were Prerna's little secret, her little revenge for when Karanjit had let her drive his Maruti and she had scared her sister half to death. Manish most likely thought she was having an affair, but that was so far from the truth—Prerna laughed to herself every time she thought of the idea—though her driving teacher was handsome and age-appropriate. Did he like Indian food? She wanted to get her licence so that Manish wouldn't be forced to drop her to the ferry or take her wherever they went.

'Ready to drive, Prerna?' asked Harold Ostasio, her balding but handsome and upbeat Dominican driving teacher.

'Harold!' said Prerna. 'I am ready.'

'Let's go,' Harold said, leading his student towards the school's small parking lot.

Prerna took a nervous breath. She had made progress since passing the written test and had spent hours on the simulator. Today's drive was her driver's test. Then she would have her licence.

Together the two walked into the parking lot, which was surrounded by a chain-link fence. Harold picked out their car for the day—a drab grey Ford Taurus, with a bright red sign with big, bold letters on top, 'STUDENT DRIVER'.

Prerna slipped into the driver's side, hitching up her saree a bit so she could operate the gas and brakes.

'Okay, Prerna. Start the car but remember to check your mirrors first.' Prerna checked them obediently.

'Oops, what are you forgetting?'

'What?'

Harold ran his hands along his seat belt.

'Yikes!' Prerna strapped herself in and started the car.

'Okay, today, we are gonna take a scenic route, drive west to the West Side Highway, then around Central Park, then through midtown for some city driving practice, then through Columbus Circle to practice a roundabout, then back here. Don't forget to do everything we learned so far—signalling, etc. Defensive driving. Sounds good? You ready? Let's do this!'

'I'm ready as I'll ever be,' said Prerna, taking a last calming breath and massaging her wrist before putting the Taurus in reverse and pressing the gas. The car lurched and Prerna slammed on the brakes.

'Take it easy, lady,' drawled Harold. 'When you back up, do it very gently. Don't stomp on the accelerator—press it gently and steadily.'

'Yes, I have to press the gas like I am shaping a rasgulla with my feet,' Prerna laughed.

'What's a rasgulla?' Harold asked.

'A popular Indian dessert made from chenna . . . Sort of like a white cheese mixed with semolina dough.'

Harold rubbed his belly. 'Yum! You are a chef?'

'Yes, well, I don't call myself that. My father taught me to be humble. I'm a cook, but my restaurant shut down.'

'What was the name of your place?'

'The Curry Bowl.'

'I've heard of that place!'

'Well, it's in the past now. Time to move on.'

This time, Prerna eased down on the gas and showed good skill in doing a three-point turn in the narrow parking lot, then inched the car towards the street, checking both directions and her three mirrors. She was glad there were no stray cows to look out for here.

Soon, they were zooming on to the West Side Highway, with the shimmering Hudson on their left. It was a bright, sunny, crisp and sparkling day for a drive. So beautiful and distracting that Prerna occasionally veered across the highway's broken white line.

'Keep your eyes on the road, Prerna, hands at ten and two,' Harold said. 'Accelerate smoothly to the legal limit, drive with the flow of traffic, not against it, not behind it, but with it. That way, you'll never get a ticket or get in an accident, at least one that's your fault. You can speed up a bit.'

Prerna did as Harold instructed her to but couldn't stop sneaking one eye towards the glorious flowing river. She wished Karanjit could see her now, or better, be sitting in the passenger seat, where he would probably be scared out of his mind but might also laugh and try to reach over and playfully honk the horn, so father and daughter could have a laugh together. Here, the cows were other drivers, in trucks or cars or atop motorcycles, it didn't matter—they all seemed addicted to honking at each other.

'Why does everyone always honk at each other?' she asked.

'See, in New York City, the horns are like people's voices, it's like talking or yelling at each other. Don't pay it too much attention, just concentrate on driving.'

'Yes, sir.'

At 79th Street, Prerna took the off-ramp a little too wide, sending her and Harold's weight to the side.

'Easy, easy,' Harold chided. 'You want to follow the curve close to the inside, then relax back into the straightaway. Keep the centreline of your trajectory. You will know that because your body won't be thrown off its axis.'

'Really? You really know your stuff.'

'Been driving in the city a long time.'

Prerna straightened the wheel at the end of the ramp, and everything went smoothly up to Amsterdam, where she had to execute a tricky, lurching lane change to get in the left turn lane after being startled by a horn that seemed like it had come from a docking ship. She was aware she had lurched, but all Harold said was, 'That lurch was actually necessary, because that Mack truck was coming up way too fast on your tail. You had no choice but to accelerate. Don't worry about it.'

Prerna enjoyed seeing New York from behind the wheel—it was a different perspective of the city. It seemed smaller, less immense and intimidating. Storefronts flew past, and Prerna was taken aback by how many Indian restaurants there were. She counted two on every block! She sighed behind the wheel as she turned on a yellow.

'Yellow is okay, Prerna. Better than slamming on the brakes and startling the driver behind you into slamming his brakes.'

'And honking.'

Harold laughed.

They drove through Central Park's serpentine roads, past a marionette theatre, Shakespeare Garden, Belvedere Castle and finally, past the crest of Cedar Hill. Oh, how proud her family would be of her.

'Prerna! Slow down!' said Harold, pressing his own set of instructor's brakes. 'You are driving like a cabbie, seventy miles per hour!'

'Sorry, I was just feeling the true pleasure of driving here. You see everything so differently driving in New York.'

'Great, but slow down to the limit. Other than that, you are doing amazing.'

Prerna's excitement had carried her away. She couldn't wait to tell everyone she had her driver's licence. A red light stopped Prerna at Fifth Avenue. Then she made an effortless turn on to Museum Mile, where her progress heading south was started and stopped at green and red lights behind buses, taxis and a few bicyclists. Applying the brakes also allowed her to admire the stately buildings that seemed to hold all the art, design and culture in the world. She felt both proud and small for being here. Could food be considered art? Would her work be preserved for posterity too, one day?

'Prerna! Look out! Keep your eyes on the road! You almost hit that street vendor.'

'Oh Hare Krishna, I'm sorry.'

'It's okay, it happens to all of us,' said Ostasio. 'It's easy to get lost in a dream in New York. Assume everyone on the road is out to get you. That's the safest way to avoid accidents or traffic tickets. Got it? You're doing great. If you can drive in New York, you can drive anywhere.'

Prerna knew it wasn't true—try Old Delhi or Mumbai! *Then* you could drive anywhere in the world.

At 59th Street, she turned smoothly past the horse-drawn carriages. She drove past Columbus Circle and looked up to see Reema's high-rise towering above her. Her sister had no idea she was this close, *driving by herself*. Prerna smiled.

'You enjoy driving a lot,' Ostasio said.

'I do now,' Prerna said.

'Driving is different when you do it for pleasure and not out of necessity. Want to hear a secret?'

'Sure!'

'I don't even own a car.'

Prerna gasped. 'What? A driving instructor who doesn't own a car?'

'Nope. Too expensive in the city—parking, street parking laws, the cost of gas, etc. If I want to drive, I rent. Unless I'm teaching, of course. Then I can get my driving on.'

'Well, I live out in suburban Staten Island. I can drive as much as I want there.' Prerna laughed.

'Ouch, really?'

'Yes. Something wrong with where I live?'

'Sorry, my Manhattan pride coming out. I can see why you might want to own a car over there. You might as well be in Miami,' Harold grinned.

The light turned green, and as Prerna navigated Columbus Circle as expertly as she had made any roti, her eyes fixed on her sister's steel-and-glass luxury tower. She suddenly couldn't remember which floor Reema, David and Kris lived on. It didn't matter to her how high above the ground a person lived because, as her father always told her, we all return to the earth. And Prerna wasn't the jealous type; she preferred being close to mother earth anyway.

Prerna imagined Reema, David and Kris looking down at her waving and clapping for her behind the wheel.

'I can't believe Masi is driving around Manhattan! Look at her! And doing it so well!' Kris might say.

'She's gonna get her teacher killed!' Reema might say. 'And in a Ford!'

But who cared?

David would probably just shake his head and report to Manish what he had just witnessed. None of it mattered because she was actually driving a car now.

Soon, they were back at the driving school.

'Very good, Prerna,' Harold said, applauding as she pulled the car to a smooth stop.

'Did I pass?' Prerna asked.

'Hold on.'

'Should I drive into the parking lot?' Prerna eagerly asked.

Ostasio smiled. 'Look around you, Prerna, and check your blind spots.'

Prerna looked around. All she saw was a smattering of parked cars. 'Cars? Yes, I see other cars.'

'What else do you see?'

'Just cars.'

'It's New York City. A driver doesn't always have a lot to park in.'

'Oh.'

'Remember parallel parking?'

Prerna sighed and gulped. 'Yes, I remember.'

'Okay, well,' Harold said, gesturing for her to begin.

Prerna looked around for a big enough space between cars to successfully parallel park. 'Ah hah,' she said and shifted into reverse, lining the Taurus in the space between two shiny cars that seemed fresh out of the showroom.

'Hold on,' said Harold, as Prerna inched forward and started to steer the Taurus's rear into place. 'That Audi is too expensive. I think we'd better find a set of used cars to park between.'

'Harold, don't you trust me?' Prerna asked.

'Sure, I trust you.'

'I got this,' Prerna said, sounding like Ruchi. She adjusted her mirrors, twisted and craned her neck around to check her blind spots. She spun the steering wheel clockwise, then counterclockwise, again and again as she inched the car back and forth, expertly using the gas, brake, wheel and her sharp eyes until, with a final deft pull at the wheel, an easing of the accelerator and constant pressure on the brakes, she brought the tires within a perfect few inches parallel with the curb. Whew!

Harold Ostasio was elated and applauded again. 'Great job! I was worried!'

'I told you so,' grinned Prerna.

Smirking, Harold pulled out a notebook and made some notes. 'That. That. That. And that.'

'What?'

'Congratulations, Prerna Malhotra, you passed!'

Prerna took a deep breath, exhaled and then impetuously threw her arms around her instructor. She couldn't wait to show Manish her licence.

Chapter 15

The Mehra Family

Reema Mehra returned from her Central Park jog, strangely sweatless in her cashmere clothes. She flitted around her lavish Manhattan apartment—all steel appliances, designer furniture and floor-to-ceiling windows, decorated entirely in whites and greys. Hidden behind a pair of Gucci sunglasses, she chased her long-haired, sweetly chubby and precocious teenage son, Kris, trying to corral him for breakfast before sending him to school.

'Kris, hurry up! You'll be late for school; the driver is on his way.'

'Ma, I already ordered an Uber,' Kris said, running back to his room and closing the door. 'I want to finish watching my video. I'm giving Masi an English lesson.'

'Huh?' Reema asked from outside.

'Like I did back at The Curry Bowl.'

'Okay, but hurry up. You can't be late.'

Kris settled on to the floor and flicked on his video. There he was, a little kid again, grinning in The Curry Bowl's kitchen standing next to Prerna, wearing her usual sari near the counter, the camera shaking with Ruchi's giggling.

'Masi, ready for today's English lesson? We're doing spices today.'

'Not really, but okay.'

'What is jeera? Answer in English.'

'Cu-min,' Prerna said. 'Cumin.'

'What is dhaniya?'

'In American English, it's, uh, ci-lan-tro. Cilantro.'

'And in British English?'

'I know, Kris. Cor-i-an-der. Coriander.'

'Perfect. Just a couple more. Haldi.'

'Tur-mer-ic.'

Kris pursed his lips like a little tough guy, then cocked his head back and puffed out his chest. 'Are you ready for the next one, Masi?'

Just then, a knock sounded on Kris' bedroom door, and he paused the video.

'Kris, hurry up!' said Reema.

'One more minute! Kris pleaded. 'Masi's about to pass her English test.'

On the screen, Prerna knitted her eyebrows, took a deep breath and smiled at her mischievous little nephew.

'You sure you are ready?' he asked again.

Prerna smiled. 'Sure.'

'What is hing, in your best English? And make sure you pronounce it right, because it was hard for you last time.'

'Asa . . . Asoe . . . Asafort—' Prerna threw up her hands and grimaced.

'Masi, watch my lips.'

Prerna focused her eyes on Kris' lips.

'Asa-fuh-tee-da,' Kris enunciated.

Prerna tried again, syllable by syllable, keeping a close eye on Kris's lips.

'Asa-fuh . . .'

'Masi you will never be able to pronounce it. Watch again. Asa-fuh-tee-da.'

'Asa-fuh-tee-da.'

'Good! Now once more without thinking about it so much.'

'Asafoetida!' Prerna said correctly.

'Yes!' Kris pumped his fist in the air and held up his hand. 'High-five me!'

Prerna high-fived her taskmaster of a nephew and sighed with relief. Dilip, Iqbal, Nazim and even Parminder applauded her from behind as the camera shook with Ruchi's delight.

Kris turned off the video and threw on a crisp white, button-down shirt and a baseball cap before racing out of the room to present himself to his mother.

'I miss The Curry Bowl, Mom.'

'I know . . . Kris, cancel your Uber. Don't be silly; our day driver's on retainer. We might as well just use him.'

Kris sighed and pressed the cancel button on his Uber app, rolling his eyes. Reema flitted over to the kitchen and was soon absorbed in the view of the already bustling Columbus Circle and Central Park offered from her sweeping windows.

'Ma! I haven't had breakfast yet,' Kris reminded her, appearing at the kitchen table.

'Huh?' Reema turned towards him.

'Breakfast? You know, what kids eat before they go to school . . .'

'There's scrambled eggs and bacon, and half a bagel in the refrigerator. You can microwave it.'

'Scrambled eggs and bacon? Ma, you know I don't like American breakfast!' said Kris, yanking open the fridge. 'Can't we ever have fresh naan and curry like Masi makes?'

'There's no Indian restaurant nearby,' said Reema.

'You are just in denial! It may not be as tasty as Masi's, but there are other options nearby. Just check Yelp.'

'Kris, you are driving me crazy with your Indian food obsession. Eat fast, you have to get to school!'

Kris ate his scrambled eggs and bacon, but not without making a face.

David Mehra, Reema's husband, sat in their cavernous living room, lounging in his cream-coloured Izod corduroy shorts, above which he sported a full navy jacket and silver tie ensemble. His cropped but tightly curled hair softened his clean-shaven, chiselled face. If he were taller, he might have made a career as a model.

Wearing a wireless headset, David stared into the flat-screen computer he had positioned atop his sleek desk, carefully positioned next to an enormous bay window. His gold-green eyes darted back and forth, as he spoke in his most drippingly sincere, most precise faux-American accent in the service of his more credible-sounding surname alias (whatever it took to make a sale). He instinctively flexed his biceps under his tailored shirt. 'Miss Lisa, this is David, uh, Chopra. I am an agent who represents clients interested in purchasing restaurants, fast food or coffee shop franchises. Currently, my client is looking to purchase a Middle-Eastern fast-food franchise.'

'Mr David,' the stern and emotionless voice on the other end said, 'you do realize there are many types of Middle-Eastern franchises. Right now, vegan organic is all the rage. To really satisfy your clients and make it worth their investment, you must hit exactly the right food equation. Middle-Eastern cuisine is still very common in the city. I can email you a few franchise decks and you can choose the specific type of Middle-Eastern fast-food establishment your client desires to purchase.'

'Perfect,' said David, smooth as butter. 'My secretary will send you our company credentials asap.' David looked towards Reema, who was standing near the kitchen island, staring into space, still with her sunglasses on. He snapped his fingers to draw her attention towards him. 'Uh . . . Jennifer, how much time do we have for the London call?'

'Jennifer' was Reema, David's 'assistant'. David then nodded into the air. 'Oh really? Perfect.' David scribbled some notes on a Post-it. Reema now stepped into the act. 'Sir?' she said, in a perfect no-nonsense American accent.

'Yes? Look, I'm still on this important phone call,' said David, feigning irritation. 'Excuse me, Ms Lisa, I have to put out a fire. Too many clients these days. Sorry. Please send me those decks right away so I can forward them to my client.'

'Right away,' said the voice on the other end.

'Thanks. Speak soon.' David clicked out of Skype and called out to his actual assistant, Jay. 'Jay, text me the notes on this last Skype call. Pronto.'

Meanwhile, in Staten Island, Manish stood in his and Prerna's humble kitchen, warming up a helping of cracked wheat daliya in a pan when he decided to march into the living room to make a call from the sofa.

He hunched over his cell phone and dialled the most frequent number of his autodial: Reema.

Reema answered right away. 'Manish, hello,' she said, sauntering around her apartment.

'What's up?' asked Manish, taking bites of his daliya with the old spoon he held in his free hand.

'What are you eating?'

'Some leftovers,' said Manish. 'Prerna might have fed her patrons at The Curry Bowl the best of her food, but not her own husband.'

'That's a shame. My sister can be selfish sometimes. Anyway, all is well over here, except for Kris's obsession with your wife,' said Reema.

'He'll get over it. I'm in bad shape,' sighed Manish.

'How so?'

'Have you spoken to Prerna lately?'

'I haven't. I've been a bit busy here.'

'Something is seriously wrong with your sister.'

'What do you mean?'

'Since Sarah has left for college and The Curry Bowl closed, she has completely changed. She never cooks any more, barely makes tea or food . . . Like I said, we are all surviving on cup noodles. It's depressing.'

'Ouch!'

'And I have no idea where she's been going every day—The Curry Bowl closed a long time ago.'

'Really, Jiju? That's sad. Do you think she's . . .?'

'No idea, and I don't want to know.'

'You married her for her cooking skills, now even that's gone. I'm not much of a cook, but I have other skills,' flirted Reema. She lowered her voice to a whisper. 'David is also totally neglecting me. All he thinks about is business these days.'

'Let's not go there,' said Manish, shuddering at the thought of Reema's shopping addiction. 'Do me a favour and bring the family over for dinner tonight. I want some life in this house. It's Friday, so Sarah will also be coming home from college for the weekend. Maybe, maybe I could convince Prerna to cook.'

Reema scanned her apartment for Kris's last whereabouts. 'Kris!'

'Yes, Ma?' came his voice from the kitchen nook. 'You want to go to Masi's tonight?' asked Reema.

'Yessss!' Kris screamed. 'I love her, and I miss being with her at The Curry Bowl.' Excited, he skidded across the living room marble in his socks to the foyer, where he dashed on a stylish leather backpack and a light jacket. 'I made her a present, and I can't wait to give it to her.'

Reema smiled and blew a kiss at her son as he raced out of the door. She got back on the phone with her brother-in-law. 'Okay, Jiju,' said Reema. 'Kris is very excited; we'll be there around eight.'

'Perfect,' said Manish, scraping a last spoonful of the now cold daliya out of his bowl. He turned the TV to the day's cricket match and lay back in the arms of the sofa.

Chapter 16

Musicians at the Fountain

Prerna sat on a bench near her favourite landmark in Central Park, the Minton Tiles Bethesda Fountain, mesmerized by a quartet of musicians. They played the bass, drums, a saxophone and a sitar! The youthful musicians sounded their notes off the plaza and tunnel tiles, their music blending with the flowing waters of the fountain, which to Prerna sounded like the soft patter of distant rain.

She relished passing her driving test. Harold Ostasio had been a wonderful teacher and Prerna couldn't believe she'd finally passed the test! Reema would fall over when she heard the news. And Sarah, Kris and Ruchi would be so pleased and proud. Prerna laughed out loud. She had driven at least as expertly as her father always did in the streets of Old Delhi. And no cows to chase or dodge! After receiving her licence, or maybe before, she planned to surprise everyone with it and eventually convince Manish she needed a car. Then she would proudly invite her whole family along for a pleasure drive along the 'tourist circle' she had driven with Harold Ostasio. Or maybe she could convince Manish they should move closer to Manhattan, or at least closer to a more beautiful view of Manhattan—maybe to Weehawken.

Beside her on the bench, Prerna had strewn a small collection of things from her purse. Every now and then, in utter privacy, Prerna loved to go through her purse—weeding out trinkets and memories. She stared at the contents of her purse, now scattered on the bench: her keys with a Golden Temple keychain; assorted lipsticks and blush powder; and a string of kuru seeds from the lucky kunda mani tree, a carved ivory-coloured elephant protruding from the top seed forming ridges with its trunk and tusks, like a fancy stopper on an expensive bottle of cognac, though Prerna had never tasted such a drink. Prerna rubbed the kuru seeds when she was contemplating or worried about something. She also kept a can of mace, and so far it was still full. As she surveyed the contents of her purse, her phone chimed—her daughter, Sarah.

'Beti,' said Prerna, picking up the call. 'Where are you?'

'Just finished a class. Ma, what happened?'

'What do you mean?'

'Tell me now! Papa has been calling me non-stop, every half hour. I lied and told him you were with me, and we were headed home together!'

Prerna sighed. 'We can talk about it later. I have a big surprise for everyone.'

'Dad is finally missing you.'

'Ah, he just misses his chai.'

'That and more. Anyway, Dad says we are all having dinner together at our place tonight. Us and the Mehras.'

'Oh, news to me! But that's fine. I guess I'll see you tonight then! And I'll tell you the good news.'

Prerna's phone rang again just as she hung up; it was Ruchi.

'Ruchi, Ruchi.'

'Ma'am . . . I mean Prerna.'

'That's more like it.' Prerna smiled.

'So, did you get your driver's licence?'

'Yes! I did!'

'Oh my god! Congratulations! How did this miracle happen?'

'My third attempt was the charm. As my instructor put it, I passed with "flying colours". You must have been really praying hard to Ganesha,' said Prerna, laughing. 'The truth is I maintained hope and worked hard for it.'

'When do I get my reward for my contribution?'

'You are already in the mood to celebrate! Anything special?'

'Yes, I want to taste your food again! And I would love to taste your stuffed okra again—wait, don't tell me. Ground peanuts, brilliant red chilli powder, golden turmeric, ground cumin and coriander, chopped fresh cilantro and salt. Did I get it right?'

'Absolutely. Kris must have been helping you back in the day. He was a little culinary, what do they say, "whiz kid".'

'Whiz kid . . . that's right,' said Ruchi.

'Ruchi . . . I'm also thinking about going back to India.'

'Moving back?'

'No, just a visit. It's time.'

'India, here you come! Your daughter returns!' chimed Ruchi.

For the first time in public, Prerna threw her head back and laughed openly in delight—not caring about her teeth. The musicians, who had edged closer, glanced over in surprise.

'What's that cool music? An electric sitar?'

'I'm in the park being serenaded,' was all Prerna revealed.

Prerna glanced at her watch, an old Bangalorean HMT Janata model that still kept perfect time. 'Oops, getting late, I have to get back downtown to catch the ferry. Apparently, my sister and her family are coming for dinner.'

'Okay. Life is looking up!'

'Ruchi, beti, thank you for arranging my driving lessons. Couldn't have done it without you.'

'It is always my pleasure, Prerna.'

For the first time in a long time, when the ferry landed at St George, Manish was not there to pick her up. Prerna had never taken the public bus south to their more suburban neighbourhood. At first, she was angry and disappointed—she even pulled her phone from her pocket to call him—but then she felt as if she didn't deserve to be picked up. Manish had picked her up every night and delivered her to St George every morning for over twenty years. A lesson? Divine karma? Facing the void of no Manish and no car hurt. She missed that special little thing they did together every day, through bad times and good. Prerna hung up before the call could register. She went to the bus stop and waited for the bus, huddled with everyone else. The ride would take over an hour, and she knew Manish would worry. But then, how could he have forgotten? She was already on her way home in the bus when Sarah called.

'Ma? Where are you?'

'I'm on a bus, headed home.'

'A bus?'

'I stayed too long in Central Park. I was depressed about your brother and was trying to distract myself. Then the subway kept breaking down and I missed my ferry. You beat me home. What do they say, "That's New York for you."' Prerna laughed. 'But don't worry about me, worry about Pita ji. He didn't come to pick me up. That's why I took the bus.'

'He should have picked you up, Ma!'

'Well, he's picked me up and taken me to the ferry every day for twenty years, he deserves to take a day off. I don't think he would leave me at St George on purpose or out of spite. It won't matter after a while.'

'What do you mean?'

'You'll find out!'

'Pita ji wouldn't leave you stranded on purpose, Ma. I'll be waiting by the phone until you get here.'

Prerna hung up and put her phone back in her purse, next to her can of mace. The can was purchased at the insistence of Dr Annu after someone had followed her out of the subway, all the way to the restaurant. But now that she had got her licence, she could put these worries behind her.

The bus ride lasted over an hour and took its passengers down the eastern coastline of Staten Island, where she saw the dark inky waters of Lower New York Bay, Anchorage Channel and The Narrows, most of it obscured by the industrial docks, gas stations, grocery stores and fast-food joints along Bay Street, then Hylan Avenue, stopping close enough to their house that she could walk the rest of the way.

Why had Manish forgotten? He had been unhappy ever since The Curry Bowl started to tank, and they had started to feud with Dr Annu . . . They had been married for so many years now, always loyal to each other, even if they didn't always get along. The elephant in the room, Prerna knew, was Karan. His shadow accompanied her from the local bus stop all the way home.

Her tears for her boy had long ago dried up. She and Manish had never spoken about what happened. The hard edges of blame occasionally pricked at both of them. Her Karan. If something happened to her on the way home, well, Prerna didn't really care. Nothing could hurt as much as losing her boy. That Manish didn't pick her up that night didn't matter much at all in the scheme of things.

* * *

Manish was sitting in a massage chair, dreamily watching the stock market closing bell on Fox News when he heard the front door open. He heard ascending footsteps. When Prerna found him in the darkened room, Manish threw her daggers with his eyes.

'Wow! Queen Elizabeth is home early today. Before sunset!' Manish said, adjusting his body—which Prerna noted had gained girth in the absence of her home-cooked food—mid-massage, as he vibrated in the chair. 'Sarah and I were worried about you. Where is she?'

'She's locked in her room taking a nap.'

'Tired from school.'

Despite her husband's foul mood and sharp tongue, Prerna just smiled and exited. She descended into the kitchen, where she cleared the table of a large pile of Chinese takeout boxes, before filling and boiling a pot of water to make chai.

'I invited Reema and her family over for dinner tonight,' Manish called down.

'So, I heard,' Prerna said. She turned off the stove, filled a cup with chai and ascended the stairs again. She stood in the spare room's doorway and glared at her husband, whose body continued to jiggle as his eyes simmered along with the eyes of the rageful Fox TV host. 'You know why I invited them over?' asked Manish

Prerna said nothing; just handed her husband his chai.

'Because it was the only way I could get fed anything other than cup noodles or Chinese takeout. Imagine, a man who married a brilliant cook who never cooks for her husband!'

'Very funny, Manish. Why didn't you inform me about your invitation earlier?'

'I can do what I want. It's not as if I didn't try to call you. You just never answer!'

'I would have brought home chicken. Kris loves my chicken. Especially my ghee roast chicken.'

Manish flicked off the news and exploded out of his massage chair. 'What about what I love?' he snarled.

Prerna avoided Manish's glance by fixating on the steam coming from his cup.

'You need to answer my calls if you want to know who I'm inviting for dinner!'

Prerna briefly covered her ears to avoid his harsh tones and retreated downstairs. She gently pulled out her chai sieve and filtered herself a cup of chai. Prerna set her chai and two whole-wheat biscuits on an old but ornate tray, and carried it upstairs, placing it on a TV tray between Manish and his TV. Manish said nothing and continued to glower into the blank TV screen. He took his cup in his hands, taking a sip as Prerna took a chair at the other side of the room, which seemed as distant as another country.

'Ouch! You made the tea too hot, Prerna! I burned my tongue!' gasped Manish.

'Serves him right,' Prerna thought. 'And in the end, I will be the one cooking for everyone. Karma.'

However, she sprang up and ran down the stairs, returning with a glass of cold water to cool her husband's burning mouth. The two simmered together in silence as Manish turned on the TV again and continued his massage. Prerna too could have used a massage; she hadn't had one in twenty years.

Chapter 17

Brothers-in-Law in Armchairs

Prerna's daughter, Sarah, twenty and fresh home from college, sat in the glow of her small TV on a blue loveseat with her younger cousin, Kris. On the surrounding walls flashed posters of pop, rock and rap stars—Justin Bieber, Britney Spears, Cardi B and Lady Gaga—and the top of her desk, dresser and bedside table spilled over with flowers and trinkets. And Sarah's many clothes lay everywhere.

Sarah, fair and petite, had inherited her mother's stunning eyes—a fact that kept her mother up sometimes, wondering if Sarah would ever find the 'right guy'. A bindi dotted her forehead, and her jewelled nose-stud caught the light each time she moved.

Kris had made Sarah promise they could watch some of the old videos she (or was it Ruchi? Kris could never remember) had shot of him and Prerna at The Curry Bowl.

'I get so sad when I remember that The Curry Bowl is closed,' sighed Kris. 'Remember when Masi taught me how to make naan bread? So cool and I made so much money there.'

'Naan bread? Silly American boy, "naan" and "bread" mean the same thing,' said Sarah, playfully pushing her cousin in the face and laughing.

'Okay, naan, because I'm not American, I am Indian. I don't even like eggs and bacon, or even bagels. Ick.'

'Well, that proves it,' said Sarah, pushing at her cousin's face again. 'Now I know you aren't an American. And what do you mean by making so much money?'

'I used to take change off the counter. I thought that's why it was there, and Masi never said anything so . . .' Kris shrugged and smiled. Those early days at The Curry Bowl were precious, and now the two gleefully watched themselves on video in their favourite place on Earth in utter glee.

In the video, flour coated Kris's face, hands and even his hair as he awkwardly produced a ball of roti that looked more like a ear. Behind him, Sarah was more focused on seeing who was taller—she or Kris—than learning to make roti.

'Masi, can I finally make naan? You've made me wait for weeks! I can't even concentrate at school any more. All I think about is naan, naan, naan. Give me the quiz!'

'Naan takes patience, Kris,' Prerna said. 'And you have to be careful. The tandoor is 900°F. That's a very high temperature, as hot as the core of the Earth.' Prerna winked into the camera 'If you don't know how to do it properly, you'll get burned.'

She pulled up the sleeve of her blouse, revealing a patch of scarred skin.

'Ouch,' Kris's eyes grew wide. 'I see what you mean.'

'But I think you are almost ready. Let me quiz you on what you've learned so far. If you pass, then you can make your first naan. Ready?'

'I've been ready for weeks!'

'Okay, my boy.' Prerna playfully slapped Kris's cheeks. 'What is the souring ingredient required to make mango pickles?'

'Green fresh mangoes, as opposed to ripe ones—yellow, orange or red.'

'Very good! Name the five ingredients of paanch phoran.'

Kris pouted and fidgeted as he wracked his brain.

'Hmm. Fenugreek seeds . . .'

The camera panned over to Dilip and Nazim, who were watching with bated breath. The camera lens shook with the videographer's nervous tension.

'Okay. What else?' Prerna said.

'Nigella seeds, cumin seeds, black mustard seeds, and uh . . .'

'C'mon. One more spice, Kris.'

'You can do it, Kris. The tandoor is waiting for you,' chimed Ruchi from off-camera.

Kris wrung his hands. 'Hmm.'

Prerna raptly stared at her nephew as he squirmed.

Suddenly, Kris beamed and snapped his fingers. 'Fennel seeds!'

'Good job!' Prerna exclaimed as Dilip and Nazim clapped. Parminder snorted, before exiting out the side door to have a cigarette.

The two cousins sank deeper into their seats to watch Kris make his first naan. Dilip, Parminder and Nazim huddled into the frame around Kris in The Curry Bowl kitchen.

'I miss those guys, cuz, even grouchy Parminder,' Kris said, and Sarah patted her cousin's back.

On TV, Prerna laughed and clapped as Kris stretched the naan into shape, then marched over to the tandoor and threw it in, immediately pulling his hand out from the heat. 'Ouch! The tandoor heat is no joke, Masi! No wonder you burned yourself.'

'Sarah, can you rewind and replay that moment when I threw in the naan?' Kris asked. Sarah rolled her eyes—she'd lost count of the number of times he'd forced her to watch this video. 'Just a couple more times,' he continued. 'They'll be calling us for dinner soon.'

'Okay, Kris,' said Prerna, stepping back into the frame. 'Wait five minutes for the naan to cook and then use the iron skewer to fish it out of the tandoor. Then place it on the cooling counter.

You don't want to burn the customers' hands or tongues. Otherwise, they can't taste the food.'

Kris appeared on screen holding an iron skewer. He poked it in the tandoor and scraped the naan from its clay walls, as the entire city of New York seemed to erupt in victorious applause for his feat, though the applause was actually just Prerna's and Sarah's. The naan was no less than perfect. Kris beamed with pride as they all gathered around to tear into his handiwork.

'I'll never forget that moment, Sarah,' breathed Kris.

Reema's voice interrupted their viewing party. 'Guys! Sarah! Kris! Wash your hands and come downstairs. Dinner time!'

'Can't we bring the food back to your room?' said Kris. 'I want to keep watching.'

Sarah snorted. 'Are you mad? I barely eat at home any more! And it's my mom's great cooking. For reals; not on video. And it's not the kind of food you want to run away and hide with.'

'I know,' said Kris. 'But I don't want to sit around a table with our dads.'

'What's the problem with our dads?'

'Well, I don't know about yours, but mine is praising white guys all the time. He hates brown people. I don't like it,' said Kris.

'Kris, you shouldn't fear his opinion or anyone's about our skin colour. Fear will only make you feel as though you are less than others. Got it?'

'Guess so,' said Kris before flopping down to the floor and playfully messing around trying to get into Sarah's backpack.

'Green check!' said Kris, as Sarah jumped down to stop the attack.

'Don't go into my backpack!' Sarah growled, wrestling for control of her backpack.

'I have to check your green level!' Kris laughed. He had the backpack partially unzipped. A plastic bag filled with books tumbled on to the floor, along with a photograph of a tall young fellow. 'What the heck is this?' Kris pulled the plastic bag from the books and held it up with his fingertips like a dead mouse. 'Still using plastic, Sarah?'

'Not as much as before,' said Sarah.

'I wish you would have said "not any more",' said Kris. 'You need to stop using plastic. A rep from the Green New Deal came in to talk to my class about why we need to stop using so much plastic. The world is getting hotter by the minute, and if we don't stop, we are all going to die!'

'We are not all going to die, Kris. Especially from using *one* plastic bag!'

'Imagine there are a million Sarahs out there in the world who think like you,'

'Who is this guy?' Kris asked, now holding the photo in front of his cousin's beaming face.

'Wouldn't you like to know!' Sarah said, before playfully grabbing one of her pillows and hitting Kris in the head with it. '*Badtameez*!'

* * *

Downstairs, Manish and David sat sipping on glasses of whisky and watching a CNBC business show blaring out of the TV.

'You like the whisky?' asked David, dressed as stylishly as ever. 'It's a twelve-year vintage. Got a real bite to it.' David took a big gulp and winced. 'Whew.'

Manish took a smaller sip from his glass. 'I'll say. Even the fumes set my lungs on fire.'

'So, what went wrong with your accident lawsuit?'

Manish coughed as he took a larger gulp now.

David slapped him on the back. 'Take it easy, tiger! The lawsuit was that bad? From what I remember, you planned every step . . . Quite literally.'

'Look, I really did fall and break my wrist. I also injured my knee and hip. It wasn't my fault. It was New York City's. The city owes me. Who doesn't repair the sidewalks and streetlights at one of the busiest intersections in the city? That's negligence,' Manish said, suddenly standing up and thrusting his hands in front of his brother-in-law's face.

'Hey, Bengal tiger, you're blocking my view,' said David.

'David, this is important, look at my hands.'

'What about them?'

'Look at my left wrist, and then my right wrist. See the difference?'

David leaned forward and focused his eyes closer along the contour of one of Manish's hands, then the other, front and back. 'Looks like the right one is slightly more bent.'

'No! You're drunk. Look again, it's my left wrist that was broken.' Manish pushed his left wrist under David's nose and changed the angle. 'See that sudden angle before it meets the base of my thumb at the wrist? That's where all the damage occurred. Bones, ligaments, muscles, tendons. I couldn't move it for months, let alone use it for anything.'

'Must have hurt!'

'Excruciating! Why do you think I've been so dependent on my wife? It was one thing when she was working and making money for us. It was another when she closed The Curry Bowl. She hasn't made up for the lost time.'

'But what went wrong with the lawsuit? Seems cut and dry to me. The city owes you millions.'

'I had enough pictures of the intersection, the cracked sidewalk, if you can even call it a sidewalk, it was more of an open pit, and of the dark lights that never went on at night as they were supposed to, but I didn't have enough medical reports to prove our case.'

'Why didn't you go to Dr Annu?' David asked.

'She wouldn't have helped. The situation between her and Prerna was already hopeless. She's not in orthopaedics. The damage was mostly internal. Without decent medical reports, I was sunk. What a waste to have that plaster cast on my hand for four months. I am going to appeal it. I have a better lawyer now.' Manish sat down in his easy chair and swigged down the last of his whisky.

David almost choked on his liquor as he threw his head back and laughed. 'That's my Bengal tiger!' He lowered his gaze at Manish. 'Manish, come closer, I want to tell you something. I don't want our wives or kids to hear.'

Manish leaned closer, still wheezing from the fumes of the whisky.

'Manish, my brother, you have to be better prepared for such cases, if you know what I mean. I do it all the time.'

'I wasn't faking it!' Manish felt his body tense.

'I know, I know, sit still. Yes, I believe you broke your wrist and that you deserve millions for it. It doesn't matter. You lost.'

'It wasn't my fault!' Manish sighed.

'Shh! Don't feel bad. Listen, in whatever case, you have to prepare every element. The courts are very sceptical of personal injury cases, especially with the city. The courts are part of the same network. Look at what I do. I get franchises for restaurants in different names, burn them down in a few months and claim huge amounts of insurance money. Nobody should know about it. I had tried to sell you on this idea too. The Curry Bowl was in business for twenty years. You should have burnt it down before Prerna ran it into the ground and closed it. You would have received millions of dollars in insurance compensation. A respected twenty-year livelihood in Lower Manhattan totally destroyed. That's money. Big money. Now, for your honest labour, you have nothing to show.'

Manish groaned and slumped back in his chair.

Just at that moment, Prerna called from the kitchen. 'Manish!'

'Yes, darling?'

'Have you seen my box of saffron?'

'Haven't, darling!' he called out, before whispering, 'Jesus Christ. The woman's psychic.'

'No, she's not. If so, The Curry Bowl wouldn't have closed.'

David grabbed the whisky bottle and refilled Manish's glass.

'And the best part is,' David continued, 'you could have reopened bigger and better on that money. Business owners do it all the time. It's almost like an investment to destroy your own business to the benefit of your next one.'

'That sounds crazy.'

'Breaking your own wrist sounds crazy.'

'David, I—'

'I'm only kidding.'

'Look, I had already tried to convince Prerna of your "business strategy" years ago, when I saw all the gentrification starting to happen downtown. I saw the dark horizon approaching and tried convincing Prerna of that. She's too headstrong and committed. God, I have never seen her so angry.'

'Prerna is a good cook, but in business, she's a fool. That contract she signed with that doctor was a fucking joke. Who in their right mind would give 40 per cent of their profits to someone for two decades? Women are foolish when it comes to business. Do you think I'd hand over the reins of my franchise business to Reema? No fucking way!'

'Bhai, now that you've got me a little drunk, I'm open to your bright business ideas,' oozed Manish.

'To win, tiger, you have to strike at the most sensitive issue. That's how I've been successful. If you can't, you'll stay stuck in the same place. Look at yourself, stuck in this isolated suburb for years.'

Manish turned down the TV volume. 'David, you are right, The Curry Bowl should have made me a millionaire by now. I even bought a millionaire jacket. But I could never convince Prerna. Bosh! Anyway, it's all over now. Too late. Give me another shot of whisky before we eat.'

David grabbed the bottle of vintage and filled Manish's glass.

'Bhai, The Curry Bowl was bound to fail. You know why?' said Manish.

'Why?'

'My wife used the most expensive saffron she could find to make four-dollar meals!' The two laughed until their tears ran into their whisky. 'She gets it from her father.'

Chapter 18

Sister to Sister

In the kitchen, Prerna pulled out a tray of roasted potatoes from the oven and tossed together a kachumber salad of tomatoes, cucumber, onions, chopped coriander and plenty of green chillies, mostly for Kris, who loved their bite and zest. Smiling as she worked, glad to be back in her element, she kneaded dough for fresh rotis.

'I really miss cooking,' said Prerna.

'I can tell,' said Reema, overdressed in a sequined gown with her trademark sunglasses perched on her nose. She half-heartedly sipped on a glass of merlot as she watched Prerna rummage around for a box of saffron.

Upon finally locating it, she presented it to Reema. 'Behen, please give this to Kris. It was left over from the restaurant. I saved it especially for him. I'm sure he missed my saffron milk pudding. It was always his favourite, and this is high-quality saffron.'

'He never mentioned it, but sure,' Reema said, inspecting the saffron from behind her glasses. Prerna drew in a breath.

'It was my boy Karan's favourite too . . . Anyway,' she continued after a pause, 'this reminds me of when we used to ride around in Pita ji's car. Me in the front, you in the back in your sunglasses, as Dad honked and chased cows off the road.'

'A little bit, I guess,' shrugged Reema. 'Except now, I have real brand-name sunglasses and not knockoffs like you still wear. And I have a few real cars to drive around in, not that old, beat-up Maruti.'

'Behen, that was a very reliable car! Dad had that car for as long as I've known him, and it never failed him.'

Reema sighed dramatically and changed the topic. 'So, Prerna . . .'

'Yes,' Prerna said, expertly rolling out rotis before popping one into a pan.

'Now that your Curry Bowl career is over, have you stopped cooking for Manish?'

'Why do you ask?'

'No reason . . .'

'Did Manish complain to you?'

'I'm not saying a word,' Reema said, before calling out to her son. 'Kris! Masi has some special saffron for you!'

'Reema! I wanted to surprise him!'

Reema abruptly switched tracks again. 'Sis, you remember the television series we used to watch where the heroine would transform into a snake? What was the title? . . . *Nagin ki Kahani*!'

Prerna burst out laughing. 'Reema, my god, how much we used to laugh at that show. I found the DVDs yesterday while cleaning the house. My sides were splitting just looking at them.'

'No, no! That show was dead serious. Most people thought she was a real *nagin*!'

Manish called out from the living room, above the blare of the TV. 'What are you ladies laughing about over there? The men are hungry! Prerna, I hope you're not making cuppa noodles!'

'God,' said Prerna, rolling her eyes as she flipped the roti over in the pan. 'Manish hasn't let up for months.'

'I sense some concern in his voice.'

'I think David got him drunk,' Prerna said. 'He barely raises his voice like that in front of people.'

'Behen, I get the sense Manish is very concerned about your mental health lately.'

'My mental health?'

'Yes, he tells me you've been going out all day from early in the morning even though The Curry Bowl is closed.'

'Huh?'

'You should at least tell him where you are going. Are you having an affair?'

'Reema, c'mon!' sputtered Prerna.

'Well, what else would cause your husband to call me up asking about your whereabouts?'

'Don't be absurd,' gasped Prerna.

Reema avoided her eyes and stared at the countertop.

'It's nothing like that,' said Prerna finally. 'I do have a secret though. Want to hear it?'

'Yes!'

'Kris and Sarah conspired to get me a "retirement" gift. They gave me a gift card for a driving school in Manhattan. I was so scared, I had Ruchi sign me up.' Prerna knew full well that Karan had been the prime mover in the conspiracy, but depending on her mood, especially the mood Reema's ribbing always put her in, the pain of uttering her boy's name could sink her for the day.

Reema rolled her eyes. 'Oh, god. That's all this family needs! You unleashed on the roads.'

'Reema, be quiet. I'm not a kid any more. I really enjoyed the classes, and they train you very well. Instead of having cows and rickshaws to avoid, you have taxis and trucks.'

The two laughed.

'Anyway, that's why I was gone all the time,' said Prerna.

'I'd rather go shopping!'

'The only thing I've ever liked shopping for is spices and food, you know that. You've been a fashionista since you were a child in Delhi.'

'What's wrong with that? I like to look good and feel good.'

'Anyway, I've passed my driving test, and I'm going to surprise everyone at dinner by telling them about it!'

'That's a real achievement, Behen. Now I'm not the only one who knows what a horrible driver you are.'

Prerna thrust her hands into the cabinet, searching for her preferred spices for the family meal. 'Reema, be happy for me. I'll get my licence soon, and then I won't have to rely on Manish or anyone else to drive me around any more.'

'So, I suppose you are planning to buy a car.'

'I'm not sure yet.'

'I don't think you will find a Maruti in New York, sis. What kind of car will you buy? A Mercedes, an Audi?'

'I'll probably get a practical car. Maybe a Taurus, or a Focus, or Fiesta. If Kris has his way, I'll get a Prius, a greener car. But I like the idea of a Taurus. Kris told me the Taurus is a type of cow. This would be an honour to our father.'

'Well, I don't think Manish has the funds for a luxury car anyway. He was helping you financially anyway with that black hole called The Curry Bowl.'

'Behen, you have that wrong,' Prerna said, giving a final toss to the asparagus she had been braising in a pot. 'My husband only lent me money for The Curry Bowl when the market collapsed in 2008. And believe me, he will never let me live that down. I've been footing the bills during the first four years of the restaurant and now for the last ten years. 2008 was a bad year for anyone in business at any level.'

'That's true.'

'The Curry Bowl never made a lot of profit, but it never operated at a loss either. That I am proud of. I have our ever-practical Pita ji to thank for that.'

Reema rolled her eyes.

Prerna snatched the asparagus from the pot and expertly plated it before pouring a curry sauce over it. She let her gaze linger on Reema. 'Sis, what is it like to see the world through light purple glasses?'

Reema didn't bother answering the question. 'I think you are losing it with all this driving business. It must be making you manic. Cool down.'

'I don't like being dependent on people, you know that.'

'Sometimes, to be really successful, you have to depend on others. Look, David has been connecting with some of the most powerful culinary investors and chefs in America on some restaurant franchising concepts. Speak to him. Maybe he can recommend you for one of them.'

'I really don't want to work a franchise or some corporate kitchen. No soul, the motive is solely profit. I like to feed real people. Every time I speak to David, he tries to convince me. He even has Kris trying to convince me.'

'You know what, behen?' continued Prerna. 'Ever since I took the pictures of the Golden Temple and Pita ji off the walls of The Curry Bowl, I can't stop thinking about India.'

'David and I can't even think about going to India anyway,' said Reema. 'We've been here so long, we can't make the adjustment any more. Last time we went to Delhi, we both had to be hospitalized for stomach infections.'

Kris raced into the kitchen to hug Prerna from behind. 'I love you, Masi!'

'Apparently,' said Prerna. 'What brings on the hug?'

'The saffron you saved for me, for one.'

Prerna reached around to hug Kris back.

'I made a gift for you,' said Kris, turning to Reema. 'Mom, can I get your car key so I can get Masi's present?'

'They are in my Saint Laurent on the living room couch.'

Kris raced out of the kitchen and appeared with Reema's stylish purse.

Reema dug around in it and produced the key to her Audi. 'Don't drive off, Kris,' Reema snidely joked. 'It's easy to get lost in the Staten Island suburbs.'

'I'm too young to drive. But if I did, I'm sure I could find my way back,' Kris said, snatching the key from his mother's hand and running out.

'What did Kris get me, and why?'

'Not sure, but he still won't stop talking about The Curry Bowl. It's as if he never quit working there. I practically have to pull him away from all the videos he took there.'

'I loved having him there. In the early days, he always helped me with English, and it was a pleasure to teach him how to prepare Indian food. He really took to it.'

'You've been a bad influence. Your Indian food is all he talks about. Masi's food this, Masi's food that.'

'And I'm making special bharwa aloo, especially for you, David and Kris tonight.'

'Sis, I already told you, David can't eat Indian food any more. It upsets his stomach, and he can't take the spices. He gets indigestion. If he eats it, he'll end up in the bathroom all night.'

'I can leave the red pepper out and only use the yogurt, ginger, peas and buttermilk. The mild version.'

'Not sure he'll risk it. Especially with all that whisky he's drinking with Manish.'

'Manish is drinking whisky?'

'Yes, David brought a very expensive bottle of twelve-year-old Scotch with him.'

Reema reached for her purse. 'Let's take a break and go out back,' said Reema, which Prerna knew meant she was itching for a smoke.

'Just for a few minutes,' Prerna said. The sisters exited the kitchen into the Malhotras' backyard.

Reema took out a gold and cream cigarette and lit it carefully with a fancy-looking gold lighter. Prerna immediately began waving away the smoke to keep a healthy bubble of air.

'This habit is going to kill you,' said Prerna severely.

'I have to do something to block out the smell of these herbs. I'm allergic to plants now. And I'm not smoking those cheap Russian Sobranies any more,' said Reema, taking a deep drag in the evening air. 'I only smoke Treasurer Golds now. David has them special delivered all the way from Burbank . . . Also, Dadi smoked. And look how long she lived!'

Reema smirked before taking another long drag. 'My smoking is like your driving; a habit that will kill someone.'

Prerna watched from the outside as Kris rambled around the kitchen, waiting for them to come back in. 'He's so tall,' she said fondly. 'Growing so fast!'

'Karan would have been just coming out of puberty around this time, sis,' said Reema quietly, blowing out a fresh plume of smoke.

Hearing her son's name threw Prerna off. She struggled to contain her feelings and cleared her throat. 'Kris is starting to look a lot like Pita ji now!' she said, hoping Reema wouldn't notice how emotional she'd become. 'I've been missing Dad a lot lately. He taught me so much. Pita ji was a real saint.'

'We're in America, just call him "Dad" will you? And saint? He left my mother, didn't he? And by the way, if you cared so much about him, you would have helped me with his cremation. You left me to take care of everything myself.'

'Reema, you know I had a limited time to have my green card sponsored. Pita ji insisted. You also know that after 9/11, it was a huge risk to leave the country!'

Prerna's mind reeled, struck by recollections of her life from almost two decades before. She was younger, smoother-faced, in her thirties, sitting on the dusty floor of her and Manish's small, one-windowed Queens apartment, clutching the phone to her ear with both hands while little Sarah skipped and played nearby, and Karan kicked at her stomach from inside her womb. Manish had been out hustling courier work that night she called Karanjit in Delhi sobbing, 'Pita ji, I've sent you the sun every day I've been in New York. Have its beams reached you?'

Karanjit lay in bed prostrate, pale, coughing up bile into a rag, still wearing his effervescent smile, though below it, his collarbones protruded. 'I've felt the warmth of your American sunbeams every day,'

'I hear you coughing. How is your health, Pita ji?'

'I may not sound like it but I'm feeling much better,' he said, stuffing his bile rag under his pillow.

'I miss you, Pita ji. I am considering coming to visit you,' Prerna said.

'Beti, please don't. I don't want you to risk it,' Karanjit said, failing to prop himself up again in bed and collapsing on to his pillow. On the phone, he had sounded so weak.

'I can hear you wheezing, pita ji!'

'It's nothing, beta. Don't worry about your trusty dad,' Karanjit said. 'Please don't risk leaving New York now. Reema and David are arriving in Delhi tomorrow.'

'Yes, I know . . .' said Prerna.

'After you get your green card, then you can visit, and we can all go to the Golden Temple in Amritsar with both your children. Promise me you'll come then!'

'I promise,' Prerna said, almost out loud, right there in front of her sister in the backyard.

'Sis, sis! You're drifting off. Snap out of it.' Reema clicked her fingers in front of Prerna's face impatiently.

After a while, Prerna spoke up again. 'Reema, what you said about me not wanting to 'be there' for Pita ji isn't true. You must remember. Before I got The Curry Bowl operational, I was living literally barefoot and pregnant. That was just after

Sarah started walking and talking, and Karan was still in my stomach. I called Dad one day and begged him to let me visit him on a parole visa. He was so sick. You and David didn't have the same problems or risks I had then. I was adamant about visiting him, you know that, but he was more adamant that I didn't risk it. I made every decision to not give Dad a heart attack. And I wasn't going to ruin his dreams for me. So, I settled here to get the restaurant going. That was his dream too, and I wasn't going to break my promise to him or let him down. And I certainly wasn't going to travel with Karan. It could have affected his health.'

'And look what happened to him.'

'Don't you say that! I might have not been allowed re-entry. I would have done anything for Pita ji, and you know it.'

'Come on, Prerna, you could have got a parole visa if you wanted. Suddenly you care about him?'

'Pita ji meant the world to me. When I visit India, I plan to stay in our childhood home.'

'Which home?'

'Our home in Old Delhi.'

Reema's mouth flew open, causing her expensive-looking cigarette to fall. She stamped it out quickly under her Gucci boot into the soil of Prerna's garden.

'Reema, please don't put your cigarettes out in the garden. It's bad for the plants.'

Reema grasped Prerna by the arm at the door. 'So, this is why you and your husband arranged dinner tonight. To scheme about Dad's house. I get it now. I was so ridiculous to not have seen it before.'

She strode into the house without a backward glance at her stunned sister.

Chapter 19

The Dinner

You could cut the tension between the sisters with a knife. 'David!' Reema called out, striding towards the living room.

'Yes, hon,' David swaggered out in his stylish shirt. Reema grabbed him by the hand and led him into a corner to whisper something in his ear—about the family house, no doubt.

'When's dinner ready?' yelled Manish from his chair in the living room, slurring his words from too much whisky.

'Manish, tiger man, it's your lucky day. No more cuppa noodles!' David said, returning to the den.

'Dinner's almost ready!' called out Prerna. 'Turn off the TV. Sarah! Kris! Kar—' She froze. It had seemed so natural! She was so sure that he would be upstairs with his sister and younger cousin. Prerna pulled the pallu of her saree over her mouth. She just had to get through this dinner somehow, and then she could think of him again.

She busied herself at the table, simply to forget.

A small thunderclap of footsteps descended the stairs. 'Ma, it smells delicious!' said Sarah, as Kris, who was just behind her, said, 'It's like we're back at The Curry Bowl. I'm starving!'

Then Manish lumbered in, eyes red from drink, looking rough around the edges.

'Manish, you smell like a distillery,' Prerna exclaimed.

'Blame David! He brought me some fine old whisky . . . Shome fine whishky . . .' he trailed off in his mangled brogue.

Reema pulled David down to the seat next to her and pushed her chair closer to his.

'Masi, what did you make? I can't remember how long it's been since we all sat down as a family to enjoy your amazing food.'

'You sound more and more like an adult, Kris,' Prerna smiled as she presented her dishes—roti, naan, bharwa aloo, asparagus, yellow dal and raita. 'At The Curry Bowl, we were always so busy serving the customers. Our extended family. And I always kept you busy teaching me how to correctly pronounce the names of spices in English, so I would have more credib . . . credibell . . . credib—.'

'Credibility? Masi? You didn't need more credibility; your food spoke its own language!'

'Kris, you always make me smile, even when I feel down.'

'Why do you f-feel down?' asked Manish.

'I can't keep my mind off Karan tonight for some reason. Everyone is here but him.'

Manish reached over and gave his wife a drunken, rare hug.

'I love you, Prerna.'

Prerna blushed and set down the dish she was passing along.

'Masi, these rotis are better than I ever tasted at The Curry Bowl.'

'Enjoy every bite, darling,' said Prerna, ruffling his hair.

Manish bit into his roti. 'Even with a numb tongue, my wife makes the best food. Hands down.'

David reared back in his chair and waved his finger. 'Manish, everyone can cook. Prerna is an okay chef. But it's the white chefs, you know, French, German, American, who know how to prepare the top cuisines. Plus, they understand business much better than these homegrown Indian chefs.'

David had both his son and sister-in-law clearing their throats, sneaking mischievous glances at each other.

'Really?' said Manish, having the drunken gall to be interested, as he gobbled down his roti. 'When I taste my wife's food after so many years, not sure I agree with you, David.'

'Hear me out. Bengal tiger, have you ever even been to a Michelin-starred restaurant?'

Manish pretended to think, even as he devoured another roti. 'Can't say that I have.'

'Then how would you know?'

Kris lowered his gaze, picking at his roti carefully as if eating fish from its bones. He leaned towards Sarah's troubled face. 'Here he goes again.' Both laughed, as Prerna sat stoically staring at the two macho men discussing the merits or demerits of her food, as they gobbled it down.

'Brother, have you tasted the quality of food at restaurants like Eleven Madison Park, or Daniel?'

'No. Too stuffy for me.'

David suddenly turned to glare at his son. 'Kris, these are the restaurants and chefs you should look up to, not Indian cooks. Cooks are not chefs, understand? There is a difference.'

Kris swallowed. 'Dad, to me, Masi is a chef.'

'What? You must be kidding!'

Now Reema piped up. 'Masi's a good cook of course, but Kris, there are chefs out there who run places like Le Cirque, Jean Georges—and Per Se, right across the street from us. And I've eaten at all of them. I mean, they're so close to where we live. And you have too!' Reema looked at her sister.

'You like the food, Reema?' asked Prerna quietly.

'Yes, delicious as always.'

'Kris is right, Chacha,' Sarah finally said.

'Call me uncle, Sarah, please.'

'Uncle David, the world is changing . . . Indian food is becoming more popular now because of chefs like Mom—'

'I don't think I will be able to digest tonight's dinner,' David cut his niece off. 'It's too much spice for me . . . Prerna, do you have any milder food tonight?'

'There's the roti and the aloo. I left the hot peppers out of it. And the naan, of course. Kris helped with that.'

'Really, son? You helped with the naan?'

'I pretty much made it from scratch. You didn't notice the mess I was making in the kitchen earlier in the evening?'

'Huh!' said his surprised father.

Sarah scooted closer to Kris. 'Do you know the coconut syndrome?' she whispered.

'No, what is it?'

'It's when brown people think they are actually white, just like a coconut.' The two muffled their sniggers behind the bowl of raita.

David wasn't finished. 'You might disagree, Prerna, but in a way, it's good The Curry Bowl closed. Little insignificant mom-and-pop, or in this case 'mom' restaurants are degrading the image of Indian food. No Indian cuisine rainmaker has appeared on the scene, and I doubt one will.'

Prerna almost choked on her roti. Her arched brows began to knit, and she felt pain rising in her wrist again.

'They are too individualized and local. That makes them less valuable in the franchising world. My clients would never invest in a place like The Curry Bowl. Too small. Not enough potential.'

'Want another potato, Uncle David?' Sarah asked, trying to change the topic.

'Sure.'

'Masi has potential. I know because I used to work there, Dad,' said Kris, before turning to Sarah. 'Sarah, how much did we used to steal from the register every day?' Sarah covered Kris's mouth with her hand. 'Kris! Don't tell Ma about your constant embezzling!' The family laughed as Kris playfully hit her head. 'Oops! Now everyone knows.'

He suddenly put on his best Prerna imitation, down to the constant massaging of her wrist. He placed his pinky and thumb to his chin and ear. 'The Curry Bowl, how can I help you? Sure. Lunch special $6.95, comes with rice. You want naan, a dollar extra.' He made Prerna sound like a mafia moll. The families laughed again.

'You kids,' said Prerna, approaching the counter to plate another serving of roti for everyone. 'Kris, Sarah, you are both lucky I don't have any tears left. I'd be weeping by now otherwise.' She slapped a roti on to Kris's plate and kissed the top of his head.

'If it wasn't for Ma, you would have fallen into the tandoor that time you tried to make naan with Parminder. Remember?' asked Sarah. 'Lucky Ma and Ruchi were there to grab you by the belt and save your butt.'

'Parminder certainly wouldn't have saved him!' Prerna smiled.

'So,' David suddenly spoke up again, sounding deliberate. 'Sister-in-law, there's a rumour going around the family that you are going back to India.'

'It's not a rumour, it's the truth. It's been a long time since I've been home.'

'Prerna! When did you make the decision?' Manish pushed himself away from the table, teetering on his whisky-loosened legs. 'Nobody in this family tells me anything any more! Where they go, what they do—'

'Tiger, relax, sit down. You drank too much.'

Manish sat down again and turned to Prerna.

'Why didn't you tell me about this, Prerna?'

'Did Prerna also not tell you she got a driver's license?' asked Reema snidely.

'What? Prerna! With a driver's license?' Manish gasped, as Kris and Sarah applauded gleefully.

This wasn't the way Prerna intended to drop the news, but she looked at Manish tenderly and said, 'Manish, I wanted to surprise you. That's why I've been going to Manhattan all the time. Kris and Sarah had gotten together and got me a driving school gift card years ago. I had to use it. You don't know how guilty I felt, making you pick me up all the time. You deserve a break.'

Kris leaned over and gave Prerna a huge side hug. 'I'm proud of you. When can we go on a road trip?'

'After I return from India. Deal?'

'Deal,' Kris said, raising his palm for a high five, which Prerna returned to Manish's dismay. 'When are you planning this India adventure?' asked Manish, folding his arms. 'And I suppose you are going to drive yourself back and forth from the airport now, too.'

'Manish, don't be ridiculous. I don't even plan on buying a car—'

'How would you? The Curry Bowl didn't give you any huge payoff. You'd have to come to me for the money. If you had agreed with me about how to make the business profitable at its peak, then maybe you could afford a few cars like the Mehras,' said Manish, placing his hands on either side of his empty plate.

David snorted. 'Tiger's got a point.'

'The most we can afford now is a used car! Last year's model,' continued Manish. 'And I'll have to go back to eating cuppa noodles and oats again. I don't want to go backwards in life.'

'Darling, we won't go backwards. You are overreacting.'

'Riding with Prerna even in a fully loaded lux vehicle would be bad enough, riding with her in a used car would be a death trip,' said Reema, sweeping her purse off the floor. 'I already need another Treasurer.' Reema slipped another cigarette from her purse.

Prerna smiled, but her eyes flashed. This was supposed to be a table full of adults, but you wouldn't believe it, given the selfishness on display.

Sarah stood by her mother's side, placing her arm around Prerna's shoulders. 'Pita ji, don't worry so much. We can take care of everything we need to when Ma's gone. She deserves a vacation after running The Curry Bowl for so long.' Everyone at the table had to nod at this; the fact was undeniable. 'And, Ma, we love you,' said Sarah. 'You must go. It will help you recover from closing The Curry Bowl and . . . Well, you need to see new skies and breathe fresher air.'

'You certainly won't find that in India,' said Reema, laughing.

David laughed too. 'Prerna, Reema tells me you are planning to visit her house,' David continued.

'Reema's house? It's *our* house.'

'No, it's not. Let me be perfectly clear right now—you can't visit Reema's house without our express permission.'

Prerna started massaging her wrist.

'David Chacha!' interjected Sarah furiously.

'Call me uncle, Sarah!'

'The house is Ma's house too! She grew up there.' In her anger, Sarah hadn't realized when she stood up and leaned towards her uncle. 'She has an equal share in Nanaji's property.'

'Relax, Sarah,' said David dismissively, turning to Manish. 'Bro, you really are raising a little tiger here. Sarah, the truth is, the house was placed only in Reema's name. I saw the will last time we went to India. That house only had Reema's name on it. Plus, it's a wreck, so I'm not sure if it's worth anything, but . . .'

'I don't believe it,' Sarah said, slumping back in her chair. 'I just don't believe it.'

'Believe it, Sarah.' David finished off his roti. Kris's lips had started to quiver. Prerna stood up to embrace him, placing her cheek on top of his head. 'Our adult talk is upsetting Kris. Let's enjoy the rest of our meal and forget about the house for now.'

Kris's eyes glistened. 'Kris, don't get upset,' said Prerna. 'Why don't you go up to Sarah's room? I'll bring you more food later.' Kris shifted out of his chair, wiped his eyes and fled the kitchen. Everyone at the table fell silent and listened to Kris's steps until Sarah's door slammed shut.

'Oh, boy,' said Reema. 'Sister, if you were so concerned, why didn't you go back to India with us?' She held her cigarette between her thumb and forefinger, bouncing its end beside her plate to pack the tobacco. She glanced sharply across the table at Sarah. 'You need a reality check, Sarah. You know that Didi is not Nana's real daughter. He picked her up from the street, and he left nothing for her. Let's not talk about the Delhi house again. Your mom didn't even go to our father's funeral.'

Manish slammed his hands on the table and moved closer to defend his wife. 'That's enough, Reema. Stop speaking to your sister like that! Not in her own house.'

David stood up from his chair to glare at Manish. 'Relax, tiger, don't talk to my wife that way. You've had too much to drink as it is. Look, sorry, but Prerna's not the legal heir to Karanjit's house. It's just the way it is.'

Reema was not done either. 'Sure Manish, now that you need money, you finally support your wife. Eyeing our—my—ancestral land!'

Manish exploded. 'Bullshit! You and David took advantage that Prerna was pregnant with Karan at the time and couldn't go to India. You transferred everything to your name behind her back.'

Prerna clasped her hands together and sighed, and now she stared blankly across the landscape of a half-eaten meal and family dysfunction. She knew that Reema and David knew she couldn't attend Karanjit's funeral because her visa wouldn't allow her to come back if she did. She wouldn't break and she wouldn't cry; she couldn't. But it would break Karan's heart to see her in this situation. She had to stay strong for both of them.

'You guys are too much,' said Reema, taking out her gold lighter and standing up, 'David, let's get out of here. I need a smoke.'

'Let's calm down and be reasonable. It's simple. Prerna wasn't the legal heir. She was adopted!' David said. 'We didn't want to lose the house.'

Prerna very slowly started to shake her head, her eyes darkening as she felt pain shoot through her wrist. She started to massage it and kept staring. 'I couldn't visit our father before he died because of visa issues, Reema, you know that. I would have lost The Curry Bowl. Dr Annu was my sponsor—both she and Dad advised me it was too risky to leave the country at that time.'

'Why are the Malhotras always so greedy for money? Didi, you also lost your son because of this greed.' Reema made to light her cigarette.

Prerna's eyes became slits. 'Reema, you can't say that. And no smoking in the house.'

'Fine. Let's go, David.'

'I don't want to go yet. Manish and I were planning to watch cricket replays.'

David! Let's go!' Reema grabbed her husband's arm as if it were another purse and led him out of the room across the living room to the front door. 'Call Kris, David.'

'Kris! Time to go!'

Kris dragged his feet down the stairs. 'I haven't given Masi her gift yet!' said Kris tearfully.

'Masi doesn't deserve a gift,' said Reema, wheeling around, lighting her cigarette inside just to annoy Prerna further. 'Masi is not your Masi. I'll explain after we leave this boring suburb.'

The front door of the Malhotra house slammed shut. Manish and Prerna sat together in silence at their dinner table, not uttering a word. The silence was finally broken when Sarah began to weep.

Chapter 20

The Morning After

Prerna woke up in her bed the next day wearing an uncharacteristic scowl. She thought going downstairs would improve her mood. She could hear Manish's loud snores all the way to the bottom of the stairs. At the last step, Prerna's eyes caught the picture of Karan she kept near the bannister, on the living room wall. She had placed it there so she could see it—see him—any time she departed or returned to the house, which until recently, had been every day. In the picture, Karan was gleefully winking into the camera. It was probably taken just before her troubled boy playfully misted Prerna's face with water, before saying to her, 'It's raining.'

As she stroked his cheeks in the photo, she thought she heard a phone ring. And it wasn't just any phone. It was the old model that rang in The Curry Bowl that fated day.

That day, Prerna had been in her restaurant's bathroom, washing her hands before preparing the special buffet for Durga Pooja, a holiday commemorating war—not any war, but a protective and fierce maternal form of war waged to combat evil or negative forces that threaten peace, prosperity, or, as Prerna liked to believe, love. Karan had called her in the midst of a frantic day.

'Mommy, are you busy?'

'When am I not busy, beta? I'm at work. It's Durga Pooja today.'

'I need help.'

'With what?'

'Come to my school, please.' Karan's voice cracked, reducing to a whimper. 'The other kids won't stop bullying me and calling me names! I'm trapped in the bathroom stall!'

Prerna froze amid her buzzing staff, who were more active and occupied than she had ever seen them, preparing and slinging all the foods destined for Durga Pooja's special buffet.

Her boy was a sensitive kid, and it wasn't the first time he had called her in a panic.

'Karan, take a deep breath and calm down,' she told him gently, making a mental note to make his favourite dinner to cheer him up. 'Be brave. You are a grown-up boy! I'm in the middle of getting the buffet ready. Call your father right now. I'll call him, too. He can come right away.' Had that been all Prerna said to her boy that day while she checked on the buffet and made the final adjustments to the pooja decorations on the tables and in the lobby? It had been.

When the phone rang next, Prerna answered in a monotone, 'The Curry Bowl, can I help you? Today's buffet special is inspired by Durga Pooja, aloo posto, shukto . . .'

'Hello, I need to speak with Prerna Malhotra. It's important.'

Prerna lowered the phone from her ear, cradling it as she closed her eyes. She took a calming breath and placed the phone back to her ear. 'This is Prerna Malhotra, who's calling?'

'Mrs Malhotra. This is Richard Debin. I'm calling from PS 43 in Heights Manor. I'm the principal here. Mrs Malhotra, I have some bad news.'

Prerna shuddered on her feet. 'Yes?'

'It's your son, Karan . . .'

'What about him?'

'It's better we talk in person. Can you come to the school?'

'I'll be there right away.'

She hung up the phone. 'Iqbal! Dilip! I have to go! It's an emergency!' Prerna tore her apron off her sari. 'My son is in trouble.'

'Ma'am, what happened?' Iqbal ran from the back of the kitchen and caught up with Prerna in the lobby. 'What happened?'

'I'll explain tomorrow. I have to go. Make sure Durga Pooja goes smoothly.'

'Don't worry; The Curry Bowl will be in good hands.'

Prerna raced down the streets, pain twisting through her right wrist. These were ill portents—not once had she left her restaurant before closing time. She was always the first one in, the last one out.

Lower Manhattan and the ferry ride back to Staten Island flashed by. Reaching St George and bolting out of the terminal, she luckily found a waiting taxi, which she, for the first time in her life, flagged down screaming, 'Taxi!' She'd never done that in her life before. The taxi dropped Prerna off in front of her boy's school. An ambulance and yellow police tape cordoned off an area alongside it. The police canvassed the area as hundreds of schoolkids stood outside murmuring. Someone had the gall to laugh.

As Prerna ran forward, she heard someone whisper that a boy had jumped off the roof.

A mother's worst fear swept Prerna through the double lines of yellow-and-black police tape, which she threw above her head as she whisked past in her sari.

No one needed to tell her—she knew it was Karan.

'My boy! My beautiful boy! I'm his mother! Let me through!' Prerna screamed, 'What happened to my boy?'

In the centre lay a small body, shrouded in white. She had been in America long enough—and seen enough crime shows—to know what being covered in a white sheet meant. Paramedics rushed the white bundle strapped to a gurney into the back of an ambulance.

Two sturdy police, a man and a woman, at first blocked her entrance. 'Lady, we need your ID. Then we'll let you through. Are you the mother?'

'Yes.' Prerna thrust her hand into her purse and pulled out her ID. The policewoman checked it against Prerna's face. 'Okay. Ma'am. I'm sorry,' she said softly and lifted the last barrier of tape so Prerna could pass under.

'My boy, my boy . . .' she wailed, sinking into shock.

A bearded man in a suit, Principal Debin, ran to Prerna's side, trying to calm her. 'Mrs Malhotra. I'm so sorry. There's nothing we could have done.'

'He called me and said he was being bullied!'

'I'm sorry . . . I'm sorry,' he kept repeating.

The last thing Prerna remembered from that day was sitting in silence next to Karan's tiny body in the ambulance.

* * *

'Good morning, Ma!' Sarah blared behind her, making Prerna jump. She didn't know how long she'd been sitting on that last step, clutching Karan's photo.

'Are you okay?' her daughter asked, sensing at once that something was wrong.

'I'm fine,' said Prerna mechanically.

'Right. Dad sure was drunk last night.'

'Shocked me too, but he's been depressed. He needed to let off some steam.' Prerna pushed herself up from her knees and walked into the kitchen. Sarah followed and stood behind her mother as she stared out of the window. Prerna put her arm around her daughter, wrapping her into a tight hug. She let her go only when Sarah yelped that she couldn't breathe.

'Last night was a disaster,' said Prerna, filling her cup with water.

'Except for your food, of course.'

'Food is easy.'

'For some. You, and maybe Kris.'

'Maybe.'

'Mom, I saw the way you were sitting on the stairs under Karan's picture. Stop blaming yourself.'

'For what?'

'You know!'

Prerna wanted to say something, but she couldn't find the words.

'Ma, a quirky kid like Karan isn't easy to raise, especially out here in the suburbs. You always tried to inspire and encourage him. I can testify to that.'

'I should have been there.'

'No, Dad should have been there.'

'Maybe. But his bullies were just awful.'

'I know. As I said, it's not your fault. It's the circumstances. No one would blame you for running the restaurant. Someone had to make ends meet around here. You deserve all the credit for this family. And I love you.'

Sarah pulled Prerna into another tight hug.

'I saved something, Sarah,' Prerna said, pulling away. 'A message you left me months ago. Listen.' Prerna found her phone and pressed play: 'Hi Mom, it's Sarah. Twenty years of running a restaurant in New York is totally epic. Most restaurants close in the first few months, but you kept The Curry Bowl going. On your own terms. As a cook, and a strong woman, you should be so proud of your achievement as both an Indian chef and a strong woman. You inspire all of us. Muah.'

'I hate hearing my voice,' Sarah said. 'But I meant every word.'

Prerna glanced out of the window at what was left of Karan's Court. 'I tried to support him.' She dumped the water from her glass into the sink, sighed and massaged her wrist. 'What kind of mother am I?'

'Mom, it wasn't your fault. Life has to move on. Stop punishing yourself.'

'But Karan called me that day in a panic. I didn't take it seriously. I thought he was just being his usual sensitive self. I should have met with his school adviser earlier.'

Sarah pressed a finger to her mother's lips. 'Maybe it would have helped,' Sarah said. 'Maybe not.'

'At least I still have you.' Prerna smiled and reached across the sink for the moka pot, trying to brighten the mood. 'I'll make some coffee so you can wake up properly.'

Sarah stopped her. 'Coffee's fine—necessary even—at college. But today, I want to have chai with you. And I'll make it. Hope I don't screw it up. I didn't inherit the cooking gene.'

'Beti,' Prerna said warmly, watching her boil the water and filter it.

They took their teacups to the table.

'You're not going to let Reema and David stop you from going to India, I hope. That's your home. Your real home, and home is home. You have the right,' said Sarah sternly.

'It's just talk. Those two always talk and scheme and get each other "up in arms"—that's how you say it, right? It drives me crazy, but my sister and brother-in-law have better intentions than you might think.'

'Could've fooled me.'

'They always have to appear upwardly mobile.' Prerna reached over and stroked Sarah's hair. 'Adults always find a way to ruin things.'

'Great,' Sarah said dryly. 'Every adult except you.'

'I have to go to India; I promised my father I would bring him some sunbeams when I could. I promised to do a few other things too.'

'Good, Mom. Well, I already texted Ruchi. She and I will help you with whatever you need. Packing or organizing or filling out your documents—anything at all. We'll even carry your bags to the airport. And don't worry about Dad. I'll make sure to feed him and cheer him up, because I'm sure he'll miss you.'

'Really, beti, that's sweet, but—'

'Mom! We already decided. And don't forget to drive on the left.'

'I'll wait to drive till I get back here,' laughed Prerna.

Chapter 21

On the Bench with Siri and Kris

Days later, Prerna found herself back at her favourite bench in Hamilton Park, across the Hudson, overlooking the shimmering Manhattan skyline. Kris sat next to her—miraculously, Prerna had convinced Reema to let him tag along, taking public transportation no less, before she left for India.

'How do you like my new happy place, Kris?' asked Prerna.

'It's beautiful,' Kris said, hypnotized by the sight, which shimmered like a mirage across the rushing waters.

'They say the best views of Manhattan are across the river in New Jersey. Do you agree?'

'Huh?' Kris was too enamoured by what he saw to reply.

Prerna sat back, remembering the first time she'd seen the Ganga. She had been as mesmerized then as Kris was now. It was then that she heard the notes from a piano struggling to find their tune. She knew who the musician was at once. And she knew of the anxiety the young musician felt. She remembered the young musician telling her about it over the phone when she was feeding customers one lunch hour at The Curry Bowl.

'Mr Houston says I'll never learn to play the piano!' the young man had complained.

'Really, why would he say that?'

'He says I don't practice enough. But the truth is he gives me pieces that are too hard for a beginner. Like Chopin! And he never shows any expression. He's cold. He just orders me to play and then criticizes me. I get nervous and screw the song up. When I practice alone, I do fine.'

'Well, maybe we can have your father talk to him.'

'Ma, Dad won't talk to him. *You* should talk to him.'

'Karan! My boy, you know how busy I am trying to put food on our table and everyone else's.'

'It's getting serious, Mom. Mr Houston told me he can't teach me any more. He says I have too much anxiety. But it's he who is giving me the anxiety.'

Sitting on the bench, the notes gave way to a soothing hum. The melodious humming, she recognized, coming from her boy's lips, had happened one night in the upstairs bedroom of her home, as she tucked him into his arrangement of pillows before he mischievously misted her with water. The hum was reminiscent of Chopin but had the crisper intonations of Ravi Shankar's sitar. There was a brilliance in the hum no anxiety could quash.

'Where did you learn that?'

'First in my heart, and then on my phone—it has a virtual keyboard in it. I want to add some beats later, maybe rap over it.'

'Rap! My god. Do you have lyrics to the song?'

'Working on them.'

Prerna never did hear or read the lyrics Karan had intended for his tune.

She sat up as the Manhattan skyline came into focus again. 'Do you miss Karan, Kris?' Prerna asked, as the young boy took videos of the park.

'Yes. I do.'

On the bench, a slight brackish breeze blew both of their hair back.

'Masi, can I show you one of the videos from The Curry Bowl? Karan is in it.'

Prerna cleared her throat, took a breath and leaned over to watch.

In the video, Kris was teaching Prerna to ask Siri questions. Karan stood laughing behind them.

'Like this, boys? I feel ashamed talking to a computer,' Prerna huffed in the video.

'It's the way of the future, Masi. Better get used to it.'

Prerna playfully tousled her nephew's longish locks, glanced at her son to secure his support and posed her first question. 'How many degrees in Celsius is 100 degrees Fahrenheit?'

'One hundred degrees Fahrenheit is 37.7778 degrees Celsius,' came Siri's cool voice at once.

Kris and Karan spun delighted circles on the balls of their feet and clapped their hands together while they laughed. 'See, Masi, you can learn as much from Siri as you can from me and Karan and Sarah.'

'I'm not sure . . . This is so embarrassing.'

'Try another one,' Kris insisted, as Reema ambled into the frame and began filing her nails.

Prerna dropped her phone to her side. 'Do I have to?'

Kris looked at Karan. 'We insist.'

'Go for it, Mom!'

'Okay, only for my persistent boys. I'll ask Siri on your behalf. What should I ask?'

'Ask what a Michelin Star is.'

'Really?'

'We insist!' repeated Kris.

Prerna groaned and again raised the phone to her lips. 'Siri?' Little tea lights appeared in her eyes. 'What is a Michelin Star?'

On the video, the staff froze and listened to the answer too. Parminder grabbed this moment of silence to go out for a smoke.

Siri spoke: 'Michelin Stars are what the Michelin guide uses to rate the quality and consistency of restaurants. One star means a good restaurant, two stars mean an excellent restaurant, and three stars mean an exceptional restaurant. The red Michelin guides have been published by the French tyre company of the same name for over a century by André Michelin.'

In the video, Prerna looked utterly mesmerized by Siri.

'How many stars do we want, Masi? One, two or three?' Kris laughed.

'Yeah, Mom,' chimed in Karan. 'Tell us!'

'Karan, Kris, this is silly,' Prerna said, instantly putting her phone away.

'Masi, I promised you. One, two or three?'

'Let me think about it.'

'One day, I will get you three!' Kris was saying in the video.

On the bench, across the Hudson, Kris and Prerna sat still, not knowing what to say to one another.

'Siri?' Kris asked suddenly.

'Yes?' cooed Siri's soothing voice, as Prerna's eyes darted back and forth between the screen and the river.

'Where is Karan?' asked Kris innocently.

Siri sent Kris's map app on a wild global search, first in New York, where its red inverted teardrop locked on the many stores of a famous designer, and then dizzied and disappointed Prerna by racing to ping her lost boy all over the world, from London to New Delhi, and finally to Mumbai, but to no avail. Karan was nowhere to be found, and Prerna had to accept it. Her boy was gone, but at least she had Kris.

'Masi,' Kris said, leaning his head on Prerna's shoulder. 'I'll miss you when you are in India.'

No water leaked from Prerna's eyes. Instead, she adjusted her sari and wrapped her nephew in her arms.

Chapter 22

City of the Uncelebrated

Mother India.

Prerna walked the same dusty old streets and the maze of lanes in Old Delhi as she had with her father so long ago. Squeezing the produce at the many markets, sampling herbs and smelling flowers, and drinking her favourite sugarcane juice, which was still so violently squeezed from its stalks between the barbaric iron jaws of gears even a quarter century later.

Prerna entered Delhi's back alleys and plunged into the spice market. If only Staten Island had Delhi's spice markets—no neat racks or bottles of spices here, but huge mounds of freshly harvested or perfectly dried, crushed and ground spices. Khanna and Sons or Patel's were never a match for the real thing.

Gone was the joy and relative luxury of riding in her father's Maruti. Even with her new licence, she'd still never drive in India—she imagined driving Reema through these streets, honking at cows like her father. How she'd shriek in horror! Peals of laughter erupted from Prerna's mouth, but she quickly covered her mouth with her pallu to stop.

Soon, Prerna came to the very intersection where she, a poor flower-selling waif promising rain by closing her eyes, had been saved from the streets. She had a destination in mind: to visit the house she grew up and learnt to cook in. If the house was in proper shape and would accept her, perhaps she would stay overnight. Prerna took the last turn, the one that led straight to her house's oversized colonial doors and rosewood archways.

It was now in decrepit shape, partially destroyed, with large holes in its old tile and bamboo roof.

A passerby circling on a bike, a thin and gaunt man with skin as sun-darkened as his turban was white and a patchwork beard, as if someone had sewn it on his face, saw Prerna staring at the place as though she was looking at the face of a god. 'I don't know why anyone would want to, but you want to go in?' he asked. 'This is the house where Karanjit ji lived. The story is that one of his daughters sold it the day he died.' The man snapped his fingers. 'Just like that. They did not even wait for a day. I circle by this old house every day and there is something so strange about it. Nothing flourishes here! The new owner abandoned it and it's up for sale again. So far, no one seems interested. As if the house is waiting for the right person to give it the proper care.'

'Oh really?' Prerna's eyes flashed and she turned to the man on the bike with a waving motion of her sari.

'Perhaps that person is you, sister.'

'Do you think the ghost of Karanjit ji would mind if I take a look? I might be interested,' Prerna said, smiling and covering her mouth.

The man smiled back. 'I'm sure it's fine. No one watches over it. The new owner hasn't come around for years and, well, why would a ghost mind having mortal company for a few hours? It's just an old house. Just be careful where you step.' The man smiled again and rode off.

Prerna's eyes traced the peeling blue paint on the home's facade. She fit one eye to a crack in the door to stare into the dark, neglected expanse. Something in the darkness, some light of life seemed to stare back at her.

A rush of the bright afternoon, dusty golden Delhi light carried Prerna inside the place—she hadn't set foot here for decades. She stood between two pillars, welling with sentiment. Her father on one side, the pillar who had imparted to her everything that mattered to him, and now mattered to her; and her step-grandmother, Devi, the pillar who had done everything to dissuade both him and her. But Prerna had taken root, much like a seed that sprouts in the harshest conditions, against all odds. Like a plant that finds the smallest crack in concrete to grow, Prerna had flourished.

For Delhi, the family house was a relative mansion, with multiple rooms on the ground and first floor, and back then, a front yard lined with flowering plants, and a backyard like a small, private vegetable farm—her father's, sprouting every size and shape of Indian vegetable, from eggplants to squash to okra to bitter gourds to cauliflower. Reema's room was on the first floor with a well-lit view of the courtyard and its many flowers. Reema always believed she held some advantage by being allowed to use her grandmother's larger and more luxuriously appointed room, which had a similar but more expansive view of the flowers, a view Prerna never enjoyed because she was forbidden from entering Devi's room.

Prerna was given a small, moonlit room in the back of the house with no particular features, whose only saving grace—a blessing, really—what that its door led directly to the kitchen. Prerna could be found here at all times—either learning from Karanjit or trying new recipes herself. She drew maximum comfort from this room—heading there at the crack of dawn to make chai, or, on the nights she couldn't sleep, drawing in the heady smells of spices to give her peace.

Prerna lingered in her new-old surroundings, her eyes fluttering as they always did before she got emotional.

Her family had a small portable tandoor in which they practised baking naan and stuffed breads, usually on Sundays. There was an old spice box in the shape of a swan, which was Karanjit's favourite. He was offered a lot of money to sell it or create a replica for it, but he would always reply with a smile, 'This is for my daughter Prerna. She is one of a kind—like this spice box.' Karanjit kept a great collection of antique pots and pans fashioned from brass, steel and clay earthenware, all collected by him during his travels. India's diversity and history never failed to inspire him, though he also owned modern pressure cookers, strainers, a mortar and pestle, rolling pins, and pots and pans of fine copper. Everything Karanjit had, he intended to share with Prerna. It was too bad that he had died so suddenly.

Prerna studied the back of her hands, then turned them over to survey her palms. They were scarred, scorched and callused, but still small, soft and tender in the right places. Prerna's were the same hands Devi had always called black. To Devi, Prerna's hands were so untouchable that she refused to eat or even be near anything they touched. Even so, Prerna was determined to carry Karanjit's legacy wherever it might lead.

Standing there, in the house of her youth, Prerna recalled one cool winter's afternoon—a memory that still caused her knees to shake.

Devi had been relaxing in the folding bed, a traditional charpoy she had Karanjit and Reema set up for her in front of their house, so she could lounge about and while away her time by drinking chai in the winter sun. That day, Karanjit had decided to have Prerna make aloo jeera, his favourite dish, and one Prerna had been practising over and over. Aloo jeera was Devi's favourite dish too, especially during winter. Potatoes always warm the body, and Karanjit knew this particular recipe was his cold mother's only weakness.

Prerna put everything Karanjit had taught her into that special bowl of aloo jeera.

She boiled and peeled the potatoes, then cut them into perfect half-inch pieces. She poured mustard oil into Karanjit's best wok and smoked the oil on high heat to reduce its pungency, just as her father had taught her. She waited a minute before adding asa-fuh-tee-da (even in her memory, she couldn't pronounce the word—where was Kris when she needed him?) and cumin. Karanjit taught her how to pound garlic in a mortar and pestle, so it released its flavours while retaining its texture. Prerna did the same for this dish. She grated ginger into fine slivers and added that in.

When the garlic began to caramelize, Prerna added the potatoes and stirred them in with a generous sprinkling of salt that reminded her of rain. It was magical to see the potatoes drink in the salt thirstily. The smell wafting up almost reminded her of petrichor.

As Karanjit always did, before serving the potatoes, Prerna scorched their skin at the edges to create a crisp texture, like a shell protecting the lusciousness inside. With the potatoes absorbing all the flavours—mustard oil, smoky cumin, pungent garlic and aromatic ginger—what Prerna realized was that it was often harder to properly cook simpler dishes. Sometimes, the most complex curries, with multiple ingredients and steps, were far easier. All of that labour, skill and consideration went into pleasing Devi that day.

When Prerna proudly submitted her dish to the bent toes of Devi's reclining feet, all she heard again was, 'Black hands!' and Devi's usual irritated grumbling between her sips of chai. 'Karanjit! What did I tell you?' she growled.

Karanjit appeared in the doorway, behind his skittish daughter. 'Mother, Prerna is turning out to be quite the cook; just give her a chance.'

'Never!' snapped Devi.

Prerna had grown into her skills and refused to give up. She edged her potatoes closer to Devi's feet, close enough that Prerna risked getting kicked in the face. Just as she retreated behind Karanjit to protect herself from certain violence, nature worked her magic. A cool breeze drove the aloo's warm aroma past Devi's nose, compelling her to gather her sari around her and, to Prerna and Karanjit's shock, reach down for a morsel. She placed a small morsel in her mouth and chewed on it thoughtfully. Then, a second miracle happened. She reached for another morsel, even setting her chai cup aside, nodding as she chewed and swallowed. Soon the plate was empty and old sautelee dadi didn't know what to do next, stunned as she was that the black hands she detested so much had prepared this. Much to father and daughter's astonishment, Devi put her hand on her chest as if she was having a heart attack and wept. Prerna's food had made her cry.

Prerna's vision returned her to the old, crumbling stone wall that marked the perimeter of her father's yard, where she saw a small blade of bright green grass twisting through stone, a sprout that had once been some random seed. Nurtured by the elements, the seed had sprouted into a stalk that had broken through thick stone to flash its green hope. In its yearning to become a plant, the seed had not given up. Just as Prerna hadn't, transcending the limitations of her skin colour, caste and 'illegitimate' birth.

The once stray 'dog' suddenly felt like a peacock, a *mor*, showing off its feathers before all the world. Despite Devi's foul attitude, Karanjit had always backed her. And here she was, making him proud by putting her food out there, allowing the world to savour it.

In the kitchen, Prerna dug out the old rolling pin, remembering how she'd roll out rotis and naan under Karanjit's watchful gaze.

For her, the excitement began right after the mid-April Baisakhi harvest festival, when Karanjit would come home with jute bags bursting with wheat germ. After the threshing, people could fill up their bags with wheat germ as the farmers prayed to the gods for granting them a bountiful harvest.

Baisakhi signalled the onset of the summer monsoons, which in turn witnessed the harshest, most unforgiving sun seen in Old Delhi—the same sun that provided the perfect temperature to dry the family wheat germ on the rooftop of their house.

Prerna would help Karanjit lay down the white cloth sheets on the terrace, so they could spread out the germ in a single layer to dry. The germ would then become the dough that Prerna loved rolling out. Despite the heat and Karanjit's scoldings, Prerna protected every grain, posting herself nearby to shoo away any crow that tried stealing bits of their precious grain from the roof.

'Prerna! Don't bother with the crows!' Karanjit would chide her. 'There will always be enough bread for everyone! A grain or two stolen by crows won't matter. They need to eat too!' At this point, Devi would inevitably shout from the courtyard, 'Under the sun, your black waif will get even darker! Dark as a devil! Just as well, then I will have even less reason to even look at her!'

After their wheat dried, Karanjit and Prerna would pack their dried grain into the same jute bags and, usually on a Sunday, head to the local grinding mill. After getting the flour ground, Prerna and Karanjit would load their sacks into the back of their old Maruti and drive to the local gurdwara to share the first bag, before taking the rest home for their own use.

To Prerna, this cycle of receiving and giving was the highlight of those sweat-drenched Sunday afternoons. It felt like a harvest season unto itself. At the gurdwara, Karanjit would help Prerna remove her sandals before removing his own. They would cover their heads, cleanse their hands at the entrance, and only then enter. The gurdwara was usually filled with worshippers. The humble, open way the community kitchens operated and the simple food they offered anyone who entered, no matter what their religion was and what they did, evoked in Prerna the same joys she felt later when she ran The Curry Bowl.

On their way home, Prerna would insist that her father tell her all the tales he knew of the Golden Temple. Karanjit just indulged her, if only to see the goosebumps rise on his daughter's arms. 'Beti, the Golden Temple has four gates welcoming everyone from every corner,' Karanjit would begin. 'Tens of thousands of people are fed twenty-four hours a day, seven days a week, so that no one will ever go hungry.'

The idea of taking care of people by feeding them really appealed to Prerna. Was it even possible? How did the Golden Temple do it? How could *she* do it if she wanted to?

Once they were back home, Prerna would help Karanjit unload the flour and place it in the dark, slightly musty coolness of their pantry, where they also stored lentils, peas, loose vegetables, bags of basmati rice, spices, plus their larger pots and pans, and some utensils and equipment they rarely used.

Since the pantry was perpetually dark, thanks to frayed wires and a fickle bulb, Prerna learnt to navigate the space by feeling her way to the right grains or vegetables or spices for whichever dish she and Karanjit had decided to make.

When Karanjit thought her heart, head and hands were ready (and when he thought he could avoid the wrath of his mother's tongue for both their sakes), he taught Prerna the intricacies of turning flour into dough. Like an apprentice to her master, Prerna would enter the pantry, fill a container with flour and then bring it to Karanjit, who would be stationed at their kitchen prep table, readying his hands for the kneading to come. First, Prerna learnt to make the dough by gradually adding water to the flour, to the ratio of three to one. But this did not always produce the proper quality of dough. The ratio was not always accurate. Karanjit would challenge Prerna to add all the water at once, according to the same ratio. Still, this method did not always yield the best results. The dough might be too watery and Prerna had to go back into the pantry for more flour. Other times, it might prove too sticky—which sent Prerna not only back into the pantry for more flour, but also to the sink to clean her hands.

Then there was the case where the dough hadn't absorbed enough water, and it would fall apart. She would have to quickly correct it by adding more water. What Prerna learnt was that the quality of the dough could vary based on the age and quality of the flour, a subtle variation in the exertion of her hands, their pantry's temperature or quality of light, and even that day's weather. Prerna perfected her dough over time, using a combination of her observation and ratios, with her instincts, feel and touch. The dough required all of it, plus love, to become the perfect naan.

Once, Prerna saw Karanjit press his hands in prayer before tossing a small piece of dough—too small to fill even a mouse's stomach—into their tandoor. Curious, she asked, 'Father, why did you throw that tiny bit of dough into the tandoor? It's too small to feed anyone.'

'All people are nourished by the sun, rain, winds, farmers and the fire,' said Karanjit. 'This, the dough, and the flour, which is from wheat, and the water from the rain, it all belongs to us, collectively. But without the fire, we have no naan. The fire is as much a part of the cycle of nature and the seasons as we are.'

Then Karanjit provided the key to the riddle of why they always took flour to the gurdwara before bringing it home. 'We offer the first bag of flour to the temple, so they can feed everyone, especially those who cannot afford their own wheat. Before baking our proper naan from our flour, we offer a small piece of it in gratitude to the fire god, Agni, the god of not only sun and fire, but lighting, and the hearth. Similar to why we offer flour to the temple before using it ourselves.'

Making naan was no simple thing!

Dough, as if by magic, could assume various forms. Once, Prerna saw Karanjit roll the dough in a different manner and shape and, instead of cooking it in the tandoor, pressed it into their tawa, where it puffed up with air like a cloud—she saw it as a breath of God. The simple magic of science and the cycle of nature, the gods and Karanjit, gave Prerna endless delight.

Another time, Prerna witnessed a swarm of ants who had infiltrated the kitchen bite into a tiny piece of bread, hoist it over their heads and carry it proudly back to their anthill (no doubt to feed their community and their queen). Ants and people were not that different, Prerna had thought then. Nourishment is best delivered by cooperation.

Chapter 23

News of a Particular Spice

Kris was sitting in his room, half-dressed, preparing to transmit his home videos to his bedroom flat-screen TV from his Bluetooth tablet when his mother entered without knocking. He flipped his tablet shut, threw it on his bed and walked immediately to his window to stare down at the traffic and pedestrians peregrinating around Columbus Circle. He stubbornly folded his arms, still fuming about the way events had unfolded at dinner at the Malhotras'.

'Kris,' said Reema gently, from behind him.

'What?'

'Don't be angry. I'll get you the cookie mould, apron and rolling pin you always wanted. And we can go to Abundant Foods and get that special flour Masi told you about. Okay? I promise.'

'Whatever,' Kris said. He pressed his nose and palms against the floor-to-ceiling windows.

'Kris! Don't get fingerprints all over the glass,' she instructed, still standing by the door. 'And your nose! That's disgusting. I'll have to call the maid again.'

The angry boy glared at his mother, then turned himself back to the window. 'There are too many cars out there. The cars are destroying the ozone layer and creating global warming. There should be more people on bikes. Look at all that carbon being emitted! We are all gonna die someday because of all those cars.'

'Don't be silly.'

Kris faced his mother. 'I'm serious. How many MPGs does your Audi get?'

'I haven't the slightest idea. I just drive it. Or get driven in it.'

'I didn't like the way you talked to Masi at the dinner. You embarrassed her.'

'I was just telling the truth.'

'The truth?' Kris hit the window with his hand.

'You want me to call your father? Calm down!'

Reema sighed and approached Kris until she was standing right next to him near the window. 'A lot of traffic today,' she said. Reema walked to Kris's bed, found his tablet and hit the video app. 'Let's see what you have on video.'

'Hey! You didn't ask my permission.'

'Kris! When do you not love watching your Curry Bowl videos? You practically grew up there. Come sit next to me and we'll watch together.'

Reema was right on both counts. Kris huffed and reluctantly joined his mother on the bed.

'Oops, there you are, all of six months old. Look at those cheeks, chubby as they are now. And your hair! Even a hippy back then.' Reema pinched her son's cheek and Kris pushed her hand away.

On the screen, confused and wide-eyed baby Kris stared up at Sarah, Karan and Prerna, kicking his legs and swimming in the air with his arms, overwhelmed by their laughter, before rolling over and trying to scramble away—but not before Prerna caught him by the ankles and spun him around. She then pressed her lips to his chubby cheeks, for their usual end-of-activity kiss.

'I can't watch this.'

'You were the cutest baby in the world, and everyone told me so.'

The scene changed to Kris's tenth birthday. Ten-year-old Kris, still chubby with even longer hair tucked into a chef's cap, stood around a high prep table in The Curry Bowl kitchen surrounded by staff and family, behind the flames of ten birthday candles, which were stuck in the shape of a circle into the thick frosting of the special cake Prerna had made for the occasion. 'Happy 10th Birthday, Kris!' read thinner frosting of another hue beneath the candles.

Leaning against his mom, Kris had to comment, 'I look happy, but also kinda confused and sad.'

On screen, Prerna began the song:

Happy Birthday to you,

Happy Birthday to you,

Happy Birthday dear Kar—Kris . . .

Happy Birthday to you . . .

It was typical for Prerna to confuse her boy's name with her nephew's, especially on Kris's birthday. Both started with 'K' and sometimes it shocked her how similar in character they were. It didn't bother Kris—it kept Karan always in his birthday wishes—but he always wondered if Prerna confused their names because she saw so much of Karan in him. Each year made his cousin's absence a little harder to bear.

Kris squeezed his eyes tightly shut to make a wish, while the rest concluded the song (rather off-key, except for Karan) and applauded while Kris filled his chest with air for his biggest breath of the year.

The camera zoomed in on Kris, just as he was about to blow his candles out, and he reached across his mother's lap for his tablet, turning off the video and leaving them both suddenly staring at fuzz.

'You didn't blow your candles out yet!'

Kris shrugged.

'Kris! What did you wish for?'

'That's between me and Masi,' said Kris, turning on to his stomach.

Reema playfully cuffed the back of her boy's head. 'I hope you're not having one of those juvenile identity crises. Maybe that's between you and Masi, too.'

Kris twisted his head around to glare at his mother. 'That's not it! I know what I want for me and for Masi,' he said.

On the floor, Reema spied the gift her son had taken to the dinner at the Malhotras, still wrapped in its pink-and-lavender paper with a gold bow adding a flourish on top. Reema picked up the gift and stared at it.

'I didn't have time to give it to Masi because all of you were being so mean to her,' mumbled Kris.

'Shush, we weren't being mean to her.'

'You were.'

'Can I see it? We can take it to Macy's and get it re-wrapped and give it to Masi when she gets back from India. Deal?'

'Okay.'

Reema carefully unwrapped the gift intended for her sister, a crude but charming painting of Prerna in her best peach and burgundy sari, with the words: World's Greatest Chef—Masi! brushed in at the bottom along with the artist's signature. Kris had certainly captured Prerna's soft yet steely eyes, her hesitant mouth and her baby cheeks right. He had captured Prerna's essence.

'Aww, Kris. That's so sweet. I'm sorry you couldn't give it to her that night. Really,' Reema said. She wrapped Kris in a tight hug. 'Turn around, dear. Give your mother a hug.'

Reema pulled away and took in her son. 'I am sorry for what I said. I know how much you love Masi.'

'It's okay . . . I guess.'

'Kris, let's talk.'

He didn't respond but begrudgingly moved closer to his mother, staring at the top of his tablet, at his 'Save The Planet' decal, which featured playful dolphins in the ocean waves at sunrise.

'Your Masi is a magician!' said Reema gently, still trying to get her son to forgive her.

'Yeah? What kind of magic tricks does she know, besides food?'

'Our Papa used to say that she could magically call rain just by simply closing her eyes and wishing for it. And you know what? Karan was just like her in that respect.'

'How?'

'Karan could always make Masi laugh—and that's not easy. She doesn't like to show any emotion, really. Karan and your Masi were best friends. When you were just a little boy, Karan would always insist on taking her to Central Park to feed the pigeons, after lunch service at The Curry Bowl, of course, when her work was done. Then he, too, would act like a magician! Pretending to call out the rain. And that's when Masi would stand up and behave like a person you'd never seen. Like a child again. She would run around in circles, laughing and staring into the sky, pretending she was being drenched by the imaginary rain Karan had called down for her. Your Masi loves rain. It was their special moment together.'

'Did it ever actually rain after Karan called for it?'

'Never!' Reema laughed. 'All the years they played this game, it never ever rained. For some reason, she still plays the rain game. Again and again, even though . . .'

'Even though what?' Kris's eyes were wide with curiosity.

Reema didn't answer. Instead, she stood and went to the door. 'Another time, Kris. Time for school. Better get ready.'

* * *

Later that day, an unimpressed David sat by his computer in his sports coat, tie and boxer shorts, video chatting with Lisa, his franchising rep. Her expression barely changed as she gave him a speech. 'David, we are seeing a huge market shift now, and that, frankly, shocks me. The interest in Indian food . . . Indian cuisine we should probably call it now . . . is going to spike.'

David leaned out of Lisa's view and mouthed the words, 'Indian cuisine', at Reema, who was putting the finishing touches on Kris's surprise lunch—finally an Indian-style wrap with tuna, cumin, mayo, tomatoes and spinach. David leaned back into view. 'Sorry, I had Jennifer take a note.'

'Quite all right, David. All these migrants coming to the US from the Middle East, South and South-east Asia, and the rise of the Indian engineer and CEO in Silicon Valley are really increasing the popularity of this cuisine. Americans have been going to the UK and coming back as Indian food converts. British-Indian chefs are gaining market share, and there are more and more popular food ambassadors talking about Indian cuisine in the media.'

'Really? I don't think so, Lisa.'

'You didn't see today's *Times*? Full-page article in the Food section, big colour photo, some legendary Indian mom-and-pop place downtown on Fulton, run by a woman chef, some Prerna—can't pronounce her last name—who lost her lease after twenty years—The Curry King.'

'The Curry Bowl?'

Lisa snapped her fingers. 'That's it, The Curry Bowl.'

David waved Reema over.

Reema reluctantly sauntered over to her 'boss,' hands tightening her Hermès belt around her waist, and now sporting her sunglasses du jour, smoke-coloured Gucci's.

'Jennifer, can you grab me today's *Times*? The Food section.'

'Right away, Mr Chopra,' said Reema, sauntering away to retrieve the paper. She suddenly yelped upon opening it and raced back with her mouth wide open. There it was: 'The Uncelebrated'—featuring a full-colour, half-page photograph of her sister, humbly standing in her usual sari and wearing her typical cautious smile amid a beaming throng of appreciative customers and Prerna's loyal staff. They scanned the byline: Ruchi Srivastava.

'Oh. My. God,' said Reema, visibly shaking. 'Kris will faint when he sees this.'

'He'll probably do more than faint,' said David, as he quickly scanned the article. 'Ms Lisa, this is an amazing article. I know the writer.' He actually didn't, but he knew someone who did.

'She's an up-and-coming. Apparently, she used to work for the woman.'

'Oh, really?'

'The point is Indian cuisine is going to explode and become more popular than ever with a higher demographic. Not just this taxi crowd. You should strike while the tandoor is hot and purchase an Indian restaurant franchise asap. It's just a matter of time before there's a Michelin-starred Indian chef tied to a Michelin-starred restaurant in town—and boom! This would be a great time to get in on the action and invest.'

On Wednesdays, the *New York Times* has a section that is all about restaurant reviews, chefs on the move and chefs' stories. But no previous Wednesday could compare to this day, as it celebrated the story of a unique chef.

The Uncelebrated

by Ruchi Srivastava

New York City, home to thousands of restaurants and top Michelin Star chefs. In the glory and shimmer of this majestic hospitality world, we tend to oversee the small, the little and the lesser-known gems. Many times, women-led restaurants are undermined. They are like a drop in the ocean of restaurants in New York, a city of reincarnation.

A small bite in these mom-and-pop places brings us closer to our home, to our roots. By the time you will be reading this, a small place like this would be torn down, to be turned into another glass-and-steel corporate tower. The unknown place was The Curry Bowl, located on 141 Fulton Street, run by the uncelebrated Indian chef Prerna Malhotra. The restaurant was previously owned by a prominent Indian physician, Dr Dayama Annu, who deceived the chef into signing a false contract through which 40 per cent of the profits were taken away from her for twenty years. This did not break Ms Malhotra's spirit—she continued to cook and serve with love and dignity. Those who visited her little place considered her a mother and would swear that her cooking healed them, especially post 9/11 when the city was looking for a new identity and inspiration. But many male chefs constantly clashed egos with her while working with her and undermined her leadership.

'She healed downtown with her simple cooking for decades. She did not need an *NY Times* review or a Michelin Star, she was beyond all the accolades,' said Martin, who ate at The Curry Bowl twice a week for 20 years.

Getting in on the action and investing was all David could think about the rest of the day, as Reema read and re-read the article before going out for her daily jog and Fifth Avenue shopping spree.

* * *

In Lower Manhattan, Dr Dayama Annu, dressed in a satin housecoat, lounged on her sleek modern sofa in her small, but modern two-bedroom condo, curled up with a cup of warm turmeric. She pulled tissue after tissue from a daisy-printed tissue box. A cold had sent her home early from her office on Fulton. In her other hand, she gripped the Food section of that morning's *Times*.

> Ms Malhotra learnt to cook from her father, Karanjit, in India, where she grew up before moving to the US in 2000. Cooking was a way to express her gratitude and to keep his inheritance alive, she worked seven days a week for two decades, as a tribute to him.
>
> As this article goes to print, Ms Malhotra is back in her homeland of India. We hope that she gets inspired again to bring the legacy of great cooking to New Yorkers one more time. May the legacy of India's greatest chef live forever in the hearts of those who ate from her hands.
>
> I wanted to end this article with a quote from Rumi, 'You are not a drop in the ocean, you are an entire ocean in a drop.'
>
> Thank you, Ms Malhotra, for showing the world the difference between good and great cooking.

'How dare she,' repeated Dr Annu into her steaming tea as she read the headline on the front page. Between sniffs and sips, grumbles and sighs, her slitted eyes tore across every word of the glowing but sympathetic article about *her* restaurant written by this neophyte Ruchi Srivastava. She didn't recall if she had ever met the author or not, though her name, Ruchi, sounded familiar. Why hadn't Prerna told her about such huge press? She could have kept The Curry Bowl open then, and the place could have finally, finally made Dr Annu a wealthy woman and elevated her status into the upper classes. Even Prerna might have made it to the middle class at the very least, had she remained open and taken her advice. Naive woman!

Shifting positions on the sofa to ease her cough, it took all of Dr Annu's fortitude to keep sipping her turmeric tea and read the next word rather than tearing the paper to shreds, as she forced herself to suffer through all the libel she was reading. The Uncelebrated, indeed.

She briefly considered her legal options, wondering if she could sue Prerna, but the very thought of spending that much time in court made her shudder.

Reading the piece one last time, she finally set her thick glasses down on her coffee table.

* * *

Ruchi concluded reading her copy of the article and set it on the grass beside her and Paul. She sighed. 'What do you think?'

'Wonderful,' Paul said, more smitten than ever. Listening to Ruchi's smart and savoury voice and relaxing in the presence of the love of his life, Paul was almost asleep when Ruchi stopped. He couldn't stop smiling. 'Hearing you read always puts me in a dream state.'

'I still can't believe *The Times* thought it was good enough for them!'

Paul threw his arms around her. 'Well, they loved the piece, the readers have loved it on social media, I loved it . . . And,' he leaned in to kiss her neck, 'I love you!'

'Paul, that tickles. Not now.' Ruchi giggled. 'Not here in the park . . . Let's go home.'

Paul gathered himself and stood up, brushing off grass and bits of dandelion from his pants. He stretched, yawned, slapped his belly and reached for Ruchi's hands. 'Shall we get a mango lassi somewhere?' he asked.

Paul, the Mango Lassi Man, would never change.

Chapter 24

Midnight in India

Sarah and Manish sat at the Malhotra kitchen table huddled together, beaming over Ruchi's piece in *The Times*.

'Wow. All I can say is . . . Wow,' said Manish, taking a sip of his chai. 'I really did marry a wonderful woman.'

'You didn't realize it until now?' Sarah asked, mock-outraged.

'I always did. Sarah, this upma is delicious, although you could add more honey and red pepper. I'm not David, you know!'

'Pita ji, I don't have Ma's talent for food. Or even Kris's. Oh, let's call Ma!' Sarah said. 'We have to tell her about her article! Ma has no idea that Ruchi did her proud by featuring her in the Food section.'

'It's midnight in India,' Manish said, scarfing down his upma. 'Your ma's probably asleep already. You get to our age and you learn you're no longer a spring chicken.'

'We both know she's probably up, brooding over something. The call will cheer her up—a front-page article in *The Times*?! . . . I'm calling her. We'll surprise her with the article and read some of it to her. She'll love it!'

In the house of her youth in Old Delhi, Prerna was already fast asleep, in the dark room she'd grown up in, a few feet away from Karanjit's kitchen. Her phone buzzed away a few flies before buzzing her awake. Prerna opened one eye, then the other. A video call from America? When her bleary vision cleared and she saw Sarah's name on her phone, she feared for the worst. Unexpected calls rarely brought good news. Half in a dream, Prerna answered in the dark. Out of the blur, she could barely make out the glow of her daughter's strangely beaming face, and then the even more strangely beaming glow of her husband, who rarely smiled.

'Hi, Ma! Wake up!' squealed Sarah. 'We have good news for you. The best news ever!'

'Huh? Sarah, Manish, I can barely open my eyes. Can I get up and wash my face first?'

'Nope,' said Sarah. 'Where the hell are you? Some cheap hotel?'

'Don't ask!'

Prerna watched as her husband and daughter giggled in delight.

'I don't want to know what you two are up to. Have things got that out of control without me? Sarah, you are feeding him, right? Is he okay? He looks thin,' Prerna said, propping herself up to assess her husband and daughter. 'Manish, has Sarah been feeding you enough?'

'He's fine. He's sitting right next to me and he is very happy today, see? Father and daughter doing just fine with mother away. Not that we don't miss you,' Sarah said, tilting the phone towards Manish.

'How are you, Prerna, my dear wife?' he asked, grinning from ear to ear.

'I'm, uh, good, Manish,' Prerna couldn't help but add her smiles to theirs. 'You haven't been drinking whisky again, I hope.'

'Not at all, dear.'

'What is it, you guys?'

'Ma, are you sitting down?'

'I was fast asleep just a second ago,' said Prerna.

'Well, I'm sure you will be wide awake after this,' Sarah said, bringing the article close to her face, so Prerna could read the headline.

'What's this? You are going to read me the news? Sarah, you woke me for this?'

'Not just any news! News about you, Ma!'

'What?!'

'Yup. Ruchi published it.'

Prerna focused her eyes closer to the screen, 'The Uncelebrated. *Me*?'

'Yep. You, finally celebrated.'

'I knew that girl was up to something!' Prerna said, finding herself wide awake and on her knees. She wrapped herself tighter in her sari.

Manish pushed his face into closer view. 'Let me speak to my lovely wife. I am so, so proud of you. And I'm also a little sad,' Manish said, suddenly frowning.

'You couldn't stop smiling and now you frown?'

'Yes. You are becoming so independent and now you're famous. When you return from India, you won't need me to drive you back and forth to the ferry any more. Your licence came in the mail, and you'll probably hire a driver like your sister did, to drive you around. Either way, I'm out of the picture.'

'Dad! Mom wouldn't do that to you! It's not in her nature.'

'Manish, I will always need you. Now that I have my licence, I can pick you up from now on. But I don't understand what my driving has to do with this call.'

'*Main tumse pyaar karta hoon* (I love you very much),' said Manish quietly, making Prerna blush.

'*Main tumse pyaar karti hoon*, my darling husband,' replied Prerna.

For an awkward second, the two stared at one another, until Sarah interrupted impatiently.

'Okay, you two, shh! Stop the love fest and listen . . .'

Sarah proudly read the entire article, word by loving word, much to Prerna's delight. 'This was all planned by crazy Ruchi!' she finally breathed once Sarah finished.

'When are you coming back to us?' said Manish. 'We miss you.'

Prerna sighed, her eyes flitting the way they always did when she was deciding something.

'Prerna? Are you okay? Your eyes have that, uh, look,' said Manish.

'I need to visit one special place before I come back . . .'

Manish nodded and his eyes glistened before Sarah hijacked the phone again.

'Ma—or Madame Michelin, should I call you now? Ha ha ha.'

'Stop it, Sarah!'

'Your article has David doing a complete turnaround,' said Manish. '"Indian cuisine is gonna be on fire soon!" he'd said. He's contacting every potential backer in his Rolodex. I can't believe what's been coming out of his mouth. He and Reema are running around everywhere telling anyone who will listen that staying connected with your roots, food-wise, is going to be the only way to be successful on foreign shores. Forget franchising, David's views on Indian cuisine have completely changed.'

'How so?'

'He thinks nouveau Indian will be the next big thing in cuisine. And you know the best part?'

'What?'

'All those hours you spent at The Curry Bowl showing Kris everything you knew is gonna pay off one day. He and Reema are totally on board with supporting Kris so he can become a chef.'

'Oh my,' said Prerna, pulling her pallu across her mouth.

'Whatever it takes.'

'That's such good news for Kris. I'm in shock.' Prerna lay back down.

'If you speak to Kris, don't mention it,' Manish cautioned. 'He's been touchy lately . . . I heard he's going through some sort of identity crisis at school.'

'Probably just growing pains, but I won't mention anything,' said Prerna. Small rivers of sweat dripped down her face. 'It's so hot here in Old Delhi. Wonder if India's in for another drought.'

'Keep yourself cool, Ma. You'll be in an air-conditioned jet on the way home soon,' sang Sarah.

'Hold on, I have to go upstairs, don't hang up,' said Manish. 'Now I have a surprise for my wife.'

He stood up and raced out of the kitchen and up the stairs to his and Prerna's room. He opened the door to his wardrobe, and there, among its darker compatriots, stood a fine white dinner jacket, one worthy of a millionaire, his Millionaire Jacket—stunning and creamy white, black trim at the cuffs and lapels, and gold cufflinks. He swiftly put it on and bounded down the stairs.

Prerna threw her hands to her cheeks. 'Manish, dear. As handsome and youthful as the day we met.'

'You like it?' said Manish, twisting around back and forth to model the jacket. 'It's just a matter of time before I go to dinner in your new restaurant, and come wearing this . . .'

Sarah shook her head. 'Oh, brother . . .'

'Let him enjoy himself. Manish, you look wonderful in your jacket.' Prerna yawned. 'Your Ma is tired, Sarah. It's after midnight over here.'

'Can't wait to see you,' said Sarah. She pressed the stop button as Prerna continued to wave and smile. Sarah gently hugged her father. 'I'm glad we called.'

Chapter 25

White Like Coconut

Reema crossed the granite floor towards her son's room, holding the folded-up *Times* article tightly in her hand. 'Kris! Are you busy? I have unbelievable news. You might faint.' She knocked on the door to no response. And she couldn't hear the usual sounds of him watching videos on his table. Strange!

Then she heard flowing water, splashing and the sounds of someone scrubbing. This was doubly strange now—Kris had been an avid shower-taker of late; he hadn't drawn a bath since he was a child. She knocked on the door again, tried to open it and discovered it was locked. 'Kris, hon, open up!' She knocked on the door again, this time harder, then yanked at the knob. 'Open the door!'

'Leave me alone. I'm taking a bath. What's wrong with that?' asked a flat voice, which sounded nothing like her son's.

'A bath, now? You never take baths any more, and if you did, it's not even close to bedtime yet. Let me in! I demand it. Otherwise, I'll get your father!'

Kris refused to answer, and the sounds of water and rubbing continued. Reema fought with the knob again, until she heard a click and the door swung open. Kris stood there, covered in white paint, looking at himself in front of a mirror.

Speechless, Reema entered and stood next to him, not knowing whether to laugh or scream, call the police or take him to see a counsellor.

Reema tossed the newspaper down and closed the door behind her. 'What prank are you up to now? This is like some stunt Karan would have pulled. Is that flour?' she demanded.

'No. It's paint. The same paint I used for Masi's gift. The one you opened without asking me. The same paint I used for Masi's portrait . . .' Kris trailed off.

'It's not Halloween and definitely not the Kumbh Mela.'

'I decided I want to be a famous chef. I want to win many awards one day. For Masi.'

'What does that have to do with locking yourself in the bathroom and painting yourself white? There could be lead in that paint.'

Kris glanced at Reema in the mirror. 'Well, all Dad talks about is how only restaurants run by white chefs can win awards and get a Michelin Star. I can't be French or German, so I was trying to become white. I don't want to be a coconut—brown outside . . .'

'Kris, look at me!' Reema said in a feeble voice. 'Don't ever call yourself a coconut. Where did you learn that term? From Sarah, I bet. Such a bad influence your cousin is.'

She took her son's hand and guided him over to the rim of the tub and into a sitting position.

Kris let himself slip into the bathwater until his head was almost submerged. Reema pulled him back into position. 'Are you trying to drown yourself?'

Kris didn't reply.

'Ew. You're all wet and pasty. You'll probably destroy my Chanel, but I don't care any more. Come here, Kris.'

She began scrubbing her son vigorously. 'Don't believe everything Dad says, and certainly don't believe anything Sarah says!'

Kris nodded.

'Don't let your skin colour define your boundaries. Look at Masi. Isn't she the best chef? And she's not white . . . Not in the least bit.'

Kris nodded again as his mother continued to scrub.

'In some ways, I feel like I failed to properly raise you. Sometimes I've thought more about myself than about others. I hope to change that now. I've treated Masi unfairly, as though she was somehow less . . . This goes back to our childhood. Now I know I've been wrong. It was just the way I was raised and made to think and act. I wanted to be first. I wanted to be the princess in the family. In many ways, I was. Because I wasn't adopted, and Masi was.'

'It's okay, Ma . . . We live and we learn.'

'Out of the mouths of babes. Isn't that what they say?'

Reema rinsed Kris out until all the white paint washed away. She then dried her hands and grabbed the newspaper off the counter. 'See this?' Reema asked, unfurling the article in front of Kris's still white-rimmed eyes. 'Look who's in the headlines.'

'Masi! A full page in *The Times*?'

'Yup, it says she's the best Indian chef in New York. A culinary treasure. And look who wrote it.'

'Ruchi . . .' Kris frowned.

'What's wrong now, Kris?'

'So Masi's not the best Indian chef in the *world*?'

Reema tousled her son's still-damp hair. 'Don't be silly, Kris. That will take more time. Give Masi a chance.'

David's voice suddenly boomed down the hallway and echoed in the bathroom. 'Jennifer!'

Reema turned towards the door. 'One second!'

Kris screwed up his face. 'Jennifer? Dad calls you Jennifer?'

'Only when he's working, trying to make us richer. And guess what else?'

'Jennifer!' came David's voice again. 'Where are you? When is my next appointment?'

'Just a minute, David,' Reema called out.

Kris let his wet head droop against his mother's chest.

'What did you want to tell me?'

Reema smiled. 'Your father is also looking for a new space to develop a new Indian restaurant.'

Kris finally smiled. 'Really?'

'Really. Exciting, huh? Kris, don't ever worry about people who can't deal with dark skin, especially bullies at school. You have to stand up for who and what you are. You're a stronger kid than Karan, so I'm not so worried.'

Reema paused before speaking again.

'You and your Ma are going with your father to shortlist locations for Masi's new restaurant. Aren't you excited?'

'Where is Masi? I want to call her right away!'

'She's still in India.'

'What?' gasped Kris. 'After this great news?'

'She just found out.' Reema laughed. 'She'll be back soon.'

Kris grabbed the towel and began rubbing himself dry vigorously. 'We can't let Masi's legacy die.'

'Well,' said Reema, playfully whacking Kris's head with the newspaper. 'Do you think you can reopen The Curry Bowl? You're still a kid.'

The blinkless way Kris stared into her eyes told her it was probably true.

Chapter 26

Temple of Rain

A crowded early morning train took Prerna from Delhi to the heart of Amritsar, where she hailed an autorickshaw to the Golden Temple. In the soft light of the early morning sun, the gold-and-white structure, surrounded by water on all four sides, almost seemed to float in mid-air. This was a vision that no postcard, picture or pendant hung on a rearview mirror could capture.

Prerna lifted her white, flowing saree, one that she had purchased specially for the occasion, above her calves and dipped her feet into the pools surrounding the temple. Massaging her wrist automatically to quell her nerves, she then strode the long path towards the entrance.

As Prerna walked towards the glowing golden structure, she noticed that the sun was obscured by a sheet of grey. She walked straight to the grand white arch of the outer gate. The temperature dropped as Prerna bent her head and bowed, before closing her eyes and walking through the arch. She opened her eyes to a tiled courtyard too beautiful for words or pictures.

The savoury aromas from the temple's venerable langar service wafted in from the far end of the bridge that connected the gated entrance to the mystical place ahead. Prerna walked, head dipped, breathing in the aromas, aromas even she, someone who had cooked tirelessly for the last twenty years, had never smelled before. Karanjit had told her that anyone could partake in the meals—no matter where they came from, or what faith they followed. The temple welcomed all and fed them. To Prerna, this was the most beautiful thing.

A slight wind rippled the surrounding waters as she made her way past the main temple.

Despite the Golden Temple's obvious shimmering allure, Prerna's real interest was the langar hall. She had never seen such a massive kitchen or such huge flames—a thousand Curry Bowls under one roof. Pots, utensils, counters, kettles and the biggest tandoor she had ever seen in her life, almost like a cave for baking all of India's naan, all surrounded her. While Prerna would have been satisfied with just scraps, at the Golden Temple that day, she received far more.

She stood in line with everyone else, waiting to be served. She was the customer now but also, in a way, a servant, not of a corrupt doctor, but of god. She received her food and found a place to sit and eat inside the pillared congregation area, the ornate langar where everyone ate communally. She had travelled far to be here, but Prerna felt utterly at ease. Everything was exactly the way her father had described it to her.

The food she had that day tasted better than anything she had ever made or served at The Curry Bowl. If only Karan and the rest of her family, even her staff, could see her now—see how much she was enjoying the food that had been served with so much humility and grace.

Karanjit and Karan's spirits were with her. In the mortal world, as a mother, Prerna had not been able to fulfil her promises to her boy. She felt regret course through her veins as she ate there.

'Karan? Is that you?' she asked quietly, sensing her boy next to her in the crowd.

'Yes, Ma. I'm sorry . . .'

'No, I'm the one who's sorry.'

'We are both sorry then . . .'

After she finished, the best meal she had ever had by far, she set her plate aside, opened her mouth to take a large breath and closed her eyes.

Then Prerna stood up and walked over to dispose of her plate in the communal dishwashing area.

She pulled her sari past her knees again and walked slowly back the way she had come, relishing every step along the walkway between the pools, the golden dome of the temple reflecting in her eyes and the waters below.

Her hands pressed together in prayer, Prerna walked back to the tiled courtyard.

Suddenly, she froze. She felt drops of water pouring down.

'It's raining, Maji!' laughed Karan next to her.

A smile creased Prerna's lips, which quickly blossomed into an open, unashamed grin, as she raised her face and palms to the sky to greet the golden rain that had started to fall. A frantic group of Sikh pilgrims in their bright orange turbans ran past her, one of them bumping into Prerna. She didn't notice; she was overcome with joy swaying in the rain.

'We did it, Ma. We made it rain. See!'

'My beautiful boy, I thought you—'

'No, Ma, how could I ever? You've kept your promise. You have taken me to the Golden Temple. And look, we've made it rain now.'

Prerna laughed again. Here was one promise she had kept for her son. What Karanjit couldn't do for her, she had done for her son.

It is the choices we make that lead us to where we are now. Prerna had made the choice to keep her family's mouths fed, and in the process, made thousands of people happy with her food. Given them a little morsel of the Golden Temple all the way in New York. For that, Prerna was pleased.

She reached to grab Karan's hands.

'Have you forgiven me?' he asked.

It was all she wanted to know, but no answer came out of her mouth. Prerna felt a warm, moist kiss on one cheek and then the other. She released the invisible hands that now so warmly gripped hers and let herself weep as she let her boy go. Tears flowed down Prerna's cheeks as the sun broke from behind a cloud and set the Golden Temple on blinding fire. She closed her eyes and let the sun warm her eyelids, opening them just as the rain receded.

Prerna closed her eyes again, which blocked out the sun, and she noticed her wrist no longer hurt.

A FEW YEARS LATER

Chapter 27

A Michelin Star, the Seed of Chef Krishna

Chef Krishna Mehra, now pushing thirty, a male model gone wayward, with the slightest of paunches from his copious and rigorous taste-testing, but still dashing, strode across his chic but welcoming dining room. From its earlier days as a luxury shell, The New Curry Bowl had morphed into an airy, steel-and-glass framed palace of pink, red, orange, lavender and magenta, set with peacock-patterned booths of teak and marble, and fine tablecloths, all surrounding the massive centrepiece—an ebony table for twelve.

Tonight, Krishna wore a master-mix shade of chef smock coat, and he gripped a red plaque that swung at his hip with every step: the Michelin Star award. Krishna's battalion of assistants, waiters, maître d's, sous chefs and his publicist could barely keep up as he crossed the kitchen and descended into his office—a drab affair compared to the dining room, with a flatscreen TV of some mid-tech Korean brand mounted high in a corner. He sat down with his entourage to watch the gala he had attended a year ago at a beautiful old Art Deco theatre on Manhattan's Theatre Row.

The polished hosts, dressed to the nines in a sparkling evening dress and a dapper Armani suit respectively, spoke into a microphone on a stand in front of a backdrop of mottled crimson. The man, a Frenchman with a Parisian accent, said, 'New York's New Curry Bowl, the Indian restaurant founded by Chef Krishna Mehra, has been awarded a Michelin Star for "Best Indian Restaurant" in New York.'

The cameras swept through the churning sea of people, an audience of chefs in full regalia, white-and-high toque blanche and elegant white coats, a standing ovation from Chef Krishna's peers. Among them, also dressed to the nines in her own humble way, in an emerald sari and matching scarf, sat Prerna, looking a little squeamish among such pomp. Beside her and squeezing her hand smiled Manish in his Millionaire Jacket, and there was no more fitting occasion to be sporting it. The camera swept back to the female host, who spoke next. 'Chef Krishna has been cooking Indian food since a very young age and has since become a true ambassador of his native India's diverse cuisine.'

The camera swept again through the crowd and found Krishna's hands flying up to cover his face. Overcome with emotion, tears sneaked through his fingers before he regained his composure.

'Chef Krishna, please join us on stage to accept your Michelin Star.'

Krishna jogged to the stage, where he stood, elated and feeling slightly bittersweet, next to the hosts, where he accepted his coveted award in his hands. As the hosts embraced him and shook his hand, he found the microphone. 'All I can say is I am humbled. And thank you, Chef Prerna Malhotra, for without you, I am nothing.'

The theatre erupted in applause, and Prerna clapped harder than she ever had in life. Kris held his award briefly in the air so she could see it from where she was seated.

'It has been Chef Krishna's constant endeavour to elevate the intricacies, stature and beauty of Indian food, and give it due recognition on the global map. Today, with this Michelin Star, Chef Krishna and The New Curry Bowl have established a first in many ways. He has set a new benchmark in the industry, not only for young Indian chefs but for aspiring chefs of many backgrounds, especially chefs who are Black and brown,' the host spoke over the applause.

At his desk, Chef Krishna turned off the TV, to the groans of his staff and planted his Michelin in the centre of his desk as though he was planting a flag on the moon. 'This is for you,' Chef Krishna said, already rolling up the sleeves of his smock. 'This award is yours, not mine. You earned it.'

He grinned, 'Now let's get back to work.'

'You got it, Kris,' said his lead sous chef, Devansh, Dilip's son, a replica of his father. 'It's about the work. We have customers to serve. The Michelin is also for them.'

He led the staff out of the office.

Krishna's rolled-up sleeves revealed firm forearms, thick as saplings, and nimble fingers attached to hands that had seen several cuts, scrapes, calluses and burns—the scars of his culinary labour. He remembered the hands of his youth—soft hands rolling out a naan carefully for the first time, as his Masi clapped behind him.

Now alone with the TV off, Krishna placed his plaque on his marble credenza below an old photo of him and Prerna—a younger, chubbier Kris with crazy long hair for a boy, beaming and draping his arm around the shoulder of his beloved aunt. The two stood next to each other in the cramped steel kitchen of the hole-in-the-wall of years before. Krishna smiled, leaned back, folded his arms and sighed. More than the Michelin gala, Krishna looked forward to the private family dinner they would all share soon, their first in The New Curry Bowl.

* * *

After the last swings of the sledgehammer and wrecking ball, and much labour and renovation, The New Curry Bowl had opened on Fulton Street in the same, but much-expanded location as the old one. It was a sleek, beautiful, airy place filled with natural light from skylights above and a glass facade below. Wanting to preserve the welcoming essence of the original, Prerna and Krishna insisted on keeping the lobby intact in its traditional form. Ruchi returned the Ganesha figure Prerna had bequeathed to her and helped Prerna build out the little sandbox for candles and incense. Above it set in a gilt frame, hung prominently underneath photos of Karanjit and the Golden Temple, was an original copy of the article Ruchi had written. A Rumi quote underlined all of it, no longer handwritten but stencilled in sleek, professional painted letters.

They had reached the soft opening. The Malhotra and Mehras sat bubbling with chatter around The New Curry Bowl's centrepiece with admiring if somewhat awestruck eyes. Krishna and Prerna had managed to not only showcase but modernize all the inspirations she and he had culled from India, Europe, Manhattan, even Staten Island. Manish sat next to David, now behaving more like brothers than drunken competitors. Manish had ceased his scheming, but sometimes he still sported his Millionaire Jacket around the house.

Prerna and her sister flanked Krishna. What was better than having two mothers?

Nurturing Kris's, Chef Krishna's, dreams, then making them real while scouting for the best location for The New Curry Bowl had brought the Malhotras and Mehras back together.

Reema, still the fashionista, had transformed into a more relaxed woman over the years, and the two sisters had reconciled not by discussing who was owed what in an ancient property or who wore a more stylish or authentic purse or the latest fashion, but by meeting more as friends getting to know each over weekly tea or coffee dates at a café on 27th Street near Park Avenue, where they discussed everything from raising children to their conflicted feelings about their relationship with their father and grandmother. Prerna told Reema all about her experience at the Golden Temple.

Sitting amid the family chatter, Prerna suddenly recalled how, a few years ago, Kris and Sarah suddenly showed up smiling like Cheshire cats, at the café she and Reema were sitting at. Then, to her bafflement, a tall, dapper gentleman sauntered over and presented Prerna with a thick, colourful packet. The man looked familiar: it was one of the groups of owners or developers—Prerna could rarely distinguish them—who had visited the old Curry Bowl on its last day.

'What's this?' she had asked.

'Ms Malhotra, I read that great *Times* article about you that came out after your restaurant closed. I understand you are planning a new restaurant. Well, here is the visualization, renderings and plans. We are proud that you and your sister always visit our café, and one day we hope to visit your new culinary venture.'

'Thank you!' This was all Prerna could say as she tried to absorb what he'd just told her.

'Surprise, sis! Behold the plans for The Curry Bowl. The lease has been signed,' laughed Reema, looking at Prerna's stunned face. She opened the file, revealing a beautiful expanse of glass, wood and steel with a fully equipped modern kitchen but with just the right set of traditional appliances and a massive tandoor—the things no steel and glass can create. The pictures were gorgeous, and the layout plans looked logical and orderly, but it was the address that shocked her: 141 Fulton Street.

'The same address?' Prerna had gasped.

Kris laughed. 'Karma?'

'You deserve it, Mom,' said Sarah. 'Chachi's been wanting to surprise you for weeks.'

'When David, Manish, Krishna and their partners were poking around for a storefront, they ran into one of those developers Ruchi hated so much,' Reema explained. 'He remembered how warmly you had treated them, despite the situation with Dr Annu back then. He told them that the last business that occupied that space failed miserably . . . Some commercial art gallery selling copies of famous artists. The art bubble had burst, the gallery lost its lease and suddenly 141 Fulton was available. How could we not?'

Prerna covered her mouth with her pallu to hide her laughter. 'How could we not?'

'I mean, ever since the article and the fact that Kris is now in culinary school . . . David jumped on it and secured the place. All systems go!'

'Are you excited, Ma?' asked Sarah, hugging her mom.

'Very,' said Prerna. 'Especially for Kris . . . This will be his place soon.'

Kris leaned over and hugged Prerna too.

Coming back to the present, Prerna found that her eyes were now moist. She excused herself from the table and walked over to the kitchen. She stopped at the mandir, said a small prayer and picked up a platter on which she kept a lamp and a small pot of vermillion. Krishna had retreated to his basement office to dress in his crispest chef uniform, white with black and red trim. He ascended the stairs just in time to greet Prerna for their ceremony for two, their passing of the tandoor flame. As they prayed, Krishna cast his own mind back on his journey—obsessively watching videos of his Masi, attending the Culinary Institute of America, strong-arming his parents (with much help from Prerna, of course) into letting him attend another course in India, where he learned the intricacies of the food he loved so, working himself to the bone there, for India offered such a vast array of food and flavours, before coming back and working long hours under some of the best chefs in America . . . All until he decided that he was ready to fulfil his Masi's dream. He never wanted to be her equal; he just wanted to carry forward her legacy. For there would have been no Krishna without Prerna.

Kris also remembered his time in Paris. He knew he needed work experience in France, and after applying at several Michelin Star restaurants, he was hired by Le Goût, a place known for its creativity and stringent methods. The pressure was on. Krishna had come a long way from being his Masi's precocious little kitchen helper to working as a sous chef under one of the most revered chefs in Paris.

It was a huge disappointment.

Krishna's revered mentor, the man he had so badly wanted to please and impress, one day refused to eat a dish Krishna had so expertly prepared as a reflection of what the apprentice had learnt from the master. Why? Krishna's 'black hands'.

Kris pulled his thoughts back to the present with some effort. Well, he had shown them, hadn't he? He knew his Masi had gone through similar experiences with her grandmother, and he supposed the strongest cooks were forged by the hottest fires. He also remembered how, when his Masi and mother were once telling him about how his great-grandmother treated Masi, in a fit of anger, Kris had yelled, 'Fuck her!' His mother very nearly banned him from going back to college for saying so. Kris had to laugh at that memory now.

Prerna opened her eyes and placed a small vermillion dot on Krishna's forehead. Krishna reverently closed his eyes and bowed to touch Prerna's feet. Kris straightened his back and Prerna, in what Krishna would later recall as a feat of surprising strength, lifted him up off the kitchen floor in a hug a bear would be proud of. Only when Prerna dropped him back to earth, did Krishna feel the gravity of having become the family's third generation of great cooks.

'Can you believe what we've been through to get here, Masi?'

'Hardly, but here we are,' Prerna smiled. 'Chef and chef.'

'Do you remember our visit to the Golden Temple?' Kris asked Prerna.

Did she remember? It was one of her happiest memories—they had travelled to every major town and city in India, sampling each place's speciality, making copious notes to recreate the dishes back in New York. She'd left the Golden Temple until the very end, and Prerna would never forget the wonder in Kris's eyes as he took in the Temple and the selflessness of the langar hall.

She took Kris's hand in hers now. 'Are we ready to meet the family, Chef Krishna?'

'Never been readier!' Kris said, embracing Prerna.

They returned to the applause of their families, who were still ebulliently chatting around the grand black table, now reflecting the pink and orange rays of the setting sun.

Prerna slid in between Sarah and Reema, while Krishna remained standing at the head of the table. 'After much toil, research and inspiration,' Kris began, 'we now begin a new journey. There are not enough thank-yous in the world for me to express how I feel about you supporting me in this journey. I want to thank my parents for tolerating my obsession with Indian food for pretty much my entire life. In this respect, I wasn't an easy kid to raise.'

Reema and David raised their glasses in good-natured agreement.

'And I am probably more difficult now,' said Krishna, eliciting more laughs. 'But I did agree to finally cut my hair, so I'd say it evens out.'

David banged the table in approval.

Chef Krishna turned to his mother next. 'You always knew I wanted to be a chef. You sent me to the best schools in America, in Europe, and took me all over India and Staten Island to learn what I could never learn in school. But you never shared the true essence of the cuisine that your father had shared with you.'

It was all true.

'Most of all, I want to thank my Masi, my guru, my second mother, my Ganga, my teacher, my muse, my saviour and inspiration. Chef Prerna Malhotra.' His eyes met hers. 'I won't say too much. She knows how I feel, and I know how much she despises attention.'

Prerna covered her smile self-consciously with her pallu.

'She has done so much, worked so hard, not only for Indian cuisine, but for me personally, and for us as a family. Masi is the spirit of the place, but I don't want her to lift a finger on my, or The New Curry Bowl's account. She's done enough. It's time for her to relax.'

'But I hate relaxing!' Prerna yelped in horror and everyone laughed.

'In spirit, but not with her hands,' Krishna continued. 'Besides being the executive chef, I will assume all responsibility for management and operations.'

Everyone clapped, anticipating Prerna's response, but none came. Sarah's watery eyes caught her mother's, and they both smiled at each other.

'Masi has generously offered to help me develop recipes and menus, participate in special tasting menus and guide The New Curry Bowl's essence according to the seasons and cultural tides. The rest, we will manage.' Krishna swallowed the lump in his throat. 'Chef Prerna Malhotra. We love you.'

Chapter 28

A Needle in a Pile of Mail, in the Taurus

Chef Krishna kicked his feet atop his desk, picked up his multi-line phone and dialled a number he knew by heart. On the other end, in the suburbs of Staten Island, Prerna reclined in an easy chair in the Malhotra living room shelling peas, a brace wrapped her wrist, her grey hair was rolled in a bun.

She answered the call right away. 'Hello, Chef Krishna!'

Kris laughed. 'Masi, you can always call me Kris! Anyway, are you sitting down?'

'It's all I seem to be doing these days. Enjoying my retirement by shelling green peas. How are you doing? So quiet at The New Curry Bowl. Is everything all right?'

'I'm in my office. It's soundproofed, so no sound from the kitchen or dining room can come here. Masi, I still can't get my turnip pickle right. When do you add the mustard?'

'Kris, turnip pickles require patience. You have to be patient. No wonder your pickles don't stay good for long. This is the problem with your generation; you want everything fast. You should know when to add ground mustard to pickle so that they add sourness and shelf life,' she reprimanded him gently.

'Okay, got it. But that's not really why I called. I have great news, Masi.'

Prerna smiled, cradling the phone between her ear and shoulder, her fingers nimbly shelling peas.

'Yes? Are you finally getting married?'

Kris laughed. 'Masi, you know I'm undateable. Who has the time?'

Prerna laughed.

'Masi, today all your recipes, your legacy, all have been rewarded again. We did it. Not sure if you heard it from my parents or Ruchi yet, but . . .' Kris turned around in his chair to look at his—their—second Michelin Star on its plaque standing proudly on the credenza behind his desk.

'Today, The New Curry Bowl was awarded its second Michelin Star. You are the first person I have called. I hope you can attend the ceremony in a few months. Did you enjoy the first one? Ruchi is already pitching another article for *The Times*.'

'The ceremony was okay. What's important is that you are happy, Kris. Are you happy?'

'Yes, I am very happy.'

'If you are happy, then I am happy. But you still have to have patience when you cook. The best-tasting food requires patience, patience and love.'

'Tell me one more thing, Masi. What secret ingredients do you add to your kheer?'

'Kris, you always forget,' said Prerna, flicking a few more shells from her peas. 'Cardamom, cinnamon, star anise and a few rose petals.'

Kris lifted his legs off his desk and began taking notes.

'Rose petals. Lovely. Okay. Next question. Can I add chickpea flour to the stuffed okra?'

'Yes, but very little,' said Prerna. 'And remember to wash the okra before chopping it or your okra will be sticky.'

'Come on, Masi, I already knew that.'

'Did you?' smiled Prerna.

* * *

A few days later, Prerna was taking a break from testing a new lentil dish she wanted to share with Kris when she decided to go through the piles of mail and papers that had accumulated around the Malhotra household over the years. Somewhere along the line, she had lost her drive for organization and Manish never had much anyway. Maybe there would be some government check waiting, or some forgotten profit share from The Curry Bowl, or a winning lottery ticket, because Manish was still buying them every time he went to the local deli. To Prerna's surprise, deep in the pile, she found an unopened letter addressed to her, postmarked years ago, with addresses in a script she recognized. One of them was an address on Fulton Street.

Prerna snatched the letter from the pile and tossed the remainder of the dead wood into the blue recycling bin Kris and Sarah had convinced her to keep by the trash in the kitchen right under the mailbox. Their 'green ideas' initiative had taken hold in their household. Prerna gripped the letter in both hands, deciding whether to open it or just forget about it and throw it in the blue bin. She considered the latter option as she crossed the living room, and passed Manish, who had just returned from meeting David over some new business. Her husband, whose hair and moustache had also gone grey, had fallen asleep in front of the TV again, in the blur of the Indian National Cricket Championships, which was all Prerna could decipher of the sport. Cricket was still so many sticky wickets to her.

Prerna stifled a modest laugh at the term with her free hand and sari, whose pallu she noticed was becoming faded, and she had to admit, a bit ragged. Unlike her sister, Prerna preferred to hang on to her garments, which she grew attached to instead of replacing them with the latest fashions. She was fine with her knockoffs.

Also, unlike Reema, Prerna did not insist or try to convince her husband she needed a new car every year. She was fine with the car she and Manish had purchased for her now that she was a fully licensed driver, a few years after she had returned from India, which just so happened to be the same model of the car she took lessons from Harold Ostasio in. Prerna always regretted she didn't keep in touch with her handsome teacher after she had earned her driver's licence. Perhaps she would seek him out and invite him and his family (*Did he have a wife?* Prerna still wondered) to The New Curry Bowl one day.

Prerna's new car (actually last year's model) was a sleek black colour, an eminently practical and humble Taurus, a classier but similar model to what she had taken lessons in.

Prerna held the lost letter tighter as she re-entered the kitchen and stared out of the window at her garden, which had become lusher with more herbs and plants than ever before. Her eyes fell again to the letter, which seemed to contain more weight and gravity than a normal one, because it was from a person she had never expected to hear from, and frankly didn't want to: Dr Dayama Annu.

Prerna glanced over her shoulder to make sure Manish was still asleep, grabbed a paring knife, slipped it under the flap and opened Annu's letter as expertly as she might slice an onion into perfect rings. She set the envelope aside and unfolded the letter. The return address hadn't lied, the letter was indeed from Dr Annu, on her official letterhead. Did she still maintain her office? Her wrist throbbing again, Prerna read her former benefactor's apology and plea. It was at that moment Prerna realized she had always had the same reaction to Dr Annu as she did to her step-grandmother, her sautelee dadi Devi, the 'princess' who was anything but. Prerna had largely recovered from the damage Devi had caused after getting her revenge through food in the form of that warm, delicious aloo jeera she had prepared all those years ago and delivered to Devi's feet during Old Delhi's cool winter wind. Now Prerna stared at her hands, which were still coated with small flecks of the garlic she was slicing for the lentil dish. Black hands? What did that mean any more? As far as she was concerned, nothing, and, she hoped, it meant even less to Kris, her Chef Krishna.

Prerna shrugged and submitted to the letter.

Dear Prerna,

How's life? I see changes down the street where The Curry Bowl was. I saw your article a while ago and have re-read it a few times since then. I disagreed with some of it, but you really made an impression on the Downtown Manhattan community and our mutual Indian community. I never guessed you'd get such support and recognition from the press. After we closed The Curry Bowl, I received so many positive comments, phone calls, texts, emails complaining that I shuttered it. It wasn't me who shuttered it. Since then, I've heard many requests to open a new place to keep part of New Delhi and Punjab cuisine available for our locals. I've been re-reading it. I hope things between us are settled. From my side, they are. No hard feelings. I am impressed by your tenacity. I only wanted to get those profits up to make it worth our while. There is a new chef, a young man by the name of Krishna? Is he that curly-haired, chubby boy who used to chase your apron strings everywhere, making mischief in the kitchen? I seem to recall seeing him always by your side when I would visit.

Anyway, if you are willing to put our past behind us, I would like to invest in The New Curry Bowl, with whatever terms you are comfortable with. I want to reiterate that the terms we had before, though your husband, Manish, wasn't comfortable with them, were necessary in order to keep the original place open and recoup my investment. That's business. I did give you your first opportunity to run a restaurant, and gave you my trust, which allowed you to gain not only experience and status but also some positive notoriety. Please don't forget that.

Again, congratulations on your article, the mark you made, and for doing our subcontinent proud. I wish you luck. I hope our paths cross in the future. In business or across a reserved dining table at The New Curry Bowl, which I promise to visit.

Sincerely,
Dayama

The old letter gave Prerna a queasy feeling in her stomach, yet she read the letter twice before she sighed and tucked it into the front of her sari as she went back to the business of preparing the new lentil dish, which she and Manish would enjoy for dinner, and which would hopefully feature on The New Curry Bowl's menu.

* * *

Later, the venerable couple sat together, enjoying each other's company—Prerna drank lemon juice while Manish sipped whisky and water.

'That aged ten-year-old label David sent me has a real bite to it. Yeow.'

'Don't drink too much.'

'I won't. Those days are gone. Finally, I get to enjoy my own wife's food. I used to resent that The Curry Bowl took you away every day. Now with Kris—sorry, Krishna—running The New Curry Bowl, I can enjoy time with my wife again.'

Prerna smiled and took a bite of her dinner. Adding extra salt had really improved the taste. She would call Kris and tell him tomorrow.

'Darling, why so quiet? Something troubling you?' Manish asked between bites and sips.

'I was just thinking about the past, how far we've come, how much we've sacrificed.'

'Also, about Karan?'

'Yes. I'm his mother, I can't help it.'

Manish reached over and squeezed Prerna's good hand.

'How is your wrist doing?'

'The brace helps. But the cortisone shots have worked wonders. Though I prefer homoeopathic methods better.'

'Well, The New Curry Bowl is a hit and we are paying off our debts. I'm planning to buy another Millionaire Jacket soon. Maybe a Billionaire Jacket.'

'Manish.' They both laughed as they finished their meal.

'You deserve it. We can thank Kris, Reema and David, even Ruchi for that article she wrote.'

'Let's toast.' The two raised their glasses and smiled, Manish far more broadly than Prerna, who only smirked.

* * *

The next morning, Prerna made a round of calls to Ruchi and Sarah.

Ruchi sat banging out words on her computer keyboard at her desk in her new, glass-enclosed high-rise office when her phone chimed. 'Ruchi Srivastava.'

'Ruchi, it's Prerna. Are you on another deadline?'

'Prerna! Been a while . . .

I'm working on a new story now.'

'About what?'

'Well, after my article about you and The New Curry Bowl came out, I kind of got pigeonholed as the journalist who writes about movers and shakers who never got their due. I'm writing about a very influential Senegalese fusion chef who had made a mark but never got to enjoy it. Oh, and I'll be pitching another full-page Food section article about you and Chef Krishna's long-standing relationship to come out when he receives his next Michelin. I hope I can interview you, for it's a unique story about the cooking and continuity of Indian culture.'

'Any time. Ruchi. And how is life being married to Mango Lassi Paul?'

'So far so good. He's been working day and night as an EMT. He loves it. Oh, and our marriage is still so fun.'

'So happy for you, Ruchi!' Prerna remembered hers and Manish's rather gaudy, solemn and confusing wedding over half a century ago in Old Delhi. Prerna still thought Ruchi's low-key wedding rather odd (a 'shotgun' wedding?) if a little tongue-in-cheek, and apparently still legal in its exchanging of vows. What was the point? Oh well. Ruchi was happy and in love and that's what mattered. With a man she had met at The Curry Bowl, no less.

Ruchi's wedding had been like a Curry Bowl reunion. Manish had pulled out his Millionaire Jacket for the occasion, while Prerna draped herself in her most formal sari. They'd also been introduced to Sarah's boyfriend there—with his red beard and John Lennon glasses. Iqbal, Nazim and Dilip had wrapped Prerna in a giant hug as soon as they saw her. And much to everyone's surprise, a clean-shaven Parminder attended as well. Although he kept sneaking out for smoke breaks throughout the ceremony and afterparty.

Kris had catered the afterparty and, as Prerna walked around the room that day, she heard all the guests gushing about the food. She'd known immediately that Kris would soon be the proud owner of a Michelin Star.

'You know who cried the hardest at my wedding?' asked Ruchi suddenly.

'Who?'

'Parminder! Then he complained he needed a cigarette and ran out again.'

'Oh my god!' Prerna couldn't control her laughter.

'I was looking at our wedding pictures just the other day. The photographer dragged us out to the sunny side of City Hall for our wedding pictures. You know, it's New York, but the sunlight shining on the wall by the park makes it look as if you're in some southern Mediterranean region of Italy. Gorgeous!'

'Funny,' Prerna said. She guessed if a new couple was clever and wanted to add some romance to the story of their wedding, they could always say they eloped to Italy, what with the dry hedges and trees and amber afternoon light of Lower Manhattan's City Hall Park. Who would know the difference?

'Ruchi, I want to ask you a question.'

'Shoot.'

'I received a letter.'

'Yeah? Who sends letters any more? Snail mail is dead, I thought.'

'It's from an older person. You know her.'

'Hmm. You got me.'

'Remember Dr Annu?'

'Hell yeah! That entitled Indian doctor bitch who always exploited you. I obviously couldn't write my true feelings in *The Times* back in the day. Why did she write you a letter?'

'She wrote it a long time ago. I just read it. It was in an old pile of junk mail.'

'Just where it belonged.'

'Maybe. Anyway, I took her letter as a sort of, how do they say it? A "backhanded" apology.'

'Yes. Prerna, you have always been too nice. Giving people who deserve it, the breaks for their attitude and talent.'

'Ruchi, I can never get anything past you. She was kind of vague, but I also found out she had anonymously called David just before The New Curry Bowl's grand opening. You are right that she probably has some business agenda. But maybe she's developed a conscience finally?'

'I doubt it. People like her never change, still stuck in a caste system, even here in progressive New York. I don't get it.'

'Ruchi, I agree she didn't behave the most humanely, but she did give me my first chance, and got me off the street and gave me a job when I needed one, as much as I hate to admit it.'

'If you say so, I guess, I wouldn't know. Well, maybe the success of The New Curry Bowl can be your comeuppance.'

'What's that?'

'Like revenge.'

Prerna laughed. 'Okay, my comeuppance. If you say so. Maybe that's part of it.'

Prerna heard a phone ring on Ruchi's end. 'Just a second.'

'Okay.'

'Okay, I finally got through to the Senegalese chef, can I call you back, Ma—I mean Prerna?'

'No need. I always love talking to you!'

Prerna hung up the phone and immediately rang her daughter up. She glanced at Manish, who had fallen asleep on the sofa in front of the TV again watching a cricket match. Good god, could that man snore! It was a snore for the ages! Prerna received a busy tone and at first, she was glad, fearing the wrath of her daughter's response to her question. By then, Sarah had a very firm grasp on exploitation—she was working on her PhD in sociology—and she had grown up with her mother working as a glorified and underpaid servant all the while at The Curry Bowl. Prerna knew what Sarah's answer would be: a big fat feisty 'No way.' Yet, Prerna left a message anyway. 'Sarah, it's your mom. I'm getting bored being at home again,' she said and hung up.

Boredom wasn't the real reason Prerna wanted to talk, Sarah would know, because Prerna never complained of boredom. She always had something to do, cooking and preparing food, or thinking or planning about cooking or preparing food, or inventing new foods altogether. Now with Kris gaining stature, she had more reason than ever. Prerna's 'boredom code' always got Sarah to call back soon.

Prerna set the phone down on the counter and went back to preparing the bitter squash dish that came to her in a dream the night before. A few minutes later, sure enough, Sarah called. Prerna dropped her knife and put her phone to her ear. 'Sarah!'

'Hi Ma,' Sarah said, sceptically. Prerna could just see her raising her eyebrow as she always did. 'You're bored, are you?' Sarah laughed and Prerna did, too, like friends rather than mother and daughter.

'You know me. Without the pressure of The Curry Bowl, I don't know what to do with myself. Go for a drive or cook for your Pita ji.'

'I think Pita ji is glad to have you back. He tells me all the time.'

'Nice to know,' Prerna said, glancing back over her shoulder towards Manish, who was still roaring, rather than snoring, on the couch. 'He's so excited about my food, he's snoring. Can you hear him?' Prerna took the phone from her ear and held it like a microphone towards her husband's rasps. 'Hear him?'

'Ma, you are too much.' Sarah laughed. 'Too much time on both your hands.'

Prerna marvelled at how her relationship with Sarah had matured over the years. She was now privileged to call her daughter her best friend.

'I need to get back to my dissertation. What did you want to ask me?'

'I found an old letter from Dr Annu.'

'What?!'

'A letter from Dr Annu. In that huge pile of junk mail I hadn't got to yet.'

'That pile's been growing for years.'

'I know. She wants to meet me.'

'For what?' asked Sarah nastily.

'Supposedly to make amends, but I'm sceptical.'

'I would be too. After the way she exploited you. In a way I hold her responsible for . . . you know.'

'I wouldn't go that far, Sarah.'

'Well, look Ma, if you were making your fair share, you could have been home more often and more available for—'

'Enough, Sarah. That's my fate. Okay, let's not go there . . . Anyway, Ruchi didn't even want to hear about it.'

'Well, Ruchi's a journalist, and has strong opinions on women who exploit other women.'

'I need what people in America call "closure". I have some bad feelings I can't get rid of because of her and the situation. Her letter was politer than her speeches and admonishment when she would show up and criticize and take the money from The Curry Bowl. I was shocked by how reasonable she sounded. And did you know she called David as soon as she saw the construction happening for The New Curry Bowl? That was also shocking. And you know what? David almost offered her shares!'

'No!'

'Manish had to remind him of what had happened in the past. Then he cut her off immediately. So did I.'

Manish's latest roar nearly made the kitchen reverberate. 'Good god, your father's snores will lift our house off its foundations someday.'

Prerna hung up the phone and went back to her work, occasionally glancing out of the window at her garden and the old, crooked basketball hoop she would never take down. Despite seasons and years of weather—they lived on an island surrounded by temperamental seas and rivers, after all—the backboard still had her and Karan's names on it from long ago.

* * *

Prerna wore a red-and-gold sari with a matching scarf for her daily drive. Today, she had driven into Lower Manhattan again to check on the old neighbourhood and run a few errands, the perfect excuse to drive, clear her head and get some 'alone time' as Sarah and Ruchi called solitude. Prerna walked briskly back to her car, which even at her age she had expertly parallel parked on Gold Street. If only Karanjit, Karan and especially Harold Ostasio could see her! How proud they would be!

After strapping on her seatbelt and adjusting her mirrors, she called Manish.

'Prerna,' Manish said, yawning.

'Guess where I am?'

'No idea.'

'I'm back in the old neighbourhood, running some errands—I drove!' said Prerna, laughing as she started the car and revved the motor.

'There's something suspicious in your voice, Prerna. Why are you calling me? To tell me you are running errands?'

'Manish! Wake up! Let's go for a drive. It's a beautiful day and I want to take you for a ride that will make up for all the rides you gave me over the years.'

Prerna was really on a high, but Manish neither expressed great joy nor resistance, he merely agreed. 'Okay, I'll shower and be ready out front in an hour so you don't have to find parking. Parking is becoming a real nightmare lately in Bay Terrace.'

'Okay, love.'

Prerna was elated to drive back to Staten Island to pick up her husband and take him for a drive to her secret happy place overlooking the Hudson River and the Manhattan skyline, the same place she had taken Kris all those years ago before departing for India. Perhaps her happy place was also a lucky place and would have the same effect on her husband as it seemed to have had on her nephew.

Prerna hung up, tossed her phone on the dash and eased her Taurus out of the parking spot, making sure to check her blind spots. Thank god there were no cows lumbering or tuk-tuks racing around Lower Manhattan. The New Curry Bowl idled just down the street, but Prerna made it a point not to look. She had passed everything down to Krishna and that pleased her.

As she manoeuvred through Lower Manhattan, Prerna honked for the pure joy of honking—everyone else did it, why not her? She enjoyed joining in and no anger made her do it. It was like playing a musical instrument to her, it was fun, and it made her think of her father, as she drove through the eerie and narrow Battery Tunnel and suddenly appeared in the glowing daylight of Brooklyn, speeding down a harbour-side highway past too many islands, piers and parks to count, through neighbourhoods with names like Brooklyn Heights, Red Hook, Sunset Park and Bay Ridge, at a rate of speed that made Brooklyn seem as buzzing, intricate and maze-like as Old Delhi.

Then she took flight, seeming to float across the elongated and towering Verrazano-Narrows Bridge, which spat her out back home in Staten Island, where she finally steered herself home. Manish was already outside, dressed in his powder-blue weekend sports coat and jeans, wearing sandals on his feet. My husband has become a silver fox, Prerna thought. Especially so with the Ray-Bans he was wearing. Reema had rubbed off on him. For their drive, Prerna tuned into a staticky Jackson Heights-transmitted Bollywood AM Radio station on the Taurus's radio dial.

Despite the fact Prerna had driven Manish around a few times, he still somehow believed she was a terrible driver. This time, too, when he clambered inside, he pulled on his seatbelt as tightly as possible and gripped the dashboard like some sort of terrified cat. Prerna pressed the accelerator and they were off.

Prerna turned and motioned with her chin.

'See my hands?'

'Keep your eyes on the road!' he gasped.

'Manish, we're fine. I had a great teacher. See my hands?'

Manish looked at Prerna's hands, which still bore the calluses and scars of a chef.

'What about your hands?'

'Ten and two,' said Prerna. She honked the horn at a jaywalking pedestrian. 'Ten and two.'

'Ten and wha . . .?'

'It's what Harold taught me.'

'Who's Harold?'

Oops, Prerna almost revealed a hint of her crush. 'I never told you about Harold.'

'No.'

'My excellent driving teacher. I'd like you to meet him sometime.'

Prerna made a wild left.

'Prerna, take it easy!'

'Who are you, Reema? Relax. The longer one drives in New York, the more one drives like a Sikh cab driver. I feel at home here more than ever since I started driving.' Prerna playfully slapped her husband's knee. 'You are in capable hands, as capable behind the wheel as they were rolling out samosa dough.'

'I'll believe it when we are safely home.' Manish stared straight ahead.

Prerna laughed.

The Hudson River suddenly revealed itself in all its glistening and flowing glory on their right. 'Wow!' said Manish, relaxing his grip and leaning towards Prerna to take in the sight. 'I've never realized how clean the Hudson River is. Nothing like the Ganga.'

'Nothing like the Ganga in some ways. Everything like the Ganga in others . . . Let me take you somewhere. To the special place where I was always "cheating" on you.'

Manish lightened up, grinning as Prerna drove towards Weehawken and Bollywood tunes filled their ears.

Soon they were speeding along the regal-sounding Port Imperial Highway, until they reached a patch of green along the river, just opposite Manhattan. Hamilton Park. She steered the Taurus into the parking lot and eased the car into a spot close to the greenery.

'Where are we going?' Manish asked.

'Follow me,' Prerna said, turning off the ignition and reaching into the back seat. 'Made us a special picnic lunch.'

Manish grumbled as he tried easing his body out of the car—Prerna had started noticing how slowly he walked these days, and how creaky his joints sounded.

'Wow! Manhattan looks marvellous from New Jersey,' he said, adjusting his sandals.

Prerna appeared around the far side of the car with a bag of her prepared delicacies. 'Let's go, dear. I'll take you to, what do they call it now, these kids, my "happy place".'

Manish followed, his eyes never leaving the gorgeous panorama of Manhattan. Prerna led them to an empty bench at the highest rim of the park closest to the water. It seemed to be her good fortune that whenever she felt like sitting on it and staring across the water, the bench was always miraculously empty. Her karma, the pleasure of sitting on this bench, enjoying this view and the Hudson-conjured fresh and brackish breeze. On the bench, husband and wife held each other's hands like high-school sweethearts.

Manish squeezed her hand, and they sat in companionable silence.

When she pulled out her phone, he chided her gently.

'Prerna, we have more time to relax now. Let's just sit and take in the sights. Put your phone away. Let's spend this time together.'

Prerna kissed her husband on the cheek.

'Okay,' she said and tucked her phone away.

She set up a little dining area between them on the bench and they enjoyed a little feast, a new kind of dal with some samosas and naan. Manish inhaled the enticing aromas, and it took him all of five minutes to devour all the food Prerna had placed between them on the bench. After he finished, Manish patted his belly and loosened his belt, relaxing back on the bench to watch the sun's refractions slowly descend along the mirror of buildings across the water.

'These are our best times, Prerna. Sitting together and enjoying food. I have the world's greatest chef for a wife. I am luckier than if I had a million dollars; even my wife insists on driving a humble Taurus.' Manish reached his arms around Prerna and gave her the hug of a lifetime. He really didn't want to let go.

'Manish! Stop! We are in a public place.'

'This is America! We can act any way we want to,' Manish proudly said.

'Manish!' Prerna pulled her head away, trying to vanish into her sari, as her eyes fell soft and hazy into an almost drunken gaze. She had to wonder how lucky she felt, now that she and her husband had managed to make their way back to one another after spending so many years apart, even under a shared roof.

The sunny day started to lapse into the deeper magenta and crimson hues of sunset when from the north, up the Hudson over Manish's shoulder, Prerna saw a bank of mottled dark clouds rolling downstream over the George Washington Bridge. Manish looked up the river and saw the same encroaching clouds. When thunder clapped, Manish stood up. 'Don't want to get wet, dear. Should we go?' Before Prerna could answer, Manish was already packing up their picnic basket and heading towards the car.

'It's just a little water,' Prerna protested.

'You know I hate getting wet.'

Prerna did. Foiled by rain!

'Okay, I'll catch up with you.'

She tossed her car keys at him. 'In case it rains before I get to the car.'

Manish nodded and turned to walk across the park as Prerna pulled out her phone and turned it on.

'Siri, where is The New Curry Bowl?'

Siri spoke, 'The New Curry Bowl is at 141 Fulton and has a five-star customer rating and a Michelin Star. The executive chef is Krishna Mehra, trained by the former chef of the original The Curry Bowl, Prerna Malhotra, who was a self-taught chef.'

Prerna smiled and her eyes started to moisten, gaining back their sparkle. 'Siri?'

'Yes?' said the female bot.

'Does my . . .' she trailed off, before taking a breath and finishing her question. 'Does my husband love me?'

Siri searched but had no answer.

Prerna smiled—she knew one answer that Siri didn't. She began jogging back to the car as the wind picked up around her, hoping to beat the rain.

Prerna approached the driver's side, which Manish had already propped open for her. She threw her hips into the seat and put the key into the ignition, fired up the engine and placed her hands at ten and two, just as Harold Ostasio had taught her.

Manish's warm hands surprised Prerna on the steering wheel. He pulled his wife's hands to his mouth and kissed them. Prerna stared at her husband, placed her hands back on the wheel and cleared her throat. She checked her mirrors and strapped herself in.

'We better drive back before it rains,' Prerna said. 'Looks like one of those relentless but quick New York monsoons.'

'The road home is bound to be slippery, are you sure you know how to drive in the rain?' Manish gripped the dash and door handle like a frightened cat again.

Prerna glared at her husband. 'You've always listened to Reema too much. What do you think? And anyway, New York rains are much friendlier than rain in New Delhi.'

Manish remained too stiff and rattled to speak.

On the way home, passing through Weehawken, Jersey City with its Heights and Journal Square, Hackensack and Greenville, each time Prerna had a chance to hit the horn at speeding trucks, wayward bikes or errant pedestrians, she saw the image of her father behind the wheel of his trusty Maruti—Karanjit's beaming face as he honked.

Lost in her memories, Prerna coaxed the car onwards, as Manish gently hummed along to the tunes on the radio.

Before they realized what was happening, Prerna pulled into St George terminal.

'Where are you going?' asked Manish, peering out of the window.

'My god, for a second, I was lost in thought, and now we're here. I thought I had to go back to work! Once a cook, always a cook.'

Prerna laughed at Manish's slack jaw and righted the Taurus again towards home, muttering to herself, 'Ten and two, ten and two, ten and two.'